CLACKAMAS LITERARY REVIEW

2007, Volume XI

Clackamas Community College, Oregon City, Oregon

CLACKAMAS LITERARY REVIEW

Editors

Andy Mingo
Amanda Coffey
Trevor Dodge
Kate Gray

Assistant Editor

Heather Frazier

Editorial Assistants

Alexandra Anderson
Bryan Edwards
Jessica Erickson
Heather Frazier
Carl Graham
Angela Hardy
Jacob Kashaija
Bryan Schwab

Cover Art

Rick True, "Bell Flower Erupting"

The Clackamas Literary Review is published annually at Clackamas Community College. Manuscripts are read from April 1st to September 1st and will not be returned. By submitting your work to CLR, you indicate your consent for us to publish that work in our print journal and on our website. Issues are $13.95; back issues are $5. Clackamas Literary Review, 19600 South Molalla Avenue, Oregon City, OR 97045. ISBN 0-9796882-0-5. Distributed by Ingram Periodicals, Inc.

http://www.clackamasliteraryreview.org

CONTENTS

INTERVIEW

SPECIAL SECTIONS

Editors' Note

Dear Friends,

CLR began as a grand experiment 10 years ago, migrating towards the places that move us most, and expressing those locales through the eyes, ears and mouths of the most amazing poets, essayists and fiction writers we were fortunate enough to meet. We are proud of territory we have traversed, and thank you for your companionship along the way.

We are delighted to tell you that the experiment will continue, and that CLR has expanded its charge to include a learning laboratory for students at Clackamas Community College who are interested in careers in editing and publishing. The content you see here was selected and agreed upon by us four faculty editors, but a great deal of the mechanics and logistics of getting this issue into your hands was delegated to a small but passionate group of students. We are revitalized by the energy we see in these students, and very excited about the next ten years of CLR's ongoing experiment.

This issue is dedicated to our students, to you, and to the future. Cheers.

Amanda Coffey
Trevor Dodge
Kate Gray
Andy Mingo

A Mid-Autumn's Night
Brad Summerhill

Steve Earle was playing the Waldorf last year, played this ditty decrying capital punishment. I'm in the midst of a crowd stirring and charged. A kid holds a beer over his head, cheering the tale of a convict who's to be executed in the morning. Beside me, a young lady with oval black eyeglasses sways. She looks over. I've been seeing her for thirty minutes. It's obvious chemistry, as if my forty years of life have been aimed toward this single moment. Another college kid holds a lighter above his head. I try to remember I've been drinking, and I do stupid things when I've been drinking. She appears so smart and pretty though, the eyeglasses I suppose, nearly an object of fetish after my decade-long parade of single moms who despite life's hardships turned out puddle-deep. A one-liner enters my head so I find myself saying in her ear, "This song's so beautiful it's a shame it's playing to a house of drunkards."

She recoils with a frown to say, "What?" and chastened I bark out over the senseless hooting and bar noise, "Such a pretty song. Shame gets played to house of drunks!"

I'm sincere. It's one of those songs that's not like the shadow of beauty but beauty itself.

She hums out a tune of an answer I can't catch. I stand nearer.

"Do you think it's a shame," I persist, "such a beautiful song plays to a house of drunks?" I point at one.

She laughs!

She eases away from me. She thinks I'm the drunk.

I concede it's the last I'll see of her. The crowd is three hundred or more. She gets herself lost in it.

I said bye to friends outside after the final encore. She stood there, her breath fogging around her, also saying bye to friends. She caught my eye.

I wouldn't say she had stars in her eyes because I wasn't looking at stars. I was looking at a tight ass, long raven hair with reddish highlights, and when she turned to stare at me once again, a face that cuts to a man's heart, big eyes and soft red cheeks. The night wasn't over. She walked away from her girlfriends and I followed her across Virginia Street to the university parking lot.

She turned, "You following me?"

"Yes," I said. "Very much."

We clambered into the cab of my truck. At first we talked the true meanings behind the songs, the people in the songs we felt we knew. She kissed like she was searching for fillings. Her tongue didn't taste right from the beers we'd drunk. I licked her neck. Pretty soon the windows steamed up. Behind our curtain of steam, I held her warm crotch. People pretend it's not important how it happens. I disagree. She unbuckled my belt and worked my jeans over my hips. I thought I was in for a blow job. She's working at my boxers. She says, "Damn, you got a knife, cowboy?" I confess I do, in the glove box. "Get it for me." I hand her the pocket knife, two and seven-eights inch blade. Three inches is illegal, reaches the heart. She uses her teeth to open the blade, dives toward my waist. I ball up my fists and she says, "Take it easy, cowboy." No one's ever called me that, except to ridicule me. I've run cattle once in my life and that was more like a camping trip than a real run. She slices the band of my boxers, throws the knife onto the mat and shreds my underwear loose with her little fists.

Now, this hadn't been done before.

My hand gropes her panties as I try to think something good to say. I can only murmur. I manage to get her jeans below her knees. She orders, "Tear them off. Tear them off." I oblige, ripping away her cotton underwear.

Her pants cuff her ankles behind her. It's like a circus show. My hands scutter up and down her pale thighs.

She eases onto me, no thought to disease in my head. It'd been a long time, possibly forever, since a woman wanted me this way.

3

I nibbled her and tried singing fragments of song lyrics in her ear. My voice cracked. We collapsed together, hugging, inhaling our smell in great deep heaves. Nothing this good ever happened to me. She made me cry. She was so unexpected. As she rocked frantically on top of me, pushing her palms upward into the roof of my cab, tears streamed down my face. She took note, she cried too as we finished our love-making.

We cried together, for beauty's sake.

Only then I focused on the big rock on her finger. I'd seen it but hadn't comprehended. I thought, a little hollow, her husband is the world's luckiest man. And probably can't realize how lucky he is—that's what the Greeks called human nature. She reminded me of sunset over Pyramid Lake or sunrise over the Toyiabe Range, the entire scope of grace and beauty.

She scurried across my body, the driver's side door already open, shivering me with cold air. Fog is rare in Reno, a strange low cold front pushing in. The fog began to pale in the witching hour. Yellow lumens of sodium lights cast over her naked form as she slipped into her jeans, sans underwear. Icy halos played around her limbs.

4

"We'll go get breakfast," I said, playing the cool cowboy. "And coffee."

"I can't believe this fog," she said. "So what do you do?"

I told her I ran the family business. "Come on back in." She evaded my questions, standing there shivering, and I said, "You love him? Is it one of those for-the-kids things?" I only wanted a real conversation.

She disappeared into the fog. Somewhere, a car engine turned over. Sounded like a mid-size, maybe a Toyota V-6. I couldn't chase her down like a maniac. At least the thought didn't occur to me till too late. I went back to the club and banged on the door. Don introduced me to Steve Earle, whose hand was softer than I expected. He might've thought the same.

"Did you see this girl near the front?" I asked him. "Her name was Bridgett."

Don mentioned to Mr. Earle I was quite a political thinker. I was replaying the thing she said. "Time's up, cowboy," she told me, wiping the steam from her eyeglasses with a loose shirt tail.

My family's place on the south end of Steamboat Ditch is good land for horses. Dad left it to Mom, she'll leave it to me. We have a single bull, named Sir Walter Raleigh. Every spring we stick an electric prod up his ass so he'll spew a quart of semen we sell at the fairgrounds. We stud him out. We're gentleman farmers, you might say. I'm no real cowboy.

That's just what she called me.

The next morning I accompanied Mom to Mass, as usual. For once, I wasn't fighting off a hangover. Visions of her skin and the frantic thrust of her jaw kept me upright during the Benediction.

So I recited, "I'm forty and live with my mother." It's a depressing formula for when I'm feeling too high. I glanced at Mom. She smiled and set her hand on the pew, brushing my leg. She drew it away quickly as if she sensed hot blood rushing to my groin.

I took Communion, got down on my knees and blasphemed. I prayed to Bridgett. I prayed for Beauty. I said, "God, Jesus, Foolish Ghost, if you can even pretend to exist, send me her again." I prayed for a heavenly visitation. Bridgett, my Gal in Heaven, hallowed be thy name. I might have been nine years old again, refusing to believe any of it until Jesus himself descended from the right hand of the Father to poke young Richard into submission with his wounded hand.

5

I fantasized, as men do. I would run into her at the tack shop. She wouldn't see me. I would walk up behind her as she's fingering a nylon horse whip and I'd say, "Call me cowboy again." The day starts with a drive to the look-out on Windy Hill and ends just about anywhere. I don't need to be so descriptive now.

Reno's a small town despite the quarter million people clogging the valleys. I figured I would see her soon enough. Didn't happen. I got not much to do. I've got my angle. How many people have time or inclination to read over a barbarian princess named Medea who wanted vengeance? I reread the classics. Plato.

Visiting a private investigator is more like visiting an accountant than chatting with a cop. She's got a dye job from a bottle and says she used to be police in California.

Prayer's fine by me but action fulfills wishes. For one teary night I suspected we do live by miracle, from miracle to miracle, until we run into Death. Real Beauty—the real

Platonic thing and not the shadow form—will spin your head until you're ready to believe in miracles.

All I have is a name: Bridgett Williams.

I describe her. My description is kind of vague. Long raven hair. (I almost say 30B cup.) I guess her model of car from the sound of the engine. I stop slouching in my chair. I'm forty acting like a blushing teen. I recite my formula.

"What?" she asks. Apparently my lips are moving.

"Hair has reddish highlights," I say. "These rosy cheeks—" I pause "—I guess that's not too helpful."

"And why are we finding her?" She stops typing at the computer. "I'm legally obligated to find out. I can't abet any criminal activity."

"Oh, no, I'm in love with her," I blurt.

She stifled her snickers. We had ourselves a long uncomfortable silence.

I suppose we spend our whole lives seeking tragedy. I must've sounded pretty lonely. Maybe I'd been searching for a lost love ever since middle school when I rolled through the snake grass with Mandy Bryles a month before she moved to Napa.

So she hammers me with, "Has it occurred to you that she gave you a fake name?"

No, thought never occurred.

She suggests Bridgett's a married woman who doesn't want to be found.

"She might, she might not," I say, unable to cover the juvenile inflections in my voice. I wonder if men undergo biological changes, like male menopause? Because I was close to tears realizing Bridgett wouldn't be found.

Hell, I paid her forty bucks an hour three weeks straight till I had to admit she was right. I was wasting my money, a lot of it. I finally woke up when I had to borrow a few hundred from Mom. So I added another line: "You're forty, you live with your mother and you borrow money from her."

Steve Earle sings a song about depression. I gave it a good listen, a hundred times over, like the punishment of a rosary.

Winter provided the miracle I craved. Inside Sears. I headed toward the table saws, sick of fooling with hand-helds, when I saw her testing out a vacuum and understood we do live by, for and from miracle. She pantomimed, pushing it back and forth. There was a man with her, a young fellow—not a salesman. It was an expensive model. So was he, top of the line woolen slacks, white linen dress shirt, two hundred dollar loafers. At a certain point in life, you choose your style. Most people choose style before they have substance. I wondered about this guy. Substance must precede style. Did he have either? He looked like every kid in high school who bought the latest polo wear. No doubt he drove a sporty BMW. No doubt he was the youngest vice president at the firm. I wasn't jealous, not of his work anyway. I remember when I came home from college with nearly perfect grades and my bachelor's in philosophy. Dad wanted me to become a lawyer. "It'll be so easy for you, Richard," he told me, one of the last things he told me. He died disappointed with his son. I know this. I know what he didn't understand, something this kid of a husband didn't understand: Beauty is the only worthwhile endeavor. Bridgett ran into my arms when she wanted real experience. I saw her pushing a deadened vacuum, living in her shadow world, the world of illusion most everyone thinks is reality. Lights flicker behind us, shadow forms dance before our eyes, and we call it reality, when all along the perfect forms are behind us, out of sight. I thought of her moaning, how this rich husband couldn't even excite his wife in bed.

7

Today wasn't new vacuum cleaner day after all. She wore a print skirt and modest heels, her hair done up with pins. She had on those sexy eyeglasses. I followed them into the mall. Oh, I thought, as they walked into Victoria's Secret. He wasn't embarrassed to dig through piles of panties and racks of bras, holding up a dainty size five nightie. I purchased a Field & Stream from the mall bookstore, using it for camouflage. Spying is not as erotic as one might suspect.

The sensation is termed distraction, I think. I was far from her, and far away from myself.

They seemed to be acting out a ritual, a sterile version of sex. You can tell when a couple isn't really together even though they have all the gestures down pat. They were the shadow forms of unity and love. I couldn't see what he was picking out, but she kept shaking her head with this thin smile. I imagine he was picking out lacy stuff with frills and doo-dads when what she really needed was simple cotton panties, light blue or white.

She accepted a few of his offerings. As they approached the register, I approached softly behind. He pulled out his credit card, naturally, and I stood at the end of a short line of customers, head down, ears up.

The checkout girls whizzed through purchases. I finally caught the miracle. I heard the golden words, "Thank you, Mr. Williams."

She'd told me the truth! Her name was Williams.

It is verily impossible to downplay the significance of this fact.

One of the girls said to me, "Can I help you, sir?" I shook my head, ducking away from Bridgett. I stared after her as they left the store, and her eyes darted back at me.

I wanted to think I saw longing in her eyes. No. More like panic. Fear. Regret.

There are exactly four hundred forty-eight Williamses in the Nevada Bell directory. Suffice it to say not many of them are related. One of them knew a Bridgett who lived in Cleveland. After a month of dialing, someone recognized my description of Sporty, the husband, whose real name was listed in the directory.

Another man might've seen that look of regret and let her go, granting himself the virtue of mercy. This is a story about a forty-year-old boy becoming a man. Or I could argue, alternately, that a lesser man would let her go. One less dedicated to Beauty. I tended to agree with Plato that the real reality is behind us and that Bridgett's marriage was simply a shadow form. I only wanted a word with her. That's a lie. I wanted a date. I wanted to discover if she was an illusion. I wanted to ask about her family, her education, her views of the role of diplomacy in the post-colonial era. I wanted to recite heartbreaking lyrics.

She lived in a faux Tudor mansion hidden up beyond Skyline.

Her name wasn't Bridgett. It was Darla. You can read a lot from a name. "Darla" reminded her of her blue-collar origins and her bourgeois ambitions. "Bridgett" was a spy in the house of love.

My friend Carl plays bass at the Shy Clown. More relevant, he makes money on the side selling Electrolux vacuums, those big industrial-strength home-use products, all shiny chrome. They look like they popped out of a Saturday Evening Post ad. I offered Carl a twelve-pack of Dos Equis to give me a demonstration.

I wanted the freedom to walk up to her front door and say, "Bridgett, you broke my heart. And you can mend it too." The vacuum—those things are heavy—was my shield if he answered the door, which he did.

"Good day, sir," I said, big grin. "My name is Carl Buena, and I would like to take the opportunity today to share with you a real miracle."

He looked at the black carrying case, thinking it was full of Bibles and pamphlets.

"The Electrolux cleaning system provides miracles every day." Carl had told me not to call it a "vacuum." "Do you have any children, sir?"

I could see he was getting antsy. Carl said when they get antsy, change the subject. Keep the conversation lively and fresh.

No kids. "Pets? You have pets?"

"Cats," he spoke.

"How have you lived without a real vacuum"—I slipped up—"to protect this house? A good cleaning system is like an insurance policy. Let me demonstrate." I hid my nerves by jamming myself sideways into the doorframe.

He gave way! "Listen, I'm a hard sell," he said. "Don't waste your time. I'm watching the tournament right now."

"Golf?" I queried. Of course. A man who watches golf.

I had my angle. There was the nagging thought that, after all, they did need a vacuum.

"What a beautiful lady," I pointed to a picture of Bridgett without her eyeglasses. A studio shot, fuzzy light. Hair down. "Is she a relative? Your sister? There's a family resemblance."

"My wife," he scowled. He was staring at my boots like he'd never seen a vacuum salesman with cowboy boots.

"Um, my wife does most of the cleaning," he said. Then he corrected himself, "We have a service come twice a month. They use our old vacuum. Let me get her. Hang tight. She's been talking about getting a new vacuum. May be your lucky day."

I noticed his black hair was silvering at the temples. He had an imperial nose and a dimpled chin. Sporty was handsome, no doubt.

When she clip-clopped down the tile hallway I twisted inside, rubbing my palms through my hair and adjusting my john at the last second before she came into view. I felt like a seventh grader sent to the principal.

There are facial expressions in life worth remembering.

She backed up, like I was going hit her, her two small fists clenched beneath her chin, eyes wide and fearful, like Mary Pickford before the advent of sound—giant melodrama.

A damsel in distress.

I thought she might scream.

"Please, quiet," I spoke gently. "I'm not here to make trouble."

"How did you— Yes, you are," she snapped. "You are here to make trouble." She whispered in the yelling way of whispering.

"It's true. I am here to make trouble," I said, defeated. There are few real fools on life's stage. I joined their unhappy ranks.

Her husband tromped down the hall. I snapped open the case saying, "We have so much confidence in this product that I will soil up your best patch of carpet with coffee grounds, or even cat urine"—her husband enjoyed this impromptu detail and I thought I detected a hint of a smile playing on her lips too—"and we will guarantee the Electrolux to clean all visible and invisible signs of staining." I gestured to my nose. Carl told me to emphasize smell. "Or we will replace the entire carpet free of charge."

"Do we get to pick the color?" Sporty asked jovially.

When the commercial break was over he drifted to the den.

"Living room," she said.

It was pristine. Original artwork on the walls, mostly watercolors. The kind of sofa and chairs no one ever sits on. The sterility might have had something to do with what happened next.

I continued my demonstration.

Carl's sales pitch spilled from my mouth. I wouldn't pause to give her a word. I feared her speech. I feared this house. I began to doubt I was really in love with her. I wasn't in love with Darla. I was in love with her ideal form, Bridgett.

"Richard, stop," she said, touching me on the shoulder as I displayed a box of attachments.

"Don't forget," I said, "the engine reverses. This model actually converts to a steam cleaner."

She gazed into my eyes. I was crushed into silence. All the emotion of that mid-autumn's night welled up in me, and I whispered, "You're so young." I laughed to stop from choking up. "I'm getting on, Darla. I need to fend off death. Give me another chance. Please."

As if I had wronged her.

Then she said the most graceful thing. She said, "My name's Bridgett. As far as you're concerned." She said it kindly.

She let me kiss her. She closed one door and stared through an open archway. She let me kiss her again. I felt that Bridgett and I stood a chance. She might run away with me.

Our night together, she explained, had been a fluke. Sporty had been cheating on her. She wasn't taking vengeance so much as finding solace. Sporty realized he was on the edge of disaster, dumped the mistress, agreed to attend marriage counseling and so on. He'd been treating her, she said, like the pay-for-hire exotic dancer she used to be when they first met. She financed her tuition that way, she said. Now he pursued his new self with all the quiet vigor of a golfer who wants to improve his handicap using meditation, religion, philosophy, money, time, effort—whatever it took.

"He's been wonderful," she said with an ashamed downturn of her lips. "I believe it's for real."

"No it's not," I said, being the petty man I couldn't help being. "I can give you what he can't."

She dimmed her eyes at me, angry. She realized I was right. "No, you're wrong," she said.

"Where are your glasses?" I asked. I was afraid she didn't really need glasses, that they were just for effect. Turned out she was wearing contacts.

I tried to kiss her again. She held me away.

"Poor cowboy," she said, slithering her torso against mine. "I heard that one-liner you laid on me. I thought you were so shallow. I mistook you for any other man."

"I'm lonely for you, Darla."

"Of course you are, cowboy," she rubbed my thigh.

"I didn't realize you were so sensitive," she said, working me up. I didn't understand her at all. I could only reasonably conclude two things. First, she was sorry for hurting me and felt obligated to pay me with a memorable goodbye. Second, I really did turn her on. More than Sporty could.

"Why do you want this?" she said. "What do you think we have here?"

"It's, it's . . . ." I searched for a word, "Chemistry."

She laughed at me. "'Chemistry'? Don't you mean 'destiny,' cowboy?"

"That too. I mean love. True storybook love. Happy endings." I told her I had money. I told her I had faith in Beautiful Things.

She plugged in the Electrolux and set it to running. She led me into the bathroom. I put my hand between her thighs. She wore baggy pants, easily removed. She said, "We've got no time." She fell to her knees and fell to work on my big belt buckle. Getting a blow job right then would have been like someone sticking the electric prod up my ass, like we do with Sir Walter Raleigh. Zap and I'd spew.

"Hold on," I said. "I don't want that from you. I want everything else." I reached inside my lapel. "I've got two tickets for Maui. We'll do the divorce by telephone. I've got the best attorneys in town."

She pushed me away, cold.

"You've got cause," I said. "Plenty of them." I held her shoulders. She dodged my eyes. I pled my love.

She shuffled into the pristine living room and shut down the Electrolux. She made it profoundly and fundamentally clear that I must leave. There was an edge of threat behind her words, as if what she said was backed up by the weight of a million-dollar home, a six-figure breadwinner and the full credit and faith of the whole damn government.

She set me straight. It was the moment of honesty people dread. To face a lonely age and slow death on the heels of glorious potential.

She did purchase the Electrolux. I gave the commission to Carl. As good salesmen will, he believes in his product.

"I can see myself out," I told them. Sporty actually shook my hand. Darla gave a fearful look, as if he might sniff her scent on my hand. And this: I shook her hand too. I squeezed it. We gazed. We said goodbye.

As I limped down the tile hallway, chastened, a boy sent to his room, I found myself alone for a few seconds. I surprised myself. I lifted her portrait from the wall. I stole a treasure. I hid it at my lower back, beneath my camel hair jacket, tucked inside my shirt. I was positive Sporty had caught me. They walked side by side down the hall. I was certain they would notice the blank space on the wall. There was Sporty in one photo, them together in another, pics of Sporty's folks and her folks and siblings and even some cats, but where was Darla's portrait?

Often we miss the obvious.

I gave her a last look, as though to say, "I will see you out there."

All that last second emotion, I told myself, was just typical emptiness, typical vanity. Bridgett had ceased to exist in any tangible sense. Darla stared at the wall, noticing the missing portrait. She jerked her head in my direction, and I moved backward into the doorframe. She opened her mouth to say something then she looked at the back of Sporty's head. He hadn't noticed a thing.

I almost sat on her picture getting into my pickup. They stood in front of their big Tudor mansion, waving as if I'd shared something special with them through door-to-door sales. I'd given them a glimpse into better household living. Their Electrolux came with a lifetime warranty. I knew they had troubles ahead. I knew they would never last. They were only shadows, diminished in the bright March sun.

Every man gets one chance to fondle divinity, I figured. I pulled out for a three-point turn on the cul-de-sac when I saw her in the rearview mirror, a last glimpse.

Angels and devils drive a man down the same path, toward the same object. The goal at the end of the road appears like a Platonic form, that's means an illusion, something out of reach. Chemistry turns to real love which isn't romantic but hard work like gathering bales in the sun. What did I know about real work? We could have had our home. Offspring. I had my pastures of plenty, Sir Walter Raleigh standing in his field, chewing his cud. He's a magnificent beast, the lines on him, the muscle. The neighbors bring by a heifer, and we watch in admiration. We stand there and we watch, and we hope that something good will come from it, some ideal prize-winning cow, a vision of strength and beauty that will spring into the sunny field instantly and magically like a goddess materializing from the horns of the immortal godhead. Then I feel that I should kneel down in thankfulness and say, "I never doubted it could happen."

Her staggering form filled the mirror's frame. She sprinted in modest heels. Sporty made confused gestures behind her

13

on the driveway. I rolled down my window. She stretched to thumb away one of my tears.

"Those airline tickets one-way?"

"What'd you tell him?" I asked, somehow full of fear.

"I didn't tell him anything."

I nearly knocked her off her feet with the swinging door. Her upraised arms, her body posture, were like a diver in reverse. I wrapped her into me and prayed thanks for her rising form.

"Wait," she said, "I don't want him to think this is some sort of kidnapping." She kissed me long and deep. "Call me Darla from now on." She called an apology to Sporty. She shouted, "I'm not in any danger, honey. It isn't a kidnapping. It's difficult to explain. I think we're in love!"

Ex Eternity

Kristen Henderson

after Marina Tsvetaeva

I'd read in the obits that your grandfather died (so I broke down
and downloaded the hometown news), heard that

your brother, my nemesis, and his wife (even worse)
had triplets. You have long

since vacated Tahiti (it was the honeymoon
I envied most) and I bet you still sing from the throat.

You must spare your spouse your dreams
of me (my influence you are determined to refute).

It was and you were and we did
then you couldn't, said you never, (but it won't

go away). How cruel it is to wake
forgetting I am thirteen years into this question,

desolation become project (repetition
to overcome). I have no choice

but to forgive myself for loving an eternity
past stylish and down into the weak hours

of need. On better days I believe you miss it so,
that you feed us in your silence

(remember sucking the tears
from my eyelids).

Aura
Cris Mazza

2001

One of Tam's doctors had told her she may someday be able to recognize pre-seizure, or aura stage, symptoms. Perhaps sound fading and returning, floating white spots, buzzing or ringing in her ears. She researched methods to forestall or prevent the actual convulsion stage of an epileptic seizure. Someone — maybe Martha, or maybe it was something Gary had said to Martha — had once recommended water therapy. Did they mean one of those sensory deprivation chambers that were supposed to recreate the womb, 98.6 degrees and just the right percentage of saline? Or a little contraption that tinkled water over stones all day? Or an actual session in a pool with a therapist leading dance-like exercises or the old-lady-style breaststroke? Tam never asked. She'd stopped speaking to her brother around the time she quit swimming. She'd almost, but then hadn't gotten back into a pool with Denny. Lately, any time Denny came percolating back, she wondered if thoughts of him *were* the aura stage — as though Denny had become inexorably linked to the defective spot in her brain, and an impending seizure sent out memories of him like a smell from embers about to combust.

The aura stage was also sometimes marked by an inability to concentrate. The inability to answer a simple question while going through the steps of turning off a computer, to sort the mail while ordering a sandwich for lunch. An incapacity to focus, sort, pin down scattered, seemingly unrelated pieces of anxiety. Images from memories running across the bottom of her mind's TV screen like a weather warning: Gary pounding on the door to the swim team office where she and Denny were holed up with a mattress on the floor. Denny, sitting on the mattress, turned away and bent slightly, his long swimmer's torso and broad swimmer's shoulders all she could see, his voice saying, "I'm a bum." Another day, rising from the rigid stage, aware of her surroundings but still immobile, her body contorted around and under a desk in the swim team office, urine streaked with uterine blood pooled around her, already drying in her hair, caked in her clothes, and the foamy saliva likewise tinged with blood already dry on her face and neck where she could smell it even before she was able to move. Her wrist cracked from flailing against a wooden chair. Her tongue swollen in her mouth. A pencil broken in half, splinters in her palm. Looking up at the bottom-side of the chair where several times she had sat on Denny's lap, kissing, his hand in her skirt, surrounded by glossy action shots of stars of a swimming powerhouse university, future Olympians or world class swimmers, frozen in a butterfly's lunge or the air-intake stroke in freestyle, one arm poised in an arc over a capped, goggled head, droplets of diamonds outlining the power of the thrust. One of them was Gary. She wasn't even sure which one. One of them was Denny. That one she took, when she left, clutched under a towel emblazoned with the university mascot that she used to cover her soiled clothes.

Dear Denny,
Do you still think best in water? I wish I'd jumped in,
one of those days you were thinking. I think I almost
did. It might've changed everything … You never
saw me foam at the mouth that night, then you never
saw me again. But you're still with me, in the grand
mal aura stage — either it induces memories of you,
or else stray memories of you jarred loose by accident
(or incident) cause the aura … So far I've staved off
the next big one. But, over the years when I've
dreamed if you, who's to say I haven't gone through
the rigid stage and woken with just a slight headache,
just a little confused

A new compose-message was grayish white, the *To, From* and *Subject* lines blank. Knowing that was exactly the kind of mindset she should be striving for, she nonetheless began filling in the spaces.

> Gary,
> People would accuse me of living in the past, but you know what happened. No, you didn't cause the seizure, I've known that a long time, but it didn't mean I wanted you as my rescuer. Why did you have to pull me out and make yourself the big hero? Did that start you on your life's path? What path did it give me? I was winning, you tried to pull me back. Then there was another chance for me to be who I thought I was going to be, with Denny. Why couldn't you just leave us alone? Not everything's a race, and not every race is with *you.*

When she reduced the two message windows, the top blue stripe of both showed, with the windows overlapping and cascading, like file folders with variably spaced index tabs. *Eudora – No recipient, no subject..*
Eudora – Dennis Clarkson, no address.

19

> Anyway Denny, I have no idea why I'm dredging all this up, and feeling like I'm sinking. But why am I spiraling? And why now? I had a successful career and have no need to worry about an income for the rest of my life (I hope). I haven't had a seizure in 25 years. (But the last one was a monument. Too bad you weren't there so you could carry it with you forever too.) Maybe I just have nothing to do now. No goals, nothing to accomplish, no one to impress, voluntarily finished, and it causes one to do a lot of nostalgic retrospect — about the stuff I didn't (couldn't) do.
> But I've successfully not thought about you, and I plan to go back to not thinking about you. It's just that you were the occasion for my last seizure, an anniversary in a couple of months. Did you think it was a false alarm — that there never was a zygote? What if I told you, after you decided to abort

everything, *I* was the one aborting — it came out all
over the floor with my piss that night

A blink of her eyes and touch of a finger, she pulled the bottom
message to the front, *No recipient, no subject.*

So Gary, have you ever wondered why Martha is the
only one of us to provide more branches for the
family tree? I have *my* reasons, which you could
never know. Maybe yours are fear of eclipsing yourself
in everybody's eyes with a clone of yourself.
    I'll bet you think I should've thanked you for
arranging to put me together with Denny. As though
you were paying indemnity to me, for ending my
swimming career. I never told Mom. She would've
thought you were being so good. Looking out for
me. Rescuing me from seizure-inducing brooding.
Why couldn't you just leave me and Denny alone?
Why couldn't you just be satisfied being the center
of Mom's universe?

Then she closed her e-mail program. When the software
asked if she would like to send the unsent messages, she
chose no. When it asked if she would like to save and queue
the unsent messages, she selected no. She lowered the
screen of the laptop. The bluish light bled around the edges,
glowing less and less as the screen neared the keyboard,
until there was just a thin beam, a laser, a sunset, that went
out when the laptop made its satisfying and conclusive click.

1974
Even though she was going to ignore Gary's "favor," a note
on her pillow, which meant he'd come into her room, she
nevertheless ended up at the coach's door the next day.

Tam, since your not doing athletics, thought you might
like to stay close, this looks like a good way, a job
as administrative assistant for the swim coach, go
see him tomorrow.

The misuse of *your* evidently not sufficient to prevent him from getting a sportswriting job upon his graduation with a degree in athletic conditioning. Gary's dominance on the swim team wasn't enough to get his victories into the local city paper, and the student body cared only for football. He had completed his last season on the college swim squad, hadn't ever made an Olympic team, his eyes suspiciously red after the last meet. Their parents spoke with him, alone in the den, for over an hour. Tam had never asked what his plans were, now that his competition days were (seemingly) over; it was okay that nobody noticed she hadn't said anything directly to Gary in at least three years. It was Gary's last semester. They'd ended up at the same university for that one year, but Tam disappeared into a freshman class of 10,000.

Denny sat behind a desk that had not stacks of paper covering it but piles — as though a trashcan had been emptied in a ring around a small clear spot where his coffee cup and a chart of the most recent set of his swimmers' lap times shared the spotlight of his ancient-looking gooseneck lamp. The office door was split, so the upper half could be open and the lower half closed. But Tam was tall, so the closed door came only to her waist.

His hair was only about a half inch long, not the usual fashion of the time, but he explained — not that day, but soon afterwards — that he shaved his head for swim season every year, so the swimmers wouldn't feel alone in their abject unstylishness. His eyebrows looked shaped too, but Tam never noticed them grow or change — thin for a man, rakishly angled, matching his tight, dimpled grin, his high cheekbones, his slightly aquiline nose.

After she'd said her name and that she understood he was looking for an administrative assistant, he said "Gary's little sister" once. Only once. They looked at each other. Tam, still on the other side of the cut-in-half door, deciding whether or not to act on her impulse to turn sharply and walk away.

He never broke eye contact. As though waiting for a sign from her. How long did the moment last? Ten seconds or three minutes? His eyes didn't crinkle when he smiled, but darkened or brightened. Darkened and brightened at the same time. Slanted late-afternoon winter sunlight after a storm. A storm that had never broken. The calm after an averted storm. As though the smile was a laugh. As though it was her own smile.

He said, "Come on in." She tried the doorknob. "Reach over." He stood behind the paper-strewn desk. "Only the outside doorknob is locked." He was wearing blue shorts, as most of the athletic personnel did, with their uniform white golf shirts, school name and their particular sport in blue embroidery over the pocket. His legs were shaved. It was a few years after Mark Spitz's hairy chest with his medals spread across it adorned posters. But swimmers shaved in the late 70's.

The rest of the office was a second desk, piled with boxes, and a work table, likewise heaped. By the end of the month, when she'd organized the little room, she knew that the boxes held a variety of odd items no one could explain, like eight track cassettes of The Doors, Henry Mancini, and Christmas music, a textbook for a political science course, a cheerleader pompom, and one size ten Converse All Star basketball shoe. But the desks and boxes were also occupied by old telephones, an already out-of-date IBM Selectric, six or seven coffee cups (some with mold growing at the bottom), numerous rusty and broken trophies, wooden clipboards, boxed stopwatches requisitioned ten years ago and never used, copies of every school newspaper with a swim meet report, official time and placement results from meets — some in loose-leaf notebooks, others stacked or packed indiscriminately — and multiple bound copies of the university code of conduct for athletes for every year starting five years before and going back at least a dozen more years, from long before Denny was the swim coach. She giggled, almost chortled, sometimes had to sit right down on the floor — a strange sensation, déja vu to nothing — as Denny made up stories about the former swim coach and how he might've used some of the mysterious junk she continued to find stashed in file cabinets and desk drawers. The bar-be-cue tools, the Russian-to-English flashcards, the marching band hat.

By the end of May she'd learned to deal with an athletic program budget, to requisition equipment or have bills for services paid, had found desk organizers and a few trash cans and cleared Denny's desk of papers, acquired a new desk lamp, clipboards, a set of metal shelves, and a new coffee maker (Denny had been sending her for tiny paper cups of coffee from a machine that dispensed lukewarm colored water for 25 cents). The end of May was Gary's graduation and she sat in the bleachers of the WPA-built football stadium with her mother, father and Martha (and a horde of other families) to watch the processional march of five thousand black-robed graduates, most of whom had decorated their caps with balloons or flowers, even an umbrella, or objects indicating their major — a model of an atom, a papier mache trumpet — to identify themselves in the crowd. Gary had a contraption built over his hat with two bright yellow swim fins and a spray of blue and white crepe paper like a splash of water.

Before Gary joined them afterwards, Tam left, saying she had to go to work. Denny had asked her to help him with a personal project. "I have to visit my parents and need a buffer zone," he'd said on Friday.

Denny's car, a VW convertible, was too loud for conversation, for guessing where they were going, for laughing at the hint he gave before starting the engine, "Did I forget to tell you? In addition to ten hours a week, part of your job is to help me use my monthly pass at Club Dread. Not a free pass either, it says in the fine print, what you don't pay in time you'll give up in personal dignity." It was the way he said it, mock seriously from behind aviator sunglasses, with his geeky short hair, buckling himself into a light blue Volkswagen, putting down the vinyl top. And, beyond geeky, wearing pennyloafers without socks. Men wouldn't commonly put bare feet into leather shoes until the late 80's or 90's. She'd been jolted the first time she saw a man in boat shoes with no socks, the first time since Denny, and jolted in a different way than the beginning-of-summer smile she felt herself wearing in 1975 as she watched his bare ankles and loafers working the gas, brake and clutch of the Volkswagen.

"They always want me to be a guest at their beloved tennis club," he'd said when they arrived in the parking lot. Not an exclusive country club, it was an anyone-can-join pay-to-use facility, kin to a YMCA. "My parents call it *The Club*," Denny said. "Maybe that's the explanation — they've been pounded over the head until they're retarded."

"Come on, they can't be that bad."

"Just wait."

23

Tennis courts, indoor racquetball and handball courts, men's and women's locker rooms, and a pool. Denny and Tam went through the building, past the two locker rooms without pausing at either one, and out the back doors onto the pool deck that was surrounded by a chain link fence and boxwood hedges clipped to the height of the fence. The pool was Olympic sized, with set-aside times for those wanting to swim laps, the rest called "splash-n-dive" on the posted schedule. A few women lay in recliners, one with her face covered by a book, the other on her stomach, head buried in her arms. In the pool, two people, standing in waist-deep water. The tiled sides and bottom were traditional aqua, the water surface glinting, throwing sun spots into Tam's eyes. She fumbled for her sunglasses. The man's hair was shockingly white, combed straight back in a poofy bouffant, country singer style, completely unmussed by his entry into the water. Broad shouldered with the beginning of a paunch, abundant gray hair on his chest. The woman wore a one-piece suit with a little skirt that the water held up like the pedals of a flower around her waist. On her head a cap with multi-colored flowers growing all over it, flowers that matched the pedals of the swimsuit skirt. The water so clear, the lane lines were crisp and distinct beneath the people's feet. The woman pointed her foot and ran her toe over the smooth black stripe. Above the water, the woman and man were beaming, even laughing aloud, as they tossed a beach ball back and forth, laughing louder if they caught the ball the same time it splatted on the calm water in front of them.

"What indescribable fun," Denny murmured. Tam might've been about to stifle a giggle, when he added, "Ever wish you were adopted?"

Tam looked down, removed her sunglasses to clean them on her shirt. She was wearing the flared green slacks, sandals and pullover top she'd worn to the graduation. The polyester top only smeared the glasses. She already knew it would. The slacks hugged her butt. She knew that too. She heard Denny, as though in the distance, introducing her, calling her *my student assistant*.

"Come on in, the water's fine!" the man called in a baritone sing-song, as though parodying something. The woman laughed as if she'd learned how somewhere, maybe for a play.

"Okay," Denny murmured, kicking off his shoes. "Time for us to get in there and look like we're frolicking with as much delight and glee. Or die trying."

Tam dropped her sunglasses, bent to pick them up. Wondering if she was having trouble catching her breath. Maybe it took forever for her to gasp, "What?"

He was stepping out of his shorts. "They expect us to play with them."

"*Us*?"

Underneath his shorts, a school-logo speedo from the university swim team. "I thought you wouldn't mind playing along, once you got here. They're so stupid it could almost be funny." He removed his shirt. It was the first time she saw his chest. The ideal swimmer's inverted triangle, the ultimate swimmer's washboard, hairless, the color of light wood, not tanned to leather. But she noticed his anatomy like a fact, one she wouldn't appreciate or relish until a later day when she would ask him how he could wear the tiny, revealing speedo in front of his mother.

Her mouth was dry. She put her sunglasses back on. "You expected me to be wearing a suit under my clothes, all the time, like an extra skin?"

"I'm sorry. I forgot, most people don't."

By this time she was smiling again, because he was standing with his back to the pool, facing her, blocking her view of the beach ball game that continued above the surface of the rippled, glinting water. And he was holding her hands.

Aviator glasses on top of his peach fuzz head, his eyes at once earnest and amused, his cheeks slightly flushed, his lips halfway pursed, fighting an outright laugh.

Tam said, "You look like a pro athlete who can't do his skit on Saturday Night Live without cracking up."

"That's exactly what this is. See how you understand already? Please, Tam, I need you. Just take off your sandals and roll up your pants and—"

"No."

"—sit on the deck—"

"No." She stopped smiling. He was still holding her hands, tugging her toward the edge of the pool. "My pants will get wet."

"—splash your feet—"

"No." She tried to twist her hands free but he held fast.

25

"—pretend you've been in a dungeon for ten years and this is the first time you've seen sunlight and touched water."

"Denny, I can't—"

"*Please*. Just consider it part of your job, to ensure my mental health."

They stood frozen for a second, and he must've sensed something. He dropped her hands, used both of his to lift her sunglasses. "Tam? Anyone home?" The splashing and laughing in the pool had also stopped. When she turned and left, she left her sunglasses in his hands.

But not for long. She only sat in the warm, dusty-smelling VW for a few minutes before he got into the driver's side, dressed again in his shorts, golf shirt and loafers. She hadn't been crying. She turned to him so he could see that.

"I'm sorry," he said. "Does this have something to do with over-stepping my boundaries as your employer?"

"No." The word just landed between them like a stone. He wasn't facing at her, which was unusual. He seemed like a guy on a bad date, wishing he could disappear, so she added. "Please don't ever think— Don't think that."

He looked at her, but didn't speak. He looked miserable.

"Just a bad combination of things, for me," she said. "I don't swim anymore."

"I knew that. Gary said—"

"I don't mean competitive, I mean ever."

"I never considered anything about this to be *swimming*. Gary said—"

"Nothing he's ever said about me counts — for *anything*. Don't even tell me, I don't want to know how he described it."

"How he described what?"

She looked at her hands, folded properly in her lap. "I have epilepsy. I don't ever go into the water. I have to be careful. I keep things at an even keel. Sometimes I even wonder if all the laughing I've done lately with you— Well, anyway, they don't let me take meds anymore because it's been too long since the last seizure. But that also means I could have another grand mal at any time.

"Does water cause seizures?"

"No, but if I seized in water, after all the ugly part, I would probably drown. Didn't Gary ..." She looked away, her eyes smarting, as though she *had* gone in.

"You said I'm supposed to forget anything he said." The smile that was not quite there was pulling at his mouth.

"Didn't he tell you, if I swim when he's not there, there'll be no one to save me?"

"How about me?"

"How can you always be there? Gary, unfortunately, will always be my brother."

The bewilderment was in the half-smile he finally showed. "So you won't even get your feet wet? You get upset if—"

"Besides not wanting to drown ... not that way ... not *any* way, but not *that* way ..." Tam squeezed her folded hands tighter together, staring down at them again. "Also ... I've lost my touch, lost my edge, lost my place. I certainly wouldn't be able to beat Gary now. So I just won't go in. Period."

"Why doesn't this make sense to me?"

"I know, it's all gotten mixed up. I don't know. I'm sorry I got upset."

"Have you had a lot of seizures?"

"One was too many. But I've had two. I was 12."

"And you haven't been in a pool since?"

"No. See? It worked." She smiled, brighter than she felt, but to help him. "Anyway, maybe too much chlorine *would* cause a seizure. That pool was *too* damn clear. Beyond clear. Practically effervescent."

Denny became Denny again, his face bright, his world bursting with amusement. "Are you kidding? My mom probably rented a lab and did a complete water chemistry analysis before she let my dad sign the membership check. Believe me, there's not a single, lonely germ in that pool, or *she* wouldn't be in there. You wanna know how nuts about germs she is? I wasn't allowed to buy ice cream from a neighborhood truck because she said it was dirty."

"Did she mean the foreign-looking man driving the truck?"

"Hell no, in those days it was a white guy with a complete white suit and black bow tie! But she did tell me to always wash my hands after touching the stairway banister at my grade school. That just happened to be when the school was becoming ... mixed, she called it."

"Wow. Where's she from?"

"Didn't you hear her accent?"

"No, she didn't say anything, just laughed. And your dad, what is he, some sort of actor?"

"Yeah. Acting like life is grand, he's seizing-the-day," Denny used an imitation of his father's ornate style. "He used to do community theater and put on that bogus voice so often it stuck, just like my mom told me if I made a pig face too much my face would freeze that way. Except she says pig in two syllables. Pee-ug."

Tam was giggling. Denny's hand was on her leg. Then he took her hand and laced her fingers with his.

After that, Gary seemed more forgotten than hanging silently in the air between them. Except the one time, later, when Gary made himself impossible to ignore. He wasn't even a student anymore, but he had come back. Why was he looking for her? Or had he been following her for a while? Could he sense the aura? About a week later, Denny made his decision. And neither one there to save her from the abrupt — and bloody — finale. It could've been a baby, and the third seizure had ended that too.

The picture of Denny she'd taken from the office, she never hung it in her apartment when she got settled in Chicago, nor in her business suite, nor in the condo she eventually bought. She wanted to, or thought she did, but when she took it out and looked at it under fluorescent lights, the flicker, the buzz, 28   the glare on the frame made her drop the picture so she could close her eyes, calm her heartbeat, count slow deep breaths and soothe the menacing hum between her ears. The first, solid evidence that Denny would forever be linked with the aura stage. She put the picture away. Into a box that included her swimming trophies and scrapbooks.

1978
It did not end where the ending began. McDonalds was just off campus, but not a place an athlete usually liked to eat, especially a vegetarian. Tam and Denny ordinarily went to a Greek cafe, mostly carry-out, but a few small tables on a linoleum floor, scattered with old issues of *The Reader*, often opened to the personal ads, and Tam would read them aloud — *SWM, 9", seeks fun-loving SWF for walks and snuggles. Try-it-u'll-like-it* — over salad with feta cheese and olives, and their favorite, spanokopeta, since they had decided to become vegetarians the previous year.

"Every few years I get this craving for French fries that won't quit," Denny had said. Was his grin forced, or was that on retrospect?

"They're fried in lard, aren't they?"

"That's what makes them so attractive, the taboo, the lure of animal fat."

But he hadn't stopped with fries; he'd ordered a Big Mac with cheese. Tam tried to stay true and at least avoided the beef; she got a fish sandwich, but she knew the block of pasteurized fish flakes was cooked on the same grill as the burgers. She held it with thumb and one finger — Denny said her hand looked like a crab's claw holding a sandwich — and peered at it, waiting to see if she would feel as queasy as she knew she ought.

"Greek food is greasy too," Denny said. "That filo dough has to be fried."

"I know." She put her fish sandwich down on the tray. "I wish Kung Food would open a place nearer to school."

Denny took a huge bite of hamburger. "Is tofu really as sexy as everyone's making it out to be?"

"How about almond butter and honey on whole wheat? That's pretty sensuous."

"Sounds like sticky paste on cardboard."

McDonalds was teeming at noon on a school day. Tam 29 and Denny had one small table, not a booth, more an island on a pillar, with two stools on pillars bolted to the floor on either side. Other toadstool tables and chairs lining up beside and around them, all brisk with students, either alone and trying to balance an open textbook along with a tray on the tiny table, or in pairs and threes. The restaurant awash with mumbling din, peaked periodically with a spike of laughter, or a shout to someone recognized across the room.

"You don't like your fish thing?" Denny asked.

"I don't think I feel well," Tam had said, even though she couldn't locate any curl of nausea.

Denny looked around as he chewed, then took another bite. With his mouth full, he said, "Um ... I think ... well ... reality's come knocking ... don't you think ... ?"

"Meaning ..." She pushed a finger into the top bun of the fish sandwich, "health food's all a sham? Or ..." She looked up suddenly. One of Denny's cheeks bulged out as he chewed. His elbows on the tiny table, his hands holding the remaining portion of his burger steady in front of his face, his eyes focused there, on the food, not on her. She said, "Yeah, I know who was knocking on the door. So *what*?"

He'd been working on that mouthful a long time. "I have to ..." He swallowed but continued chewing without taking another bite. "I can't ..." He swallowed again, put the hamburger down and picked up his soda, held the cup and drank from the straw, his eyes closed, until the last of the liquid rattled. He hadn't even touched the French fries that had supposedly provoked this whole lunch.

"I just ... can't risk this," he'd said.

"*This*? What's that supposed to mean?"

With the straw, he poked at the ice still in his cup. Looked down at what he was doing as though he were fixing a watch. "That ... I think we should go our separate ways. I think now's the best time."

"Now? Now that I'm ..."

"Look, we sneak around, we ... on the floor of my office. What kind of person is that for you to be with?"

"It's a person I ..." She couldn't be the first to say *love*. She abruptly crumpled her untouched sandwich inside its wrapper.

"Look, it was fun, a *lot* of fun, but ... I ... Think about it ... I'm a big bum. You're graduating, your degree's in, what, finance?" Suddenly a succession of words coming out of him, and now he was looking at her. "You'll get a much better job at a bank or something, you don't need to be saddled with a floundering swim coach at a school considering doing away with swimming so they can give more of the bucks to football."

"Is that what this is about? You don't have to support us."

"Tam, don't. Maybe you shouldn't have been with me in the first place. If anyone had known or found out ... Maybe someone already does ..."

"You mean *Gary*?"

Denny didn't answer.

"I can't believe this ...."

"I know how bad it seems. But you'll forget this, Tam, in no time. By this time next month, you'll be able to look forward and see yourself a year from now, two years from now—"

"And twenty years from now, it'll be after 2000, so damn what?"

"Shhh, Tam, come on. We both knew ..."

By then she was crying. Actually gulping hiccups to forestall crying, but tears and snot obliterating not only her vision but any semblance of composure. She pushed greasy napkins into her eye sockets, smelled ketchup, felt a clammy shred of lettuce on her cheek and angrily snatched it away with her other hand.

"I'm sorry, but I have to think about my career going nowhere fast. If, or when, I have to get another position, I can't afford any kind of ... thing on my reputation."

"Thing? It's not a *thing*."

Maybe he didn't even understand her, through the blubbering. By then, his strategy, if that's what it had been, of doing it in public so there wouldn't be a scene, had broken down. After sweeping the trash and food from their table onto a tray and leaving Tam alone, head down, crying, to throw it all away, Denny draped her sweater over her head and led her from the McDonalds like a prisoner who doesn't want to be recorded on TV cameras. He kept his arm around her, and she submitted, let herself be guided through campus, seeing only her own feet, sunny sidewalks, and grass when Denny took shortcuts. She recognized the wooden steps to the old gym's auxiliary building where the swim team office was located. She recognized the cool smell of their dark office, the tiny aisle leading around the file cabinets, and she let her knees buckle there, curled into a fetal position on their mattress, no thought to her dignity, she wept, then quieted when Denny lay beside her. Neither of them said anything for an hour or more.

31

Then Denny whispered he had a meeting with the assistant athletic director, would she be okay alone for an hour?

Tam nodded. He didn't kiss her when he left. He rustled softly in the outer office for a moment, but didn't turn on any lights. When he left, he closed the office door with a soft click.

Tam thought she kept her eyes closed for the entire hour Denny was away, but she didn't sleep. A clock somewhere in the office was ticking. She'd never noticed it before. The air system came on and off. Students in the hall of the old building went past the door with brassy laughter and boisterous voices, swelling then receding as they passed the door. Her brain chanted in rhythm with the phantom clock, *He won't leave me, he won't leave me.*

When Denny gently returned, as though to a sick room, there was nothing more to say, but they said it all again anyway.

"I don't know why you're doing this."

"Tam, I could get fired."

"For what? You're a good coach."

"A good coach who boffs his student help."

"I thought we ... cared about each other."

"We did. We do. That's why we have to do what's best for each other now."

"This isn't best for *me*."

"It seems bad now, but look at the big picture, someday-"

"That's crap. That's such crap. You're being wretched. You're horrible."

It went on and on. She would cry. He would stroke her like a dying animal. She would calm a little. They would be quiet for a while. Then they started over. Her face was a puffy, slimy horror. Her blouse and skirt wrinkled, damp with sweat. She could smell the rank distress seeping from her pores. The aura had never been a smell. In fact, three years with Denny, four years off her meds, sometimes she'd almost forgotten about it, frequently forgot to be on guard for signs of loss of stability. So the stench of terror exuding from her body that afternoon didn't warn her. Didn't warn her enough.

32

2001

Dear Denny,

I never told you everything. About my first seizure. About Gary saving my life (and ending it). I would've beat him. It was just practice. But I was winning. After I seized and he pulled me up, he *still* hit the lip, got his time, beat me. Saved me *and* won. I couldn't let him save me -- or beat me -- again. But when he sent me to you ... maybe I let him do both. That's why now that Gary's the one who's in trouble, I
Ctrl+A Del

Gary's not winning this time, he's
Ctrl+A Del

I don't know whether I'm going back to help him or running away again
Ctrl+A Del

Dear Denny,
You were afraid Gary had found out about us. But he needed help that day. And we didn't answer his knock.
Ctrl+A Del

1978
Because she'd been crying for more than an hour since Denny left the office, when the seizure first started, she thought it was still just the wobbly fatigue of feral sobbing. For a second she may have registered how dangerous this was, this kind of unrestrained discharge of sorrow, persisting despite abject exhaustion. All before her cognizance was gone too. But there may have been five seconds, as she was drawn into the curl of a wave of lightheaded void, when her perception moved from weeping to *oh no, I can't, not now,* and then to nothing.

What happened in between, and how long it actually was, she could only guess subsequently, when she came-to in the sticky, twisted, putrid aftermath. Where had she been beforehand? She hadn't stayed sobbing on the mattress behind the file cabinets. If she had, the whole mess could've been dragged out the door and disposed of, neatly. But she'd been at his desk. Couldn't stay on the mattress that smelled of him, and of them together. So she'd walked, wailing, around the office, and ended sitting at his desk. That's why she found herself under his desk, or half under, her body cranked around and between the legs of the chair, her face glued with blood and drool to a short leg of the old wooden desk, the back of her skull in the cleft between the bottom drawer and the coarse industrial carpet. And as though someone had placed her mouth to protect her tongue, her teeth were clamped on the desk's leg. It hadn't completely saved her tongue, though. Her old scars were bleeding.

Her first awareness was only where her head was. The rest of her body not yet retrieved. Then she located her hands, at the ends of contorted arms. One arm straight but twisted almost 360 degrees, most of that arm plunged into the metal trashcan, lying on its side, her hand buried in the rubbish, as though searching for something she'd discarded but now needed to recover. Her other arm was ratcheted under her

33

back, her bunched fist was the knot she was beginning to feel against her spine.

She'd started trying to move before she discovered the extent of her body's purge. She pulled her arms in like bird wings, then pushed her palms against the carpet to slide out from under the desk. Her head hung like a puppet with a broken string. When she tried to get up or crawl away from the desk, her knees ripped away from a gluey wetness. She rolled her hips to a sitting position. Her skirt, dark and damp, was scrunched against her thighs, her skin stained with streaks and caked dried blood, and between her legs a viscous black puddle. During the seizure, her thrashing legs had spread the mess, and her hands must have been in it too, because smears and streaks painted the side of the desk, the seat of the chair, and the carpet in a body-length radius. Hands on the rug on either side of her hips, she pushed herself back away from it, her feet dragging through until she found the muscles to lift her shoes over the thicker clumps. It took every determined kernel of force she'd ever used to burn through the last 50 yards of a freestyle race, just to pull her feet under her weight and then push on her legs to stand, holding onto the back of the chair, her arms joining in the strain to right her body. Her eyes never left the stain, the disaster left under the desk. Although her guts felt heavy, leaden, pulling on her to let her body return to the floor, she also knew there was a vacuum inside her now, whatever had been in there was gone.

34

2001
Dear Denny,
He was looking for me because he thought I'd be the only one who would understand what was happening to him. And maybe I was

We Made a Run of It
Lindsey Gosma

I.
Autumn has dropped off to winter,
pulled back like the corner of the Lover's
Knot quilt you watched me piece for our bed.
We spoke not nearly as much
as I wanted while I worked. You,
content to tinker with some scrap of metal,
some bit of paper. We always had to keep
our hands occupied, mouths,
open slightly with measured intent,
like my breath, when I ran the last mile.
You watched from the window
that last day, air not fighting my lungs.
It is such a quiet task, running, a game
played with the wind and trees:
a disappearing, first, from our bed,
then, from the orchard's ear. Even now,
you see me curl in the corner chair,
muscles, I know, weakening.

II.
I felt you shuffle out of bed
cool summer mornings, before humidity
sat down like some tired fruit picker,
an old widow with calloused hands
from years of reaching, cutting, in the orchard

where you run, mornings like this, alone,
for an hour both of us nearly silent
except for the fall of breath. It is almost
sunrise now and you should return like always,
like cicadas, apple blooms, or harvests.

But today, like the past twelve weeks,
a seasons' worth of weeks, since you left
for drier heat, later mornings, a cooler bed,
you will not slip through the kitchen door,
click the lock, softly to not wake me,
restless until that very lock clicks,
for twelve weeks if that is just how long
it takes to imagine the fall of fruit,
anything to mark a presence
like cicadas or apple blooms.

Only Now, the Arriving
                    Lindsey Gosma

When I leave this place, in evening,
in summer's humid breath at dusk,
I will take with me the coming
musk of fall, wind from the mountain,
and late blue grasses. I will take
memories of whiskey my father drank
on evenings not nearly as stifling as this.

I crouch in darkness, to hide from starlight,
I will shoulder my mother's stories,
her childhood with the hint of tobacco
still in her hair. I carry
such a history in my skin, an old
hound could tell where I've been
and am off to. Even now I cannot find
the same good reasons to drift away.

I can only take what I have the keys to,
I can only leave behind what
others will make their lives of.
As I set off, there is only now
the arriving, always the turning-
over of history. I am leaving now,
the chill of the harvest at my back.

The Story I Would Tell You
                    Aaron Landsman

The guy next to me is wearing a light yellow short-sleeved dress shirt and a dark blue tie. When I first sit down he's reading a pocket-sized novel, but soon he gets his briefcase from under the seat in front of him, opens it on the tray table and almost imperceptibly sighs. He pulls out a stapled set of spreadsheets, puts the briefcase back, starts fingering charts and making notes on certain figures. *Projected Growth*, it says on each page, *Second Quarter.*

Normally, traveling, I fixate on the mundane details of other people's lives, sure that if I dig deep enough I'll discover their hidden, underneath passions; for this reason I am usually too friendly to my row-mates on flights. "Regional Supervisor," I'll say. "Sounds intense." Usually, I end up with the long details of someone's infidelities or a litany of minor workplace injustices.

This time I'm just trying to keep it together. I pull on my beard, fumble with my peanuts, the guy notices me staring, stops closing up his tray for takeoff. If you were here you'd make me wear my glasses and fix my hair.

You broke things a lot. Dishes, lamps, glass trinkets on mantles, picture frames, the occasional window. Usually it was just distraction, a misplaced elbow. You would apologize, but in a sort of off-handed way that was exasperating. I used to joke that I was going to end up with a house full of Tupperware, that soon we'd be eating soup out of former peanut butter tubs, drinking milk from yogurt containers, and every night would be a picnic or a barbecue on paper plates. I'd get calls after you'd visited somewhere, from friends who had agreed to put you up, complaining. And I'd write a check. Some of them bounced. I think it was important to me to feel myself acting like a father should, even if there wasn't anything in the account.

Mr. Sales Growth and I are pressed against the seat backs. Detroit diminishes below us. If he asked me something about myself today I would tell him this: You could say I lived for my daughters, but everyone says that about their kids; I actually enjoyed it. I liked to think I was showing them the world, but the whole time they were leading me: New York to see their old babysitter; Nebraska to see my folks; Mexico for a vacation. Hop in the van and go. They aren't twins but they have that kind of symbiosis. Language is almost unnecessary between them because they understand right away. Tessa is three years younger, more focused. She puts more pressure on herself to excel. Parker's more like me. Was. When is that normal to say?

Two days ago, a state trooper called and said that you had been in an accident and was I sitting down. He said you and two other people were killed, one your travel companion who may or may not have been your boyfriend, one in the other car. The driver of the other car walked away. You had been asleep after an all-nighter on the road, and somewhere along the line someone lost control, they still weren't sure. The state trooper said how sorry he was, and how, "We get an embarrassing amount of fatalities in New Mexico since they did away with the speed limit." He was very nice. He said it was instantaneous and you didn't suffer. "She probably never knew." You were about to turn 21.

"Folks, from up in the flight deck… We're at about 24,000 feet, heading to a cruising altitude of 35,000…. passing just west of the Chicago area…flight route'll take us over Kansas, and Southeastern Colorado before we make our de-scent over the Oklahoma panhandle and into Albuquerque… ought to have smooth sailing all the way, so I'm gonna turn the seatbelt sign off, though we do recommend that while you're in your seats you keep 'em

fastened nice and tight around you. For now, sit back, relax and enjoy the excellent service provided by our award-winning cabin crew..."

He said they found your driver's license in your pocket and I told him I didn't want to see your body because I didn't want my last image of my daughter to be a broken one. I told him I didn't want an investigation, and wouldn't press charges; can you imagine, I said, finding out a month or a year later that it had been someone else's fault. Or yours. Who would that save? He didn't respond, then said he understood. He gave me the number of the boy's parents, suggested maybe we could coordinate our pickup since we were both coming in from out of town. He said it might be good to have some company on a trip like this.

So they're cremating you, and I'll meet them and we'll rent a car at the airport and go together to get the ashes. The state trooper will not be at the morgue, and I wish he were because I want something at least a little familiar in this absolute, inexplicable situation I'm flying into. Then I'll be back home tonight, and everyone will be waiting for me. Tessa will be there. She'll stay with Kristin, their mother, across town.

The guy is napping now, mouth open, head lolling, *Projected Sales Growth* splayed on his lap. I haven't done anything this whole flight except stare. I keep imagining your last moment: headlights, a lurch, no time to even scream. A celluloid loop that becomes more and more abstract; it projects me away from the actualities.

Because if I stop and think of one real thing for too long, it will be this map of your shards that I've followed across the country, willingly, for years. I will fill an airsick bag with my tears and we will have to make an emergency landing, because the weight of my sorrow will bring down this plane.

You had a place in you I couldn't get beyond. You traveled a lot after 'taking some time off' as everyone who drops out of college says. Like I did when I dropped out. I figured I did okay, why shouldn't you? I'd get calls from places where I didn't even know you *had* friends, then I'd call Tess and she'd fill me in: You went to LA and got a job at a jewelry store, and were going to learn how to make rings. You went to Hawaii for a yoga retreat with a guy named John. You were determined so I didn't try to interfere. For so long Kristin and I were proud we'd raised an independent girl, a woman who could take care of herself.

"Folks, First Off'cer Wilcox up in flight deck...uh, we're cleared for final 'proach into Albuquerque...ought to have y'at the jetway in just a few minutes... flight attendants 'pare doors for 'rival."

I don't know how I'll recognize the parents of the boy you were with. They're coming in from Hartford. Jim and Sue Brennan. Benson? Brenneman. I stupidly tried to make small talk with them on the phone. Mr. Brenneman said he'd rent the car and we'd meet up at Avis, very authoritatively.

The reverse thrusters roar us slower down the runway. When we stop at the gate, Sales Growth stirs, wipes his eyes and his lips, shuffles his papers into a stack. He looks at me, blinking, his face asking, 'Did I reveal something?' or 'Who are you?' I can't tell which.

41

The stewardess and the pilot are standing back in the recess by the exit door: *"g'bye... g'bye!...thanks! g'bye!...bu-bye!...thanks! g'bye!..."* She catches my eye, I make the mistake of meeting her gaze, and I realize that as the truth has been sinking in more and more during the flight I must look crazier than when I got on. I half stop to say something to her and she stutters a little at the sight of me, then nods and says, *"'Kay,"* ushering me through for the sake of the line behind.

Albuquerque International is all done up in adobe and clay tile. The trinket shops are named *Spirit Gift*. Families in matching pastels run straight from the arrival gates to the Starbucks, where there's a special on Strawberry Frappucinos.

The air outside is dry and cool and I want to walk and walk so this imaginary conversation with you can go on until the sun sets. I'll go back to Detroit and my brothers will be there, my mom and Tessa and Kristin. And I'll walk in empty-handed and shrug my shoulders and say "We had a great time in New Mexico."

A friend who recently buried his father told me I had better be prepared for the ashes, because it's not a fine, gray, cigarette-style soot like they sprinkle over the ocean in movies, at least not all of it. There will be fragments of bone, teeth, maybe the metal button off a coat. I'd rather drive to my own cremation.

On the shuttle bus to the rental lot, there is a couple holding hands and staring straight ahead. They are neatly dressed, and almost totally coordinated in navy, burgundy and white, to the point where, at first they look like a pilot and stewardess couple and for a second I think to myself, *'that is so romantic.'* I imagine they have been on separate routes for a week, him covering the Japan-San Francisco run, her running quick jaunts between Dallas and Greenville. They have been staying alone in nameless airport hotels, the take-offs and landings disrupting their restless sleep; when the runways shut down it's too quiet, and the bed is so terribly empty. Finally they have scheduled a couple days getaway in Santa Fe together and now, here they are, clinging to each other with amorous expectation.

But they aren't wearing ID badges or name tags. The deep navy of his suit matches her skirt and the red stripe on her hat matches his tie. His cufflinks and her earrings. His shoes, her handbag. They look miserable. If those aren't airline uniforms, it can only mean one thing: Connecticut.

"Are you the Brennemans?"

"Mr. Wade?" Her voice is firm with effort.

"Call me Tom." My eyes well, they look away, and the bus swings around a corner, then the other way, and then we clunk across the spikes that keep you from backing out of the rental lot. I pull myself together. "So you got in okay."

"Not bad." His words are clipped as short as his fingernails.

The airbrakes exhale loudly and the doors open. Mr. Brenneman leaps out, with his briefcase, Mrs. Brenneman follows, and I come after them. I stand outside for a moment, then go in. Mr. Brenneman is arguing with the counter-person, a chubby young woman with braces. It's a two-hour ride to the morgue near a town called Torreon.

"Hey, do you want to include me as a driver, so we can share the driving?"

He turns. "Not on our credit card."

Mrs. Brenneman follows me outside. We stand and look at the sky for a few minutes until Mr. Brenneman comes out.

"Aisle 17," he says, "Tan Neon."

"How should we settle this up?"

He's walking a few steps ahead, and doesn't turn. "It's fine."

"I have cash if you want. " He says nothing, disappearing down our row.

Next to me, he drives too slowly along the interstate while I hold the map. His wife sits facing the window in back. New pick-ups rush by, jacked up on big wheels. Salvaged wrecks blow smoke across the lanes. The pink-orange mesa leans away, then turns to scrub hills dotted with caves and listing shacks.

"So, you're in accounting, I understand."

"Yes."

"That must be..." *What must it be? I don't know.* "I'm a photographer. Architecture and interiors mostly. But it takes me all over."

"Uh uh."

"It pays the bills."

Then the road settles into its surging, tacking rhythm for a long time, past the point where someone could break the silence easily to the point where someone will have to make an obvious effort. It's Mrs. Brenneman who is the most valiant of us. "There must be a lot of strong personalities in that," she tries out.

"I guess. It meant I got to show the girls a lot of the country."

After another silence she asks, "Why were our children together?"

I am in instinctive 'nice' mode, making small talk before I know it. My coping mechanism. "I think they met in California or something. Greg right? I kind of lost track of all the places she had been recently."

"I see."

"I like to think I have influence but it's not always true. I'd tell her I was worried. She'd say she was fine."

"Maybe we aren't so different, then," she says.

43

He glares at her in the mirror. "Maggie – "

She looks out the window. He's white knuckling the steering wheel. *Always the peacemaker, I ask them,* "So does Greg have brothers and sisters?"

No good. She chirps out a tiny, high sound that she clips off with her breath as if she wanted it back when she heard it. I turn around and she has a hand over her mouth, her eyebrows raised. I try to fix it. *Stupid.* "I'm sorry, I – "

"I have a daughter from a previous marriage. We don't speak," Mr. Brenneman says without taking his eyes off the road. I notice the gray at his temples, the slight thinning on his crown. He is quite a bit older than her. My mind jumps on the possibilities. *Secretary? Tennis buddy's daughter? Anything to take me out of this car into someone else's life.*

I say, "I'll stop prying...Parker was clumsy. She takes after me."

I hear ruffling. Mrs. Brenneman is composing herself, smoothing out her skirt, removing her hat and fixing her hair. "I should apologize," she says.

"No, you - "

"I wish we could have called them or something, you know. I think sometimes that you are supposed to have premonitions when something bad happens, and sometimes if it's real enough and you trust it, you just, you call in time, you just call to check in and they are fine and they think you're crazy, and you do too, and none of you ever knows that you saved your kids' life, but you just woke them up long enough to, you know?"

"Right."

"Lives, I guess. Hers too."

"Thanks."

She recovers herself and says, "Couldn't you have taught her some self-control," and half-laughs it away.

"Excuse me?"

He shoots her another look – "Maggie!"

I say, "I trusted her."

Mrs. Brenneman forces a sigh through her teeth, then says, "I think I'll just stretch out back here for a minute," And curls across the backseat.

We exit onto a smaller road that winds upward into the hills and forest. Now Mr. Brenneman seems to enjoy speeding around the curves. The kids were driving Greg's van, which I think Parker told me was a hand-me-down. He'd taken the seats out and put down a futon. I wonder if he liked driving fast, too.

Mr. Brenneman says, "I have a 733 at home that'd be great on these roads." I look across at him; he's still staring straight ahead. "I keep wanting to downshift, you know?"

"A 733?"

"BMW 733i."

"Sorry. I'm not up on cars."

"It's a lot of fun." His wife has fallen asleep, impervious to the turns. "She sleeps through anything," he says.

It's always foreign to me, what two men talk about, alone in situations like these. I say, "I like driving, too."

"What do you drive?"

"I have a van…for work. I travel a lot and the girls – I used to take them everywhere I could."

"I see."

Sage flowers line the shoulder, a lavender blur. There's a logging truck behind us, losing ground on the up hills, bearing down on the descents. Your tendency to drift drew me toward you. "I'm sorry if I said something – "

45

"Maggie wanted to have another child," he says, glancing at her. "As if that would make things easier right now."

"No. It wouldn't. I have another daughter."

"Have to tell Maggie that. I said I already had one other child and we couldn't afford everything for two more that we wanted to give them."

"I wish I had thought like that." I say unconsciously. And what, not have had Tessa?

"It does make sense to plan ahead."

I don't think I have ever had the experience of actually counting my blessings but I am doing that now. For my brothers who'll be back there at my house as soon as their shifts are over, 24-pack of Miller in hand, sitting on my couch and trying very very hard to make jokes, and cooking a big beef stew for everyone. For Tessa, even Kristin. For my mother with her soft face. For none of us ever planning anything ahead.

"When she was 15," I start saying–I want him to know this–"she came and woke me up to confess a whole list of worries. She'd been out walking around the neighborhood; it was 2:00 AM—this is Detroit, you know, not a safe place to be walking around then—but she was fearless about it—"

"Real firecracker, huh."

"She told me she had tried acid, and her friend Carla did it every weekend and it scared her. She told me she'd fallen in love with a boy who'd stopped calling, and she wondered what she'd done wrong. She was glad Kristin and me weren't together any more. All this in one long stream of words and tears. I was reeling a little, you know, but so proud of myself, that my daughter would bring this all to me. I don't know when she started keeping things to herself."

"Huh," he says, then, "sounds like you guys were real close."

We're approaching the smaller road that leads to the one morgue. I point out the turn off and Mr. Brenneman slows down a bit for the last stretch.

He says, "Do you know where the accident was?"

"I bet we could find out. Do you want to go see it?"

"I wish I had a couple days here, you know? Beautiful country."

"Mmm. You can't take more time?"

"It's tax season. At the level I'm at, it's impossible to get any time off. Part of me was even thankful at first in a weird way that the accident timed out so we were coming here on a Friday. I thought that we could stay the weekend, but then I realized we'd have the ashes with us so that didn't make sense." He's saying all this without turning to me.

"Greg seemed like a great kid when I talked to him," I say. All I remember is a sort of high voice, a little nervous in that 'girlfriend's-father-on-the-phone' way. He said, 'Parker's, uh, in the shower, can she call you back.' I said, 'Sure,' and that was it.

"He was great. He was." He turns to me finally and stops the car before the driveway we have to enter. He clears his throat. "He was a good kid. I loved him a lot." Clears his throat again. Eases the car into the drive. Scans for a parking spot and pulls up, then turns to me. "I don't want to wake her. Do you want to just do this with me? She'll kill me but I'd hate – she'd hate to have a breakdown in there, she – we get embarrassed."

"I think this is one of those things you don't want to face alone," I say.

"Well *you* are." He turns back, his hands still on the

wheel as if he's driving, as if he's got something to look at. I am unconsciously running the rental car's electric window up and down. Something to do with my hands.

"Maybe they loved each other," I say. "Maybe they were in love and they were driving east as fast as they could to tell us all about it." And out of my mouth comes a little laugh so unfamiliar it sounds like it's coming from someone else. A game show host or a used car salesman. A laugh that is politely trying to garner support for a theory, but already knows it's no use; a little 'hah-hah', already stillborn in the tan Neon's air.

He says, "Don't tell Maggie that."

You coward. You accountant. You Connecticut.

"Look, Tom." He's pleading with me. "Let's go just do this. She'll give me hell but – "

I stare at him until he trails off. He turns to face forward again.

Maybe someone will know who we are and deliver the ashes to the car like an A & W drive-up morgue. Maybe Maggie will wake up and have a scene. Maybe I will slow my heart enough to tell this man how lucky I feel. Felt. Maybe you will come walking out of there whole, your jaw set, your eyes piercing all of us with such deliberate honesty. Or was that a way to keep everyone from asking questions? I'll ask your sister about that. As it is, I play with the window until he turns off the car.

She begins to stir in the back seat, and he sits upright. She mumbles something in her sleep and shifts her legs under her. He opens the door and looks at me, gets out of the car, gingerly, then closes the door with the quietest possible 'click.' He starts walking toward the little cinder block building without looking back, like a little kid about to be caught for some infraction, hoping that if he doesn't see her, maybe she won't see him.

We would take the girls everywhere with us. When they were five and two, they were the life of the party, asking many questions, dancing to P-Funk at a barbecue. We would watch them, and hold hands, and watch people laugh. You were our entertainment, everyone's.

Mrs. Brenneman is lying on her side, her hair sprayed

and askew, her hands in prayer position under her ear, her shoes kicked off, stockings bunched at the ankles.

It takes everything in my body to do this. To not do this, I smooth my jacket and open the door of the car, pull my folder out of my backpack. Birth certificate, a photo from last year, somewhere you sent it from I can't remember. Were you still prone to headcolds? What color was your hair? Do you know how good those tomatoes we canned tasted?

I turn and look to the door of the building, then back at the woman in the car. I wish I had a copy of *Projected Sales Growth: Second Quarter.* I could organize all of this into figures.

Then I don't know what's happening. In a minute I am going to walk inside and bring you home; in an hour we'll be back on the road. But right now there is the car, and my hands and feet, punching the door, kicking at the tire and the hubcap, beating the hood, yanking the windshield wipers up on their stalks, staring at the tired, startled face rising behind the glass, her hair a stiff blob. There is the state trooper on break up the driveway walking toward me, the door to the building further and further away. God damn you are never ending. Wake up. Wake up. Your husband's inside; your son is inside. My girl is a flicker, a well, a hole in the ground, and you know nothing, lady, you know nothing. You know nothing, you know nothing, you know nothing, you know nothing, you know nothing, you know nothing, you know nothing about me.

48

Safe
John Bullock

Next-door's kids have been up and down those stairs like demented infantry since seven this morning. It's just after ten now, Sunday. The sky's a shade between slate and gravel. Rain's bouncing off everything.

I wedge a roach into a fresh joint, then light it. My throat's tight. My lungs are like bags of old shoes. On the telly some cartoon chick's trying to hatch, but it's got this long bent-up beak and it can't break the shell, so it's rushing about in a flap because time's running out, and the drill sergeant in the shape of an egg timer keeps yelling at it, and the sand's draining from the sergeant's face and filling his chest, and the chick's getting more and more desperate, but all it can do is panic.

The phone goes. I pray it's Gabby, telling me she's made a mistake, that I should burn the letter, that she's left Duncan for good, packed her things, and is on her way over. I cut the sound on the telly and answer.

"Wakey wakey, hands off snaky," says Micky, my brother. "Who won three hundred quid on roulette the other night?"

"I wonder."

"Superstar, mate. You should've come."

On Friday he'd turned up at the cottage I'm rewiring. I had all the old cable stripped and was slinging the last of it out of the upstairs window into the skip below. He waltzed in, turned his nose up, swanned about. "I'd top myself if I had to work in a place like this," he said, brushing dust from his sleeves. "You'd top yourself if you had to work anywhere," I said. He was off to Brighton with Charlie, asked if I fancied the casino. Said he could feel a win in his water. "I can't," I said. "Gabby's comin' round later." He shook his head. "Silly boy. You'll kick yourself tomorrow." Then he left.

"What you doin'?" he says.

"Nothing." There's squawking down the phone. "What's that?"

"What?"

"There, where you are. Where are you?"

"Charlie's mum's."

"What's that noise?"

"Oh," he says, "birds."

"What birds?"

"I don't know. Parrots, cockatoos. Fuck the birds. Listen. Is Gabby there?"

"No."

"Nice one. Got a little surprise for you. About half hour?"

"Not today, Mick. I'm not up for it."

"What's wrong, someone piss in your ear?"

"No."

"Then stop moanin' and put the kettle on."

The phone clicks off. I pick up Gabby's letter, reread the first lines:

Duncan's been offered a great job in Scarborough. He wants us to move up there and get married. Mart, I know you'll hate me, but I've decided to go with him. . . .

Scarborough! She might as well sod off to Lapland for all the good it'll do. Everything was fine. I mean, she had a bit of an outburst Friday night but nothing unusual. This time she hated herself more than ever for cheating on Duncan, plus for not complaining when they'd overcharged her at Sainsbury's, plus for not standing up to her pig of a boss when he stiffed her out of her bonus. Once she'd got it all out of her system, she was right as rain. But then I get back from work yesterday, open the door, and there's her letter on the mat. She must've thought about where to put it so I'd see it when I got in. Must've been the last thing she did in the house. Why couldn't she wait for me to get back, let me have my say? What really gets me is how cocksure she is about what we'd be like together if she *were* to leave Duncan, when really she hasn't got a clue. Besides, most of what's in the letter is stuff I've told her all along to help her feel better about herself, to get her to stop picking over every mess in her life just to prove how useless she is.

I stare at the telly and finish the spliff. Ten minutes later, Micky's at the door. "Put it away!" he shouts through the letterbox. I stuff the letter under the cushion then go to open the front door.

"Where you been?" he says. "I'm soaked." He looks like he's off out for the night: lilac shirt ironed, buttoned cuffs. There's a crocodile on his pocket. I look at the rain. "That's why they invented coats," I say, knowing he won't wear one on principle. Behind him I see Charlie and some other bloke opening the back of the Shogun.

"Didn't know you were bringin' your fan club."

He wipes his shoes on the mat. "My free enterprise partners."

"How nice."

"I thought so," he says, screwing his face up at the dark spots of rain on his shirt. "Bit of class."

"What, like remedial class?"

He grabs my neck in the hall, gives me one of his Doctor Spock's. "Get off!" I say, twisting to break his grip. "I'm not in the mood." I point at Charlie and his mate. "And they're not dossin' here all day either."

The rain's coming down full pelt now, and we both look out to see what they're up to. They rest what looks like a big box on the back edge of the Shogun. "Put the sheet over it!" shouts Micky. Charlie looks our way, throws his hands up, mouths something we can't hear for the rain. The tall one takes the weight of the box while Charlie covers it with a sheet.

"What's that?" I say.

Micky taps his nose. "You are *not* gonna believe this."

"I thought you hated being banged up."

"Who said anythin' about being banged up?"

He's just done a year in Pentonville, forged dollars. Christ knows what he was doing with them. Every few weeks I'd take him a half ounce of soft black, rolled into two clingfilmed bullets, ready for bottling. He'd sit there all baby-oiled up, biding his time.

I remember when they moved him to Camp Hill on the Isle of Wight. Going over on the passenger ferry reminded me of the week we spent there with Mum when we were kids. "Don't be stupid," said Micky when I mentioned it one visit. "There's nothin' *cool* about this fuckin' place. It's full of dogs."

Charlie and the other bloke wiggle the box out and lift it clear. Charlie nudges the car door closed and they start down the path, the box low and lumpy between them. Micky watches them struggle.

"Who's that?" I ask, looking at the tall bloke.

"Who, Goacher? Priceless. Useless but priceless."

Goacher's walking backwards and telling Charlie not to push. "This way, lads," Micky says, waving them in. "And wipe your feet while you're at it."

He comes into the front room, looks at the mess on the floor, then starts sniffing. "Smells like a barnyard. These windows open or what?"

I kick a few magazines to the side of the settee, throw my coat under the stairs.

"Got any Shake 'n Vac?"

"No."

"Po puree. That's what you need."

There's nothing out of place where he lives. It's like a show home. He spends all day polishing the mirrors and the coffee table, washing the ashtrays. "No one's comin' round to inspect it," I said to him once. "That's not the point," he said. "It matters. 'Bout time you took some pride in yourself."

I say we're brothers, but with different dads. Mine's Canadian. Mum met him when she worked at the airport. He was over on business. Could be anywhere now for all I know. Micky's dad Ron does the teas and sandwiches in the park caf, plus the pitch and putt in summer. He kept coming and going for years, then left for good when I was six and Micky was nine. Micky won't have anything to do with him, won't even let him see Jade, his little girl, who's eight now. After Ron went it was always just me and Micky. Mum worked in the bakers, mopped the library at night. Weekends she made wedding cakes and curtains for extra cash. Now she looks after Jade.

There's a couple of nasty shunts before Charlie and his mate finally get the box through the door. When I go to close it I see a trail of sawdust from where they're standing all the way back to the car.

"Where d'you want her?" asks Micky.

I point to the kitchen.

Micky tries to pull the dustsheet off as they walk through, but it's tucked under Charlie's hands, and he wobbles when Micky tugs it. "Don't fuck about!" says Charlie: "I nearly dropped the cunt." When they move, the trail of sawdust follows them into the kitchen. I look down and see a small pile where they were standing.

They put the box on the floor. Micky pulls the sheet off. "Ta-da," he says, presenting it.

"What is it?" I say.

"This little baby," he says, rubbing dust from the top, "is what you might call a safe." He grins. "A not-very-safe safe."

"Where'd you get it?"

"Ockley. Them stables where Donna works?" Then he says, "I'll split whatever's in there four ways."

He introduces me to Goacher, who's got one of those long round-bottomed faces, too much bone in the jaw. It must take some shaving. He puts his cell down then picks up the tea towel and dries his hair with it. Charlie's wearing the last donkey jacket on earth. He takes it off. His T-shirt's never seen an iron. There's a cartoon Tasmanian devil on the front with CRASH in broken-glass letters. "Fuck, that's heavy," he says, blowing on his fingers.

53

Micky smiles. "Good sign, good sign." He puts his cell on the table. "Where's that tea?"

I put the kettle on, pick up the mugs in the front room, give them a quick sloosh. I stick three bags in the pot. When I turn around, Micky's staring at the old tin kettle. "Why d'you always buy crap?"

"It boils water. What else d'you want?"

"Couple rounds of toast," says Charlie.

"Nice one," says Goacher, opening the bread bin. "Got any of them pop-up tarts?"

"Them what?" I say.

Now he's poking about in the top cupboard. "Them pop-up tart things. Fruity."

"No mate," I say.

"Don't be shy, Goach," says Micky, shaking his head. "No manners, some people."

Then he gets on the floor, taps the safe, listens. "Piece of piss. Right." He sits up. "We need a lump hammer and . . . what is it? Not a chisel. One of them brick things?"

Goacher shrugs.

"Bolster?" Charlie says.

"You're not gonna start crackin' that open in here," I say.

"What else am I gonna do, sit and paint it?"

"Not today, Mick. I told you earlier."

"You don't want a couple of grand? No worries. We'll split it threes. Charlie the Wonder Horse got six grand out of there last year, didn't you?"

"Yes mate, out the house," says Charlie, eyeing the safe.

"I said no, for fuck's sake!" I go into the front room, stand by the window, seething. It wouldn't make the blindest bit of difference to Mick if I was laid up on the settee with two broken legs. He'd still walk in and take over.

Micky shouts, "You two gonna stand there like a couple of dildos?" Then, "Sort it out, Goach. Keys are there."

Goacher runs out and opens the back of my van. Micky pops his head round the wall, almost sheepish. "Do something useful and skin up," he says, tossing me a bag of weed. "One of your big uns."

I get my fags and papers and sit at the kitchen table. Goacher comes back with a lump hammer and a paint scraper with some peelings still on the blade. When Micky sees the scraper he says, "Funny bolster, that. Horse, check it out will you?" Charlie goes to grab Goacher's nuts on his way out, and runs to the van. He comes back with a chisel. He'll be there all day with that.

Micky lifts the hammer behind his head, says, "God bless all who sail in her," then brings it down and gives the chisel a good crack.

"Keep it down," I say. "My head's splittin'."

"I thought you was skinnin' up," says Micky.

The bag's full of bud. It reeks. After I break a couple open and start laying the weed in, my fingers get all sticky with oil. I get my rolling mat out and build one triple-length, double-wide, and front-loaded. "Got any more of this?" I say.

"Might have," Micky says. He angles the chisel and keeps going. I can't remember the last time he used my tools. He tries to come over the old pro but he's got the shaft cack-handed and he's swinging it wrong. Trust him to make a song and dance of it, like he's going through hell just for us. It's weird seeing the hammer in his girly hands.

After a while, he drops it and sits back, shaking his arm. "Won't be long now. You rolled that number, Mart?"

"Might have." Sometimes these long ones end up tight or baggy, but this one's a peach. I toke and watch the sides crinkle, feel the smoke's easy draw. I'll hog it till Micky notices. Right now he's up and down on his knees again, attacking the safe from all sides, trying to see through the chain of small holes. I picture him making a hole big enough to worm his head in, and then getting it stuck. "You won't fit in there," I tell him.

With the next swing, he misses the chisel and bangs his hand. He drops the hammer, stares at his knuckles. "Bastard."

"I've got a nice pair of tin snips," I say, laughing out smoke. I cough up what feels like an oyster.

"Serves you right." He sits back on his haunches, holds his hand out for the joint. I pass it to him. He wants to know what happened to the tea. When I look at the kettle there's steam spouting from it. I grab the handle without thinking. It's burning. I drop it back on the cooker and rush to the sink, hold my fingers under the cold water. "Make the tea, Charlie," I say. "Use Goacher's towel on the handle."

"How's work?" Charlie says to me, pouring water into the teapot. It's all he ever says. Because we're both in the trade – even though he's a labourer and only works when he feels like it – he talks like we're Masons.

55

I dry my hands and sit back at the table. "Plenty of it," I say, blowing on my fingers.

He nods, mulling something over as he stirs the pot. After a while he says, "Bit tucked up meself. Bottom's fallen out of it."

"Listen to 'im!" says Goacher.

"What!" says Charlie, all offended.

"You wouldn't know a day's work if it fell on your head."

Charlie smiles. "And you would?"

"What d'you mean! I work," Goacher says.

"Your mum still combs your hair."

"No she don't." Goacher looks hurt.

Charlie's looking at Micky. "Soon as she's open, I'm off down Curry's, buy the biggest fuck-off telly in there. Then I'm gonna get me a nice chair, one of them ones with the handles, goes back like, plot up for the rest of me days, bucket of weed, get fuckin' coated. Tea's up." Then, all concerned he says, "Got a cosy, Mart?"

"No mate."

Goacher goes quiet for a moment then says, "My old dear wants to see them *Cats*. Up town. Might treat 'er."

Charlie rubs Goacher's hair. "Who's a lovely boy."

"You two make me die," snaps Micky. "What d'you think'll be left of your shares after I clear your tabs?" He downs his tea, takes a bunch of tokes on the joint, hands it to Goacher. He starts banging again. I cringe as he raises the hammer. The way he's going, he'll crack every bone in his hand. Charlie takes his tea and leans against the cupboard, tongue lolling in his teeth, taking the piss out of Micky. He doesn't notice his mug tip, spilling tea on his slip-ons. "Mug," says Goacher, looking down at the mess. I can't be arsed to clear it up. I get the Hobnobs out. "Goach," I say, and throw them to him.

"Plain chocolate. Blindin'." He takes two out, dunks one.

Charlie goes over to Micky, leans down, whispers in his ear.

"He don't care!" Micky says, looking at me. "Horse wants to chop some lemon. Got a mirror?"

"Yeah."

I run upstairs.

In the bathroom, my heart's going like an abattoir at Christmas. When I close my eyes, I get a tingling in my head, a spirally blackness. My brain feels like a walnut tossed in the corner. A moment or two later the wave passes and I pull out one of the small sliding mirrors from the cabinet. I hold the mirror up. My chin's flabby, my eyes puffy and shot. Pleurisy, I think. Lumbago. All of that. If Gabby was here, she'd make me lie on the settee and put a quilt over me. If Gabby was here, Micky wouldn't be.

Last summer comes to mind. I'd been telling Gabby about the duck pond in the park, about how when we were kids we were too scared to go out to the island because it was haunted. So one night last summer, me and Gabby went down to the pond, stripped to our skivvies, and swam out to it. We sat there waiting for something to happen, but nothing did. Then we had our best shag ever. Even she said it was romantic, lying there after, just her and me on that tiny island with the stars twinkling above.

"Duncan wouldn't be seen dead doing this," she said.

We'd been with each other a year then, but it was the first time I really thought of us as boyfriend-girlfriend. I think that's why I told her then about Micky and Ron. "At least he's got a dad," I said. "If mine worked in the park, I'd be down there every day." She said it was hard for her to understand because her mum and dad were happy. But she tried to imagine. She was nice about it and everything.

"I want to have a party," I said, "on a boat. You can hire all different ones, just for the day. Mum, Ron, me, you, Micky, Jade, anyone. Summer's day, loads of bubbly." When I got choked up, she didn't laugh or anything, just held me while I let it all out. Later I told her I'd given Ron a couple of photos of Jade that I took on her last birthday. One of them was of Micky lifting her nurse's cape over her head. Ron said it was very thoughtful of me. I don't think he knew when to stop looking at them, or what to do with the photos after.

Halfway down the stairs I nearly lose it. I've got all this Gladys Knight stuff going on, lines of embarrassing songs. My eyes go blurry. I blot them with my sleeve, wait for a moment, then go back down.

Charlie's opening a wrap at the table. His face lights up when I give him the mirror. "Nice one," he says. He taps powder onto it and draws more out with his Stanley blade. He sits and admires it before hunching over all crafty. He chops, snakes it around, chops on.

"Line us up, Charlie," says Goacher.

"Sorry mate, members only. You buy it, you snort it."

Micky's cut through about half the door. He uses the chisel point to free up enough of the lip so he can bend it back. "Give us a hand, Goach." Goacher gives Charlie the joint and takes the chisel. Micky gets up, comes over to the table, wets his finger.

"Easy," says Charlie, bobbing about in his seat, checking Micky's finger. "It don't grow on trees, y'know."

"Cheeky git. You ain't paid me for the last bag." Micky dabs the powder, licks it off his finger, runs his tongue around his mouth. He sits at the table. "Nice flowers," he says. "You buy 'em?"

I say "Yeah."

"Tasteful."

He takes the Rizla, strips a Benson, lines the tobacco in the fold. "It's all work," he says, throwing me the Rizla. "How's that Gabby then? Do anything nice?"

I'm slumped, digging my thumbnail into the edge of the table. "No."

"Remind me not to ask again."

"I will."

"Ain't you got nothin' to say for yourself?"

"Yeah. When are you lot goin'?"

When I first told him about Gabby, he called her a slag for going behind Duncan's back. Still calls her that now. "You don't go shaggin' other bloke's birds," he said. I mean, he's right and all that, and I know he's got this big thing about it – I think something funny went on with Jade's mum Lisa, but he's never come right out with it – but me and Gabby were serious. It was never just slipping her one on the side. "Hark at Mister Morality here," I said. "It's the first rule of decency," he said. I laughed. "What, and you'd know about that?" Then he rammed me against the wall, pinned me with his forearm under my chin. "I'm not tellin' you again," he said. I could feel his words on my face.

When he was banged up, I tried to talk to him about Gabby during my visits. "Forget her," he'd say, "she ain't worth a wank." Then he'd say stuff like, "You always get in a mess with birds. You're too serious. It ain't love every time."

Charlie wipes powder from the blade and starts shaving off little bits of thumbnail. They're full of muck. Then he says to me, "I don't mind doin' a couple of days, if you need someone, like."

"Charlie," I say, "I wouldn't phone you if there was a tiger in the house."

Goacher's stopped with the banging and is leaning back on his haunches, hands flat on his thighs. He's staring at something in the corner. "For the first time in my life I feel satisfied with the direction my career is heading."

"Your career what?" Micky says.

Goacher turns, looks like he's just come back from a dream. "Oh, just some posh bird on the telly."

Charlie jumps up from the table, cocks his leg and farts. "Get out and walk," he says. It smells of beer and peanuts.

"Pig," says Goacher. "Can't take you anywhere."

Charlie sits back down, waves the smell away. "God bless," he says, then takes a long line up each nostril. He holds the back of his head tight with both hands.

"Is that your brain fizzing?" says Micky.

Charlie clenches his teeth; all the bits in his neck stick out. Then he juts his neck high, draws his lips back tight, and bares his teeth. "What am I?" he says. His hands are at his chest, flopped over.

"An embarrassment to your own mother," says Goacher.

"A cryin' shame," says Micky.

Charlie gets into it, shaking his head left and right, doing something squirrely with his cheeks.

"A rabbit with myxomatosis," I say.

"What's wrong with you lot? I'm a meerkat. Haven't you seen 'em on telly? Best animal ever invented."

Goacher's given up with the safe and is gawping at the big black-and-white ballerina print on the living room wall. The girl's standing on one leg and holding the other straight up past her head. I feel like falling over just looking at her. Gabby took a fancy to it when we were in Athena, so I bought it that week and hung it in the front room for the next time she came over. It went down a storm. I might take it outside later and burn it. "That your bird?" he says.

"Yeah," I say, "but she's yours for a tenner."

"Nah. Women are crap." He bends down, tries to see up her dress. "Just stand about waiting for you to tell 'em what to do."

"He's got a brain on 'im, that Goach," says Micky.

"Look at 'im!" Charlie says. "Can you see 'er minge?"

"He's a genius," says Micky. "Works it all out on the quiet. Int that right, Goach?"

Goacher doesn't say anything, but he looks pleased.

"Oy Goach," Micky says. "When was the last time you had a snifter?"

After a couple of seconds, Charlie says, "He had that old spunker, Bev."

"That was years ago," Micky says.

"Wasn't," Goacher says, wounded.

"I wouldn't touch 'er with yours," says Charlie.

"Anyway, look at 'im," says Micky. "Who in their right mind would fuck that?"

"I would," says Charlie, "in that dress."

"Nice one, Charlie." Goacher smiles. His face is always busy.

Micky lights his joint. I light mine. "We just gettin' the one tea then?" He's eyeing the Hobnobs.

"I thought you weren't stayin'," I say.

He looks at Goacher and then Charlie to see if they heard, but they're not listening. "You were sitting on your arse when I phoned."

"It's not the point. You stroll in here like . . . like the King of bloody Sheba, leave your shit everywhere."

As I get up from the table he says, "I'll ignore that."

"Please yourself."

I walk past Goacher, who flashes me a nervous look before picking up the hammer and chisel again and getting on with the safe. I cross the kitchen and stand with my back to the fridge. In no time he's torn half the door open, enough to get his hand in. Micky sees him fishing around. "That's where you stop," he says, then jumps up from the table and takes over. He's got half his arm in the safe now, but he's not saying anything. Goacher stands over him. "What you got, Mick?"

"I'll tell you what I've got when I've got it, all right?"

Goacher tokes on the joint, goes cross-eyed when he inhales. I give my joint to Charlie.

Micky pulls his arm out. I can tell something's up. Micky's got his hard-done-by face on, his little boy lost. He's up to his elbow in sawdust. There's still some in his hair. Something's not right. I can see it on his face. I feel bad for him, same as always, whether I like it or not. If there was one thing I could change it'd be that: to not know how he feels.

"Want me to skin up?" I say.

There's sawdust all over the floor. The safe looks torpedoed. I start to put the papers together and strip another Benson. Goacher's laughing at the mess Micky's made in the kitchen. Then he takes the last seat at the table. "What happened?"

Charlie looks at Micky, reads his face. "You're jokin'!" says Charlie. "What about me telly?"

Then Goacher says in a retard's voice, "It ain't empty is it?" and bangs his head with his knuckles.

"All right, Einstein!" shouts Micky. "Why don't you show us what a genius can do with a dustpan and brush? Ay?"

"I mean, who'd stash all their notes in a stable?" adds Goacher.

Micky slams the table. "I told you!"

Goacher goes sulky. I make the joint and give it to Mick. He puts it in his mouth and I light a match to it, then I sweep the spilled bits of grass and tobacco into the ashtray. He works his way through most of the joint, saying nothing. Charlie's laughing at Goacher, who's doing a mad jerky dance by the window. Then Charlie pats his pockets. "Where's me lemon?"

The small clingfilmed wrap is next to the vase of lilies. "Here," I say, and toss it to him. He's rummaging. "Where's me blade?"

I stick more Rizla together. Just then, out of the blue, the waterworks start. My eyes load up and go blurry again. I'm trying to put the joint together but I can't see what I'm doing. Any minute now they'll leak like mad and there'll be nothing I can do. I can't look up. I've got my head down when all of a sudden the room goes quiet. Not a word. It feels like there's a crowd around me, watching.

"You all right?" says Micky.

I don't answer.

"What is it?"

"Nothing," I say.

"That's a funny nothin'. Come on."

"I'm all right!"

"You're not."

Charlie starts singing: *My girl Lollipop, b-doot boop boop, you make my heart go giddy-up, b-doot boop boop . . .*

"Give it a rest, Charlie," Micky says.

Goacher steps in. "Rain's stopped," he says cheerily, rubbing his hands.

"Tell you what I fancy," says Charlie. "One of them steakwiches at The Nelson."

Micky says, "I told Big Ian The Coot. The Coot it is."

"Sunday," ponders Charlie. "That Lorraine'll be workin'. Oy Goach. It *is* Holsten in The Nelson, innit?"

I look out down the garden. Rainwater's dripping from the shed roof. Bet it's raining in Scarborough. Always does up north. Any money you like, in a month or two, Gabby'll look out her window at the rain hitting the sea and wonder why she ever moved up there. As for Mick, he'll buy me a beer in The Coot to make up for the mess. Six pints later, he'll slur when he tells me what it means to be brothers. We'll be mates again, for a while. We'll probably hug. And that'll last till sooner or later I mention Dad – mine, not his – which I always do, without meaning to. Then he'll lose his rag. "You're like a scratched record," he'll say, or, "Give it a rest." And then, same as always, I'll ignore him, maybe for months. And he'll tell Mum it's all my doing, that there's no getting through to me. That it's about time I grew up.

Atrium
Deborah Narin-Wells

They say *atrial fibrillation*
and I imagine your heart
fluttering like the sleeves
of your favorite red shirt
when we hike Three Sisters.

They say *cardiac* and I think
of the invisible cord that binds us,
that core deeper than language,
irrevocable reach of trees
toward sunlight

and it's aerial
not atrial I hear,
magic of flight,
your visionary heart
reaching sky-ward

the way we climb over
lava to alpine meadows,
thousands of wildflowers
where we lie down,
my ear against your chest,

the slow murmur
of your heart

like rain water
collecting in a clear pool
of an atrium,

courtyard of a Roman
household in the book I read
to our son years ago,
the safe walls, someone drawing water
from the well, children playing:

your wandering heart
finding its way home.

I Cut Up the Flag
Dianne Stepp

The nurse that tends the stoma
in his neck they feed him through
since he won't eat, she glares at me
behind the plastic tubes,
but I don't care.

I snip Old Glory into little squares
as I sit beside his bed week
by week, stow them in a grocery bag,
stitch them back one by one
to eight-patch squares.

When they prop him in his chair
his head hangs like a baby bird.
The white gauze, cinched tight around his neck,
blinds the ordinary air.

The doctors skirt my chair,
they know by now a mother's grief.
And I know their job's to keep
the kill-count down, keep this war
hidden from the public eye.

Which is why, our first excursion out
to practice real life,
when they send three young aides, all smiles,

to help his Dad and me
learn to care for him, I insist
to drape my patchwork flag across his knees.
Sitting at the restaurant table,
I tuck a cloth beneath his chin,
scoot close as I used to do
before he knew words.

That woman staring by the window—let her weep.

Pointing, one by one, I pronounce:
knife, spoon.

What I Know About War
                    Dianne Stepp

begins with a photo of my uncle
standing on a beach on Tarawa,
jabbing the tip of a Japanese sword into a helmet
washed up at his feet like a ripe coconut,

and curving behind him,
the detonated shoreline, one lone palm,
jagged in the distance,
at his feet wavelets, licking his boots
like an afterthought.

And under the brim of his helmet,
his eyes, sun-blasted into shadow.

This is the uncle whose wife divorced him in 1944,
who never remarried,
whose son we never saw,
who appeared holidays only,
a twenty pound bird under his arm,
who disappeared into the garage
with my father and a bottle,
who told me when I was seven,
there was a Jap head inside that helmet.

The uncle who drove me to the corner market
one Thanksgiving when I was a teenager,

when the rain ran down the windshield like tears,
and the wind pelted the trolley lines,
and the last-minute shoppers
hunched under umbrellas in the parking lot,
fumbling for keys.

Who drew from the glove box
a packet of photos of a naked woman,
who watched, under the brim of his cap,
for my reaction as she aimed at me,
from inside the pinked edges of the photo's frame,
the white torpedoes of her breasts,
the sticky-pout of her lip-sticked mouth,
the dark wounds of her nipples.

anxious pleasures:
after a novel by kafka
an excerpt
Lance Olsen

The author living alone in the flat directly below the Samsas' coughs wetly in his sleep and rotates his head a little to the left. Lying on his back in his neatly made bed, hands fisted on belly, he dreams of an elderly couple lying side-by-side on their backs in a neatly made bed in a hotel room on a rainy island off the northwest coast. They are awake, holding hands in the dark, waiting, although they have forgotten what it is they are waiting for.

Their names are Neddie and Nellie. Two weeks ago they got into their small red Fiat to drive several kilometers to a party hosted by friends. At the second T in the road, they turned right instead of turning left. Their careful little lives fell away behind them. They had tidied their house, put out the rubbish, locked the windows. In the boot were two small dented leather suitcases. They meandered along narrow back roads through the night. To keep themselves awake, they sang songs popular when they first met. Dawn dusting the landscape, they pulled into an inexpensive hotel, rented a room, and slept. They used false names and paid in cash. In each town through which they passed, they stopped at the local chemist to purchase over-the-counter drugs they read about in a special book they ordered from America. The only way they remembered to do so was by taping to the dashboard the instructions they had written down.

After traveling like that for nearly a week, Neddie and Nellie ran out of land. They took a ferry across to an island, drove until they reached the far side, took another ferry, and so on. Before long, they ran out of ferries. They took a room at this hotel, a whitewashed rectangular box with a dark slate roof set atop a barren promontory overlooking a sea the color of slick stones and opals.

Three heartflutters ago, they awoke from dreaming the same dream. In it, an elderly couple noticed one day they had begun losing weight. They had been quite fit. They ate well. They got plenty of rest. Yet no matter what they did they couldn't help it. They shed the smallest amounts at first. So small, they took unspoken pride in their unintentional accomplishment. But the losses mounted. Each morning they stepped onto the scale to discover there was just a little less of them there than there had been the morning before.

Then it struck them: they were not losing fat. They were losing memories. Every day a handful more burned away like so many unwanted calories. In the beginning, it was nothing to get alarmed about: the misplaced car keys, the sack of groceries accidentally left behind on the supermarket counter. They told each other not to worry. It happened to everyone. Slowly, though, matters became more serious. The unrenewed subscriptions piled up, the unpaid bills. The couple couldn't recall the names of their friends, then of their grandchildren. They hadn't thought of their favorite, Margie, for weeks.

69

Yesterday they noticed when attempting to walk that their feet only touched the carpet sporadically. This morning the best they could do was float a little above it, as if there were an invisible floor hovering three centimeters atop the real one. Sometime early this afternoon, in the middle of a conversation about where the wife might have left her reading glasses, they were unnerved when their heads bumped against the ceiling. They had become that light. It was tricky for them to reach the dining room table to eat, but they told themselves that that was all right because they didn't have much of an appetite left anymore anyway.

They kissed with a familiar kiss only those married for many decades can fully appreciate, and, crawling upside down across the ceiling, inched their way to the window, which the husband, after a bit of logistical nuisance, pried open. Holding hands, they eased through. Up they ascended into the cool night sky blurry with stars. They became smaller and smaller as they rose, at first the size of dolls, then fists, then thumbs, then teeth, and then they vanished altogether--and then Neddie and Nellie opened their eyes in this hotel room in this whitewashed rectangular box.

They lie quietly side-by-side in a neatly made bed, trying to figure out if this is the dream or the other thing.

-Where are we? Nellie asks in the darkness.

-I don't know, Neddie replies.

He sits up cautiously and pats the air around him until he locates a light switch at the base of a lamp on the side table. To the best of his recollection, he has never seen this lamp or this room. Taped to the base by the switch he finds a list of instructions written in what he recognizes as his own handwriting. He plucks it off and reads it aloud with interest. Nellie concentrates, asking him to repeat certain phrases she finds difficult to take in.

They do what the instructions tell them: fill glasses of water at the sink in the corner and swallow the pills they bought on their journey. They become drowsy. When their muscles begin loosening, their breaths becoming shallower, they turn off the lamp and lie down side-by-side in the dark once more and, once more, take each other's hands. Soon they can no longer tell if they have started to sleep or are still awake. Neddie looks around, confused. He is positive he sees the luminous outline of a tall skinny man sitting naked in the chair by the telly at the foot of the bed. The man is watching them. Nellie has the distinct impression Neddie and she are bobbing on a raft in the middle of a very calm ocean on a very clear night. She can hear the waves lapping around them. When she starts feeling uneasy, she rolls onto her side and curls into Neddie's thin arms. She enjoys the sour-milk fragrance of his mouth.

The tall skinny man at the foot of the bed stands, approaches them, leans over Nellie and, running his fingers through her hair, whispers *heart of my heart, heart of my heart*, until Nellie no longer feels frightened. Her body seems to her less and less significant, like a large hand has begun to erase it.

-What time is it? she asks, although a second later she can't remember having just asked.

The sound of the windy drizzle outside suffuses the room and then, from a very long way off, from a centimeter to her left, from deep inside her head, a voice resonant with kindness and reassurance replies:

The Distance
D. James Smith

Besides the halo of a distant town
    or the stars netted in the tips of pines,
black, set far up on a ridge,
    there is little to report at night

from the windows of a passing train.
    You see the cold moon sails
a sea of grass someone parted with their knees,
    wading out, the line, just glimpsed, and somehow
grave because it fails suddenly so that you wonder
    who lies there, or for how long, no evidence
of he or she having trailed back.
    Didn't you, once, want to cut your own line out,
even if it was only to shout back,
    No, not this way. Didn't you
want to part the fabric of the world?
    Remember unbuttoning your girl's jeans,
a warm spring rain, and you descending
    into the brief church the tall grass made.
How did you know you'd never be the same?
    Never seventeen and soon to leave home for good.
Wasn't it in the way she kept opening
    and closing her eyes to those splinters of rain
to look at you as for the first time that scared you,
    seeing how love was too close to loss?
And hasn't it always been?
    And, now, the train hurtling the distance

and the porter smiling with beautiful teeth
        leaning to offer the consolation of a gin
though memory briefly offers you the same,
        before the windows go abruptly dark
as you fly, entering thickets and the trees.

Almost a Beautiful Place
Justin Jainchill

Look at him. George. That big-eyed boy in transit. The one who walks so quickly, little knobs of muscle tensing through his tee-shirt, eyes lit-up like movie screens, as if electricity pumps through his pupils. George is in a rush today, like always, but no one knows why, not even his mother, because he hasn't said a single word since she packed their things and moved them to the city -- the city where George is always taunted -- a place where his silence is treated like a threat. Just look around. Blown-out buildings bake in the sun, their metallic insides splayed out on the street, the bricks and beams of their bodies exposed, broken, cracked like bones and scattered around in piles. Fires flare out from trashcans, their flames licking the air like tongues. Burned-up trash releases vapor into the sky and it has all congealed, like gel, and now a jelly-thick cloud hangs over the city.

But people don't seem to notice.

They walk like George walks. Impervious. Stoic. Alone in the world by choice. Though George is the one they pick on. He can't even walk to school with anonymity. Today he tries to cross through Checkpoint-1 -- which looks like a militarized tollbooth, all metal-platted and fatigue-colored -- and the guard holds him up with questions. His uniform is perfectly stitched, starched, and the gun he shoulders looks like a polished toy.

"What's the boy who can't say boy doing in Borough Ten today," the guard says through an intercom.

George slouches under the canopied checkpoint. He looks at the guard. Their eyes lock through the glass.

"Well, I've got to write something in my book. Why don't you just say debating, or acting class, or anything else involving verbal gymnastics," the guard says.

George continues to stand there, slouching, arms crossed. A few seconds pass. Then a full minute. The people behind him start to bitch. The guard pushes a button. A sign above George flashes three times: *Authorized to Cross, Authorized to Cross, Authorized to Cross.*

George's class is learning cursive today. His third grade teacher, Mrs. Bilido, calls the students up one at a time. Together they trace the spiraling, looped lines of consonances and vowels onto the blackboard, all of them seduced by the elegance of written language, because its lithe and languid shapes are just so lovely!

Later that morning Mrs. Bilido leads the class through an exercise with blocks. Not just square and rectangular chunks of wood, but intricately cut geometric shapes which the students must first identify by name, before finding the proper mold for each new form. But George doesn't participate. Instead he plays with some blocks by himself in a corner.

When Mrs. Bilido notices him, she excuses herself from a group of girls who are whizzing through the activity. She walks up to him. "George," she says, her voice like fake-sugar, "the rest of your classmates are having wonderful time learning over there." Mrs. Bilido points at some of the boys and girls who huddle close together, shoulder to shoulder, with their backs turned to George.

He looks over at them, and then goes back to his blocks.

"Well, what are you building anyway? I can't tell what it is," Mrs. Bilido says.

George doesn't say anything. His eyes are glued to the patterns only he can see. A jumble of signs heaped together like a bad sentence.

Mrs. Bilido sighs. The air slaps out of her mouth. "Okay, George, we've got to talk." She reaches down and takes a block from George's hand, and he pulls back, as if stung by the feel of her skin. He stands up. He looks around the room. He shifts his weight from side to side, both hands cupped around his crotch.

"You need to go to the bathroom?" Mrs. Bilido asks.

George nods. He points at the door.

"Of course, go if you need to. And don't forget to wash yourself afterward."

George ambles off and Mrs. Bilido returns to the girls who are now done with their work. Ten minutes pass. An hour goes by. The students keep on working, Mrs. Bilido keeps on teaching, but George doesn't return from the bathroom. Mrs. Bilido begins to worry. She wonders where he could be. She rushes out of the classroom and into the hallway. She calls his name, but George doesn't answer. He is gone.

His school sends letters. George has five of them now. And today he burns them all. In the kitchen George drops them into the sink, followed by a match, and when the fire catches, hisses, then turns blue, George runs the water. The flames hiss out. But then he hears the front door open. Could his mother already be home from work?

George grabs a wooden spoon out of the drawer and tries to scoop up the ashes. A second later his mother walks into the kitchen. "What did you do?" she asks.

George is now using the spoon like a paddle. Ashy water splashes out of the sink and onto the floor. Smoke spirals up toward the ceiling.

"My god, George," she says.

George looks up at her, smiles, and then turns the water off.

"You found those matches I left in the cabinet, didn't you?" his mother asks, and then she slumps down to the floor. "You can't burn things, George. You have to talk to me instead. You have to tell me what's wrong."

An hour later they eat dinner in silence. George rocks back and forth in his chair. Cindy picks at something on her plate, and then she reaches for her glass of water on the table and takes the last sip. "We need a little life around here," Cindy says. "Something to lighten the mood." She looks across the table at George. "How about a pet?" she asks. George flashes a big smile at her; his teeth wink in the light. "Do that again," Cindy says. And then there is laughter, which fills their apartment like gas, and they both feel high for awhile.

George walks through the city this afternoon. It is lunch hour, which is the worst time of day for traffic. People bulldoze forward, their shoulders leveled, briefcases tucked under their arms like footballs. Yet George keeps up. He walks quickly, deftly, elbows at his side like guarder-rails. George is supposed to meet his mother for lunch at 2PM, which is only two hours from now. And he needs to go find the pet store first. He wants to show up to lunch with a surprise for his mother. But the city is like a maze today. A blur of storefronts and blinking signs. He feels lost inside a funhouse, and doesn't know which way to turn, or how to find his way. Is he even headed in the right direction? Which way is North? Which way is South? What is a cross-street? Is it the same as a side-street?

Inside the pet store George can see his reflection in a large glass enclosure, his hands pressed against it like two small bodies. In front of him there are dozens of turtles, and he wants to reach through the glass and pick one of them up. Wants to feel the weight of a turtle in his hands.

"You need help with something," says a man from behind the service counter.

George shakes his head. Both hands remain suction-cupped to the glass.

"If you'd like to handle one of them, please ask for assistance. They're very fragile."

George ignores the voice. He is consumed by the turtles. In their glass-enclosed world they squirm and jive, all of them bald and shiny like well-sucked thumbs. George taps the glass.

"Please don't hit the case, it could rupture!"

But George starts tapping the glass harder, quicker, like a drummer.

The voice begins to shout.

George keeps on tapping on.

"Stop that! Why aren't you stopping? Don't you hear me?" And then a man hurries out from behind the service counter. His long hair billows behind him, like a cape, and his glasses are strapped to his head like goggles.

George takes five dollars from his pocket and holds it toward the man.

"What's this?" The clerk asks. "I don't want your money. I just want you to stop drumming on my damn turtle colony."

George nods his head at the turtles, then at the money. He wants to buy one, wants to bring a turtle home. What's there not to understand? It's the most customary exchange.

George holds a large cardboard box as he enters the restaurant. He bumps and nudges through the crowded dining area. People nudge him back. There is a wall of televisions behind the bar. A group of business men watch in silence. They all look tired. The stools they sit on don't have any cushions.

George finds a booth in the back. He pushes his box along the seat and pulls himself up. On the table George sees a book of matches. He picks it up and runs his finger along the scratch-strip, feeling the friction, and he likes how the rough texture pulls at skin, just like a cat's tongue. Then he lights one of the matches. He holds it up to his face. The flame is like a bulbous flower, a blossom of red-blue gas blooming before his eyes. George blows it out, and then pockets all the matches.

Minutes later a waitress with wrinkled pants comes over to the table. She places a laminated menu in front of him, and opens the first page. Her tick-tack-mint cracks between chipped teeth. George hears it splinter.

"Eating alone today?" she asks.

George shakes his head. He holds up two fingers, shrugging. The waitress frowns. She rushes off toward another table.

George's mother arrives twenty minutes later. She sits down at the table. From her handbag she removes a cigarette and lights it. George watches as she blows smoke-rings that that look like broken halos. She continues to smoke while reading the menu. George already knows what he wants to eat.

"Why don't you at least look through the menu? See if there's anything interesting. Try something new," she says.

His menu is face down on the table. He reaches for it, opens the first page, and then scans from right to left. There is nothing that catches his eye. He shakes his head.

Cindy stubs out her half-smoked cigarette. "You're going to order for yourself today. I'm sick of this act. This not talking. You're almost ten years old. You need to adjust."

George leans back in the booth. He crosses his arms.

"So you're not eating today, I see. Good decision, George. Good one. Just starve yourself over this. Just to spite me, right?"

When their waitress returns she asks George for his order. He doesn't answer. She asks again, louder this time, but gets no response. "Look lady, I've got other tables. Is the kid going to eat or not?"

Cindy reaches for her pack of cigarettes on the table. "My son doesn't want anything for lunch. Eating would require him to open his mouth."

At home, after lunch, George spends hours with his turtle. As they stand there looking out the window, the turtle's eyes focus on the same distant points as George's. The hours pass. Darkness comes. Cars crawl through the streets like bugs, their headlights blinking though the distance. Below them the city looks skeletal, emaciated, a network of scaffolds and skinny buildings. But George and his turtle continue to gaze out the window, as if looking for something behind the artifice of night. The city is almost a beautiful place.   79

Their kitchen is shaped like a shoebox, and way too small, but Cindy makes do. All four burners coiled red at once, pots and pans boiling over with water, carrots and celery diced up and then added to the broth. The smell is thick and healthy and makes her feel good inside. These dinners she labors over are all for George, but he never says so much as thank you.

After dinner they watch television for awhile.

Cindy is sprawled across the couch and George sits on the floor. She reaches down and twirls George's hair. Then she traces his ear with her fingertip. "Come up, George. Come up with mommy," Cindy says, but he is off somewhere else, somewhere distant and far from here, and she doesn't know how to reach him. But, all Cindy can do is love him the best she can. "I've got a surprise for you. Tomorrow we're going to have some fun," she says, in hopes of breaking through the shell of silence he hides inside.

The circus is traveling through Borough Nine today. A caravan of wheeled tents rumbles along the street. Cindy and George watch from their stoop. They see giant clowns on metal stilts, jugglers tossing fire-sticks, acrobats flung from the arms of strong-men. There is even a midget woman, tuxedo dressed, whose top-hat is taller than a building.

All the neighborhood people watch and laugh as well. Everyone is excited for the circus that travels from Borough to Borough. Two years ago the city emptied its jails and mental hospitals and homeless shelters. All the inmates and addicts and crazies were put to work. The city trained these populations to become circus performers. And this is what they are, this is what they have become -- entertainment.

But it's still such a wonderful circus!

There is so much to see. Oddities and novelties so many wonderful deformities. Anything goes at the circus. Kids throw baseballs at swollen-faced women. Fathers show their children how to aim a rifle, how to pull the trigger, how to laugh when a shot bounces off a bullet-proofed performer. There is even a booth where rotten pies can be hurled at the faces of elderly targets. But the most exciting part of the circus is all the animal-people. Look at the man who swims in the pool over there. He looks like a shark. His face is sharp as a snout. He even has a fin.

Oh, what fun it is to look and laugh at him!

After dinner George and his mother head toward the neon lights and carnie-music. Once inside the vast network of tents, they walk amongst booths and vendors. They hear the crack of live ammunition, the cheers of children, and the applause of people winning prizes. As they walk they watch, moving without direction, until they stop in front of a fortuneteller's booth. She is all belly and breast, and bracelets cover her arms like sleeves.

The fortuneteller stands up in her booth. "That boy's got crazy eyes. I felt him coming from a hundred yards away. He's got those x-ray eyes," the fortuneteller yells at George.

There are people everywhere, and they all turn around at once to look at Cindy and George.

"That boy should be in the circus with eyes like that," someone yells.

"He must be some kind of freak," another person shouts.

The fortuneteller points her finger at the mob.

"No, no," she says. "He knows more than you, he sees everything."

Dozens of people chatter amongst themselves. Soon they start waving their tickets at George. "Tell us what you see," they say to him, "and we'll give you all our tickets."

And then a woman gets down on her knees in front of George. She's wearing paper bags which have been sown together, like a patch-work dress, and her face is ravaged, red, and rough as sandpaper. "What's in my skin? What's clogging my pores? What makes me ugly?" she asks.

George doesn't answer, and the woman looks wounded. "I want to know," she yells.

But before the woman can say another word, Cindy pushes her over, and punches the woman in the face. Then Cindy stands back up. With her keys she stabs at the people crowded around them. "Grab mommy's hand, George. Grab it real tight, and then we'll start running."

The next morning George leaves at 7am, as if going to school, and then comes back home after his mother goes to work. He plays with his turtle for awhile. He makes them some lunch. But George is bored by the early afternoon. He is ready to go outside. On his way out George checks their mail slot, where he finds a letter from his school. He shreds the envelope and throws away the scraps, and then heads for the elevator down the hall from their apartment.

Outside the city is quiet. Three o'clock is a calm time of day. There are still a few people around, but they don't seem to notice him. They walk with their heads down, plowing forward, as if speeding along a track. But George doesn't rush today. He just doesn't feel the need to.

The park George visits was once a beautiful place. There used to be ice cream vendors and plenty of pigeons to feed. In the winter a skating rink, Christmas trees, and a million shimmering bulbs that washed the sky clean. But today the park is empty. Old jungle-gyms twisted and bent, slides crimped over with age, basketball hoops hunched-over and ready to topple, just like the city around it, which is all stripped-down metal frames, broken buildings, fire, clouds, nothing.

George sits down on a wobble-legged bench. He hears a sound -- something grating, something scraping. Metal, maybe. And then George sees an old man coming toward him. George watches as he kicks a can attached to a string. The old man is skinny. His bed-pan-smell is nasty. The clothes he wears are filthy. "Boy," he says to George. "You might see something beautiful in the sky tonight. But you have to look really hard. You have to make yourself see it." The old man points a crooked finger at the sky. "It will be up there where there's nothing but smog and broken stars and all that blackness. It will be the brightest thing you've ever seen. Will you be able to look at it?"

George looks up into the sky, which is clear and blue and cloudless today. But when he turns back around the old man is gone. A breeze blows where his body had been. Leaves loop through the air like kites.

When George gets home his mother is waiting at the door. She has the letter he threw away in her hands, which she pieced together with tape. George tries to walk past her but she reaches out and grabs his arm. She holds him there for a second. He looks up at her and smiles. "That baby face isn't going to work," she says. He shrugs, and then yanks his arm free. "You and I are marching down to that school tomorrow," she says. George makes his hand into a fist and shakes it at her. She shakes her head. Then he flicks her off, and so she flicks him off, and for a while they stand like this, saying Fuck You with their fingers.

George lets go of his mother's hand. He rushes over to his turtle and picks him up in his arms and walks over to the door. Cindy follows behind him, with her hands on both of his shoulders, pushing him toward whatever comes next.

When George gets home from the park he collects all the paper he can find and piles it in the middle of his room. From his pocket he removes a book of matches. He strikes one match, then another, a third, and then a fourth. He drops them all onto the pile. The fire begins to hiss. The papers burn. Smoke thickens around him. He losses himself in the hazy heat, which makes him feel good. So good he wants it all to burn. Maybe the whole city. Flames thrown from his hands as he snaps and cracks his knuckles, making fire dance and skid in every direction, while George and his turtle stand here, silently, like two stoic witnesses left to ponder all that remains -- the minutes, the seconds, the time it takes to destroy everything around them. Their shells will repel the heat; flames will bounce and spin off their armored bodies. And what will be left is beautiful. The pristine silence of such a grand aftermath, the wordless knowing of an apocalypse, the muted beginnings of rebirth.

A few minutes later Cindy smells the smoke.

She drops her knife in the sink and runs toward George's room. The door is locked, but Cindy shoulders through it. The impact levels her. From the floor she calls for him. "George, fire, George," she's says, now out of breath, and trying to focus her eyes.

George emerges like a ghost from the smoke. He reaches down and takes his mother's hand. She stands back up. Together they wade toward his window.

"What is it, George, what's burning? What's on fire," Cindy says.

They stop in front of the window. George grips Cindy's hand. With his head he points out toward the city. Cindy squints, steps closer to the window, and then she sees what George sees, for the first time in months, and it is truly beautiful. The sky is like a paint-dripped canvas, explosions of chemical-red, a stretch of atomic pink, a nuclear orange powders the sky like snow. Colors flare through the night, detonating like fireworks in front of their eyes, and the effect is almost blinding.

They stand in front of the window for awhile. The smoke grows thicker. The fumes began to flood their brains. With each breath they slip further and further away. George looks up at his mother and smiles, but Cindy knows they can't stay here.

"Let's go George. We need to leave. I want to get you out of here."

Burn Through
Greg Nicholl

My father writes from Barrow, Alaska
sends pictures of whale bone forced into sand,
an arch on the beach, each rib a sanctuary.
Pictures of boardwalks built across bogs,
of meat left to cure on cedar planks,
fibers tinged green by fog, salt off the ocean.
He sends them, because I ask
to be reminded, to hear of forests
that open into oceans. Of travelers
who cross mountains; how they stood
on a cliff to watch the head of a seal
surface on the water, to trace its retreat.
Anxious. Afraid. As anyone who first comes here—
the rain at night, so constant, can sound
like gunfire. The fits of gray so depressing
in its weight that only fire can burn
through. Those fires, like the ones
they built on the ice the week the harbor froze;
it was 1927, and they eased the Ford
down the shore just to drive it half a mile,
the tires spinning on the snow, one man
behind the wheel and a dog cowering
in the backseat. Give me that winter.
Give me rain and the thickest fog and a green
so consuming, you cannot help but enter.

The Confluent Dreams
of Eveline and Gretta[i]
Cindy May Murphy

(to be read vertically the first time and horizontally the second)

	beneath the dripping tree
he stands	he sings
calling	my name
from the rail	from the grave
and i	i gladly follow
descend into a sea	rendering to what no one understands
deeper than his hands	his eyes
until suddenly we have escaped	have traveled
beyond dublin	beyond death
my world is	closed
safe from you	forever
father	

[i] Eveline Hill and Gretta Conroy are characters in James Joyce's book of short stories entitled *Dubliners*. They appear in "Eveline" and "The Dead" respectively.

Interview with Paul B. Roth
Diane Averill
(5/20/06 to 8/05/06)

Paul B. Roth has been the editor and publisher of *The Bitter Oleander* since 1976, publishing contemporary poetry and fiction in translation, along with essays and interviews. Cyrpress Books will publish his collection *Cadenzas by Needlelight* in 2008.

DA: I have finished carefully reading each and every prose poem in *Fields Below Zero*, and I will read it a couple more times. One thing I've strongly felt about your work is that it reveals a sense of mystery more than any other poet's work I've read. One irritating and confining thought about concluding a poem is that it must provide "closure," or some kind of ending. I think of the film Rashoman and the different perspectives it provides on the same "reality." I don't believe in "closure." I think the word is psychobabble.

I love the line in "Preparing for the Self" where you say "Sounds guide you so well where it is moonless that you sense tiny variations in the wind just by listening to nests fill with snow inside thick underbrush." There are two schools of thought regarding prose poems: one advocates using line breaks at the ends of the long lines whereas the other says to just run each line to the end and see what you've got. I'm not sure which you subscribe to.

Finally, I'd like to ask you if a direct approach to social/religious garbage in our society holds value for you in the work of other poets. Does it? "Pentecostal Locksmith" is an example of my attempt to do this, and people really respond to it in readings. I have several such, but many I've discarded as too polemical. They are hard to write. I feel the responsiblity to point out these issues to the general public, however.

PBR: I don't know nor do I adhere to any particular schools of thought when I write prose poems. I only know that I want them to reflect continuously changing states of mind created by stimuli primarily found in the natural world. I used to write in longer sentences than these, but have worked hard to be more cogent, more direct. Sound is such a huge part of the pieces in *Fields Below Zero* and the format allowed me to expand sounds I could not always accomplish in line poetry because of its greater inclination to brevity. Not being much of a narrative poet, I have to appeal to the ear more than one whose story-line accomplishes that in its stead. If there is any mystery at all, it's a matter of accustoming your sight to see in the dark with my eyes.

I'm not exactly certain what you mean by "social/religious garbage" but for the most part those who write about it are stuck in both the past and the present. Controlling universes is playing god. I don't like to listen to most folks' thoughts since they are mostly all the same litter especially concerning these topics: religion and society. To be a real skeptic, I think one has to have the ongoing choice to defy belief in what is taken for granted, whether it be in language or the perception leading to that language. Since most people are in love with being ignorant, none of the important issues are their concern. They are in denial. Look at our choices for leaders!!! Can you ask for a better example of our own demise? I guess I just think there may be more important things to think about rather than the same socio-political conditions that plague every era, every society and every individual through time up until right now. Nothing goes away and for individuals, life doesn't get any longer.

DA: My male poet friends say that this poem embarrasses them, then all criticism stops there.

My Whole Life

Making love with you is a stone thrown
into the earth's one river, sending spirals
along my whole day. Your imprints remain,
fingers like minnows on my skin,

rain on water. Iridescent ducks
skim my thoughts; my dreams are wings.
Surface water sparkles like my breasts.

You have parted
my curtain to the world.
You have entered me,
dropped down and down
and I swelled, river rocking you.

I sometimes see sunrise,
clitoris pink, rose
spreading above me, as you did.

And now, can you tell me again about our "sex life"?

But what about Miller, Ginsberg, Whitman? They wrote about their bodies, so why can't women? The point I'm trying to make is that my partner, Jim, uses the term "sex life" as if it was in a separate category from all the rest of life between lovers. Any thoughts on this would be appreciated. Women tend to respond in a positive way to the poem.

PBR: It's a good question because it dates way back to the one thing we're all trying to hedge in our own lives: religion. For the most part, religion has destroyed the senses, made it almost impossible for anyone to achieve any true happiness on earth because of their conviction that true happiness rests in an abstraction (heaven or hell) or with an abstraction (God). If you pursue the religious path, the one that says you must give up the senses, then the beautiful aspects of life are immediately removed, and your left believing in a here-after that doesn't exist no matter what anyone tells you. It disturbs most men to see or read the way you wrote these two pieces because they're still attached to the principle that life depends on giving its best parts up, nor do they especially like having a woman put it right back in their faces. I'm not talking about going debauchery here, maybe just a little more self-controlled hedonism without obliterating the sexes or each other's desires. It is not even societal now that religion has bored deep into it like a toxic disease. Our provincial attitudes are merely a cover-up for the more seedy side of life that exists in cities, in villages, in townships and outposts from here to Inner Mongolia. The reason women like your poem is because they are not embarassed by your beautiful image. Men are, because they have to face the reality that is not guarded from them by the glossy pages and celluloid formats of pornographic magazines and films respectively. It makes them compare and debase because most men are raised wrong, are raised to be insensitive and competitive. Parents and school contribute nicely thank you!

DA: I like the mythology inherent in religion and like to use some of its symbols: yin/yang is one example. You play with religion too, right? In your older book, *Half-Said*, I especially like the twist in the poem "Open Hand." The space before the last line is just right, and "a prayer to survive" has a double meaning. Secondly, why did you choose to write an entire book of prose poems? I'm interested in them, but they are a departure from your earlier book.

PBR: My thoughts on religion go very deep, but what I meant was that even the use of symbols can sometimes act as preconceptions of thought rather than original thought, thereby confusing the reader (writer too) as they search for their individualized path of perception and try to find an original, an authentic, and intimate experience in all forms without leaving language as exempt. I understand the symbols, but unless they are in tandem with some kind of particularized vision, they are just that: symbols. I too enjoy mythology although I have found religion to be more of a burden than an asset, even in my own work. Early on in my writings, I believed my attraction to it meant I could speak through its symbols as well, but I've learned that I have to create a new symbolism for any of the "real" thought religion possesses to have any vital impact on me and my senses. It's a hard issue. It's not one we are alone in addressing, but it has its place in many interior dialogues.

I suppose I wrote the prose pieces because I just write longer lines anyway. My mind works that way, and I wanted to put it out there as far as I cared to go. I probably have close to six or seven individual and unpublished manuscripts of prose poems dating back to the mid-eighties or so. It just feels natural for me, and I always feel most comfortable in that kind of focus. Plus, I'm not a very narrative poet and that medium of language has been helpful in being a springboard to a new kind of narration, if you will.

DA: Why do you do interviews in *The Bitter Oleander*, and on what basis do you choose the poets you choose to interview?

PBR: I choose poets to interview because of their poetry and because I like getting inside the head of the poet whose process may be radically different than I imagined. Once I start an interview, I dig for an essence of the poet, for something that will still be relevant in the future. I keep digging until a sprout pops up in my hand which is when I know I'm getting somewhere. The poets I choose have usually passed a lot of their work in front of me at my request and having been involved in it for a good period of time, I start to either feel intense attraction to it or none at all. What I truly enjoy is uncovering specifics about this or that poet's methodology, how he or she percieves reality, defines perception individually and responds to forces other than the commonplace, media-driven reality under which we suffer in our society today. The primary reason we do such interviews is to help preserve for the future the way a particular poet thought not so much about the usual things but about things that will always matter about their work far into the future.

DA: I just wanted to tell you of a couple of instances in which technology got in the way of direct experience of nature. (This is partly in response to your *Editor's Note* in Volume 11 Number 1 of *TBO*, and partly in response to some remarks made by you in our dialogues.)

A friend visited Yellowstone Park last year and saw parents positioning their two children in front of Old Faithful, backs turned to the geyser, fronts to the video camera. When the geyser ceased to spout, the family went on to other areas of the park and did not come back to Old Faithful. Absurd, isn't it, that the children never got to see the geyser spout in real life, but only later on video!

I like to hike, and I also like to stay for quite awhile at various beautiful locations. In the Columbia Gorge, there is a spot known as Beacon Rock, where one can see mountains, forests, clouds passing, and the Columbia River. My partner, Jim, and I stayed there for a long time---about 45 minutes. Most people who climbed the rock only stayed there for about 5 minutes. The worst situation, in our minds, was when two women got to the top and asked us to take their picture together with fists raised in triumph, so that their husbands waiting below could see that they had made it to the top. After that, they didn't even look around, but just started back down!

PBR: I'm used to all those things. And more...my poems comment on them continuously...for most folks, it's all about the success, the achievement, the accomplishment, the memory, the photograph instead of having to perceive and absorb anything. Ultimately, their children learn nothing, hate everything and wind up looking for ways to replace their parents with drugs, sex, tv, ipods, cd's, dvd's, video games, drugs, gambling, alcohol, and so on and so forth. It makes you wonder if anyone sits still in silence any more? Don't our lives allow us the opportunity anymore to be pleased and delighted by the greatness in all that surrounds us in teeming numbers? Instead, it seems that everyone has to be talking to someone, their cellphone clutched to their ears as if they were getting by-the-number instructions on how to perform a rare surgical technique or something...I could go on ranting forever about everything...my poems help control it, but a lot of what I say in my personal essays do not...

DA: I sometimes fall into a very light sleep, and images come to the fore which seem to be unconscious choices leading me to what is significant. Psychologists call this a "hypnogogic state." My Buddhist friend seems to create a similar state in a process she calls meditation. Do any of your imaginative images come from a form of consciousness such as any of the above?

PBR: It's well-known that all moments couched in relaxation and a lack of responsibility enhance the process by which images come forth. In my case, I have had these moments but rely on first hand recognition of things through my senses which I try to keep finely tuned so as to be illuminated terrestrially. The clarity of the literal world is so provocative if we would only see through the veil of limited subjectivity forced upon us by society's need for categorization, conformity and agreement. We'd have no interest in believing in abstract deities, after-lives, or other levels of dwelling eternally. When I notice a small blue flower with a five sectioned center of yellow blossoming in abundance by the roadside, I'm in that kind of "state" of image-making, because its beauty, its purpose against all possibilities is so evident. But again, it's not a "spiritual" process at all, as some may claim, but more, as I've said above, a terrestrial experience, an earthly rapture, a tellurian reality. If a person pays close, close attention to things and stops depending on their common meaning, reference or preconception, things begin to look very different and life has an excitement, a delight to it that no technological advance can ever offer us as human beings.

DA: I often find that your work recalls Koans; that is, it attacks the rational, or leaves me feeling as if I've asked the

wrong question. For instance, in "Birthday Poem," there are the lines

"I sit alone
behind an open door
and think this is the darkness
and the silence I have sought."

"When I look outside I am still completely blind."

Does the term Koan, or this sense I have of your attacking the obvious, the rational, resonate in any way with you?

PBR: I love the Koan but don't presume to understand the way it works. It fascinates me that we are so blind to actual reality and never give it a second thought when faced with the strange, the new or the unusual, to react in a way only our previous experiences allow us to act because we have no basis for understanding other than that which is, ultimately, useless. Cultivating a way to see things means destroying an entire world of preconceived notions, all types of mimesis, and most importantly, shared feelings or the agreement that says a group can feel exactly the same way about any one thing and totally abdicate their emotional base for something bland, matter-of-fact, robotic, etc. I think the poem's lines you quote here are indicative of my belief that no matter what the setting, no matter what the ultimate living condition, I am still blind to any and everything. Perhaps all this effort means nothing if I've tried too hard.

DA: Do your poems attempt to find the source of words, first by silence, and only then by speaking?

PBR: I don't know how words arise. I don't logically seek the extension of one word to the next. Doing that is like trying to make the distance between each pulse in your body the same whether running off a cliff, diving into icy water or walking up Everest without oxygen. I think the experience itself, and the associative power of that experience, creates a language that must first be totally absent until it gradually fills with a sound or sounds that channel themselves into a solidified kinship with words. The words are only messengers. They contain no source, to speak of. Yet, contradictory to this, if there is any source of words, of their sound, it may very well be in their absence.

DA: I definitely want to know why you started *The Bitter Oleander,* a light for many of us.

PBR: I started *TBO* simply because everything I read for over thirty years was depressing my sensibilities. I could not tell one magazine from another. It seems that confessional narrative type poetry was the rage or Bukowski tirades of language were some sort of oracle of alcoholism and lost promises. The void was huge for poetry that had depth, that had a strong and purposeful affinity to nature and, above all, one that was serious about every single word that was written. When I began this back in 1974, that was and still is my main interest: to undominate the market of its sameness and try to reach as many people as possible with a vital, exciting, unique kind of poetry that makes you emote instead of ponder what you already know or feel half-amused.

DA: Could you elucidate on what exactly the Immanentist movement is all about?

PBR: Movements do not interest me personally. Immanentism is, at best, a vague term Duane Locke has used to talk about poets who write from the superconscious, but because it represents a huge individual perspective and not a common, generalized one, it could never be a movement based on total agreement because it has no solid foundation except in that language must fit your perception and your perception alone for it to be a true one. The rest of the work is on your own. As far as imaginative versus deep image, I think the term "imaginative" has been given poor regard because most folks feel it means fantasy or comic book fiction. If you read back to William Blake, and then come forward to the present, there are poets in every era since then who subscribed to the imaginative in order to make sense out of their own private and sometimes hell-driven realities. So, nothing's changed.

DA: Since poetry is such a venture into the unknown and unexpected, does it ever become scary for you? There wouldn't be another person there with you; the way you write strikes me as if you were on a long, somewhat dangerous hike, alone. What is the impulse---I like your word-pulse-rate analogy---to go into these unknown language spaces and place words there?

PBR: I guess that's the whole point, that it be "scary," that this venturing into new experience not be burdened by old experience so that you actually get your eyes opened instead of being dull to the experience because your conditioning's telling you that it's a similar experience as before. Since nothing stays the same, it stands to even the most limited of reasons, that learning is unlearning what you've been taught in order to learn something new. The impulse to venture into these unworded spaces is, at least for me, to find a place (as often as possible) that gets me out of the suffering that's my life, your life or every single person's life on this turbulent planet. Of course, the simple beauty of putting words out on the page, naked and trembling, thrills me to no end. I'm preoccupied with it.

94

An Aspect's Aftermath
Paul B. Roth

Circular

staircases curl

each single

blonde strand

of her hair

Old secrets

kissing

in dim hallways

embrace

neckless perfumes

Dreams

never recalled

for their clothes

appear naked

in black and white

spaces

Even

her underarm's

curvature

resembles

a sleeveless moon

Strewn

across bedsheets

are wrinkles

96   her missing shape

scrawls

Music in Silence
Paul B. Roth

Dawn's

white fragrance

of apple blossoms

strings

with its delicate

pink-orange hairs

a silent violin

whose music

honey bees tune

with their soft

blossoming hugs

buzzing

and touching

nothing less

than every

weightless petal

Secret Tomas
Gina Frangello

Things to do on 27th Birthday:
1) hit Louis Vuitton to get replacement foot for one that fell off tote
"Mmm, your skin's soft as silk."
2) if I leave straight from here I can afford a cab . . .
"Tell me what it feels like in there."
3) but if I don't go home first, it'll be hours before I can check the mail . . .
"Come on, baby, talk to me."
4) shit, say something: "Mmm, yeah. Feels . . . full . . . good . . ."

Brent's climax hits abrupt and silent. Over his shoulder, through his bedroom window, Annette watches the ferris wheel at Navy Pier inching its jerky rotation to nowhere. Brent's body reclines upon hers, restraining the movement of her neck, her view of the kitschy, touristy merriment, only for a moment. Then he is up, shaking his skin free of her, heading for the shower.

5) There are some phones in Ghana. Go home first, check mail and answering machine . . .

Mid-step, Brent's eyes trail to the window and back to her breasts, which, in repose, have perhaps already started to roll a bit more towards her armpits than they did at twenty-six. His eyebrows gather. "Well, now I know how necrophilia feels. Thanks. Look, I'm leaving straight from work tonight, so . . ."

"Can't wait for another trip to the morgue?" Annette turns onto her side.

"Yeah, well, I hate to leave when I've got a stiff body right here at home . . ." He half-laughs. Then: "She's making me go, you know. I don't care how damned hot it is outside, the water will be freezing. You can't swim in March—what's the point?"

Annette sighs.

"Look, why don't you go to the gym today, get your nails done or something?" He turns back towards the bathroom. "Get a good night's rest. Cheer yourself up."

As if she has another option. "Thanks for the advice."

"This ain't no charity service, lady," he growls with false jocularity—disappears behind the door. "I expect to get what I'm paying for."

Morning mimosas could be the answer. She should have told Brent it was her birthday—then there would be the two of them here, maybe a blue Tiffany's box tied with a billowy white bow, two plane tickets under her coffee saucer, roses on the breakfast table. Instead, there is only Annette lingering naked in Brent's bed chiding herself for being a bad lay, and worse, pathetic. She rises, hoping the champagne from last night isn't too flat to ruin the vibe she's striving for. Sometimes, something like this—an image of herself in her mind as a nude, sexy, mimosa-drinking woman on a rich man's leather sofa during business hours—is enough to replace whatever other ugly image has been dominant. She wishes Brent's city apartment had fresh-cut orchids or a grand piano or something romantic, but those touches are no doubt reserved for the real home he shares with his wife in Lake Forest. Still, this clubby, masculine atmosphere might work too, in a different, more torrid way. She pirouettes towards the fridge.

100

A window washer is looking right at her.

"Fuck!"

Annette staggers, half-falls back through the doorway separating Brent's bedroom and living room, then, in a panic that somehow the window-washer can still see her (though she can no longer see him), scoots on her bare ass into the bathroom where there are no windows, and throws on Brent's robe. Cross-legged on the floor, heart pulsing in her ears, she listens as though the soundproof walls might give something away. Her watch is on the coffee table; she has no idea how long to wait, the duration of time it might take to clean such a gargantuan window and whether he was almost finished or had just begun. Her stomach growls impatiently. Brent has no food, though the mimosa would have calmed her hunger. She shouldn't have jumped, shouldn't have freaked out—should have strode right to the refrigerator and poured herself a drink, raised it towards him in a salute. Then she could have come back into the bedroom and gotten dressed and left like a woman entitled to be here, not like some perverted cat-burglar who takes to undressing in the homes of her victims and prancing about like a fool. Annette bursts into tears. It must be hypoglycemia. She has not eaten since half a tuna sandwich yesterday for lunch.

By the time she emerges, the tears have only made her feel silly. From the way she bolted, he probably guessed she'd run cowering to the bathroom to bawl like a baby. It doesn't matter now anyway. The window-washer is gone.

Every afternoon, the butterflies in her stomach are the same. The turning of her key in the rusty mail box; the flutter rising up her esophagus as she sorts through envelopes, scanning for a foreign stamp. Every afternoon, so part of her always thinks *today* cannot be the day—good things have to catch you unaware, you cannot be caught waiting for them. *A watched pot never boils.* Once, Annette forced herself not to check the mail for four days, certain that her self-deprivation would magically produce a reward, but it produced only more bills Brent had to help her with, a jury summons, a letter from the INS addressed to her grandmother who has been dead for twenty years and never lived in this apartment. The way her hands perspired when she finally allowed herself to check the mail—key slipping from her grasp like a slimy bar of soap—embarrassed her sufficiently that she resigned to indulging herself with her daily fix of nausea and disappointment. Since Nicky has been in Ghana, the progression has been from frequent long letters to sporadic postcards. He has been gone two years. Even his mother has more sense than to spend every day *expecting*.

Today is the day. Clutching what looks like an actual birthday card, Annette's heart surges violently forward, the rest of her taking a moment to catch up. She is almost angry:

usually Nicky's holiday greetings arrive weeks late—now she will never know when to calm down. Unable to wait until she reaches the privacy of her own apartment, she rips it open in the foyer, ankle-deep in discarded coupon pages, flyers and advertisements. *Netty Baby!* But after that, she—Annette—disappears amidst: . . . *we got them to donate some old computers and I've spent the better part of a month trying to sort them out, most were archaic.* Is relegated to the role of blind spectator: *I call our best student "Powder" because she's always covered in dust lighter than her skin, but her father won't let her come to school anymore since her mother had another baby and Powder has to take care of him while her parents work . . .*

When Annette got dirty as a child, Nicky called her Pig Pen. *Her* dirt—Chicago dirt—was not imbued with the drama of Africa. *Her* absences from school were not because her working parents made her take care of the home, but because they were too busy to know or care where she went—and so she went with Nicky. Maybe she was never enough of a victim for him; all the time she was struggling to keep up, maybe she should have let herself fall so he could rescue her. Maybe then he would not have needed to go halfway around the world to feel important. Maybe then "archaic" would be written with irony—with an implicit wink, *Remember when we would've called that a ten-dollar-word?*—instead of carelessly, as though he had forgotten he was not addressing one of his Peace Corps buddies. Or maybe then, they would just both be where they had always been: on drugs, in trouble, stagnant.

How can she explain to anyone—her mother, Brent, least of all Nicky in his campaign to save the world through the civilized means of computer training—that she wishes the brutal, crazy race towards death they once shared had never come to an end?

The window-washer's jaw seemed vaguely Czech, she realizes. Square and animalistic, like the author of that novel she tried to read once—not at all like the actor who'd starred in the film version, ethereal Daniel Day Lewis. *The Unbearable Lightness of Being.* She thinks it's still hidden under a mattress in her parents' home, like porn. Annette remembers a scene in the movie where Day-Lewis' character Tomas, a doctor by trade, is forced out of his practice by oppressive Communists and has to become a window washer to make a living. Tomas systematically beds the housewives inside the homes whose windows he cleans—including the wife of a high-ranking Communist official (played by a flat-chested, pug-looking actress.) The scene intrigued Annette even before having a window-washer of her own to think about, because it showed a man in a chick role—without money or power—using sex the way women had to: as revenge, as an equalizer. Though if she remembers right, Tomas-The-Powerful-Doctor was a player to begin with (easy since every woman wants to fuck a doctor), so maybe she doesn't get the point at all. Still, it makes her want to ask who ranks higher on the urban food chain: a financially dependent, poorly educated mistress of an influential married man, or a young, blue collar window-washer, possibly of foreign descent, who has, regardless of other obvious social deficiencies, a dick?

She is not Brent's wife; it is not her apartment; fucking her would offer, in the sad, bottom-line truth of it, no revenge on the alpha males of the world.

But her square-jawed, secret Tomas knows none of this.   103

Once upon a time, Annette and her cousin Nicky were partners in crime. He introduced her to every illicit thing she did; she dated the Mafioso wannabes he traveled with, snorted the coke he sold, hung out at the club where he bounced. Before that, when he was nothing but a punk in the hood, a fourteen to her ten, she worshipped him, trailed around behind his fellow gangbangers until the scummier among them, who could not get fourteen-year-old girls to make out with them, would settle for French kissing Annette behind the shelter court in the playground, groping up her shirt for breasts that wouldn't be there for three years.

She was prettier than other girls. It was her currency in the neighborhood, where being female or smart or ambitious didn't count for much, could be a liability. Guys liked her, and since she was an only child, Nicky was her stand-in brother, protector and pimp in one. He guarded her virginity ruthlessly at first—threatened to smack her around if she drank or got high with anyone but him. But by the time she started high school it was as though his mission was accomplished, and like a hippie dad overeager to relive his own youth, he hastily drew her into his fold as a full initiate. Her school acquaintances amused her with their adolescent antics; by then she was going out with Nicky's best friend, a nineteen-year-old dealer; she got her coke for free. Even the sex didn't seem to bother Nicky anymore—when her first lover tired of her, there were a string of others, all stamped with Nicky's seal of approval, all in the club scene, all small-time aspiring gangsters in an era before *The Sopranos* made Guidos chic, all with a plethora of drugs and occasional free tickets to Vegas, all with hard, lean bodies and pissed-off pricks and a disgust for the female menstrual cycle that bordered on Hasidic.

In Nicky's world, her closest girlfriends were the rotating parade of girls his friends fucked. Women existed only on the fringes. She was really the *guys'* mascot; their team whore on a one-at-a-time basis. They trusted her, told her about the break-ins, the occasional shootings. She hid under the bed when somebody came trying to kill Nicky over a deal gone awry. It was a family.

"Blood is thicker than water," Nicky always used to say. "You're the only one I can talk to." He was that cinematic breed: the soulful gang-leader, his hair, in a sea of brillo-pad Italian-boy heads, fell in loose locks into his eyes. They made such a beautiful pair that, hair wet, in skimpy swimsuits on Oak Street beach, people gawked. But out in public, in clothes that grew progressively more expensive the more Nicky sold, a certain gaud easily distinguished them from the *righteous* affluent, those whose establishment she and Nicky gladly skirted. Women averted their eyes; men tightened their grips on their wallets. Nowadays, even though it has come back in fashion, Annette refuses to wear gold.

The facts: it was a Friday when the window washer first arrived (or rather, when she accidentally flashed him and noticed his existence—he has probably been at this job for some time.) So, each Thursday night she makes certain to sleep at Brent's, which is easier now that his wife and their three children are in South Haven for the summer and Brent drives up from Friday night to Sunday morning. Thursday evenings, he is desperate to see her, desperate to fuck her brains out, even though he admits he and his wife *do* have sex. "It's easier than having to talk about why we never screw," he says. Clearly no brains will be hitting the headboard in South Haven.

Annette sat, a tight coil besides Nicky's sprawled-wide legs. He was purposely bored, having only come as a favor to her, one he wasn't intending to let her forget. Annette had read a review of *The Unbearable Lightness of Being* and *needed* to see it. She nursed a fantasy of herself as the kind of girl who liked foreign films, but the prospect of getting anyone she knew to sit through subtitles was nonexistent, and this movie—in English, but with its European stars and director— seemed a possible compromise. "You'll like it," she'd begged Nicky, "It's supposed to be sexy." To which he replied, "I don't need to go to the movies to get off." He'd smuggled in more candy than they could eat, just to make a point.

This was the only cinema they'd ever visited together. Childhood movies they both loved—*Grease, Saturday Night Fever*—they'd seen separately, or on cable, getting high around the glow of somebody's mother's old TV. Yet he was here. It occurred to neither of them that she should go alone.

Nicky's every squirm and twitch jarred her. She imagined him berating her in his head for not reading the part about the movie being *three hours long*. When the credits finally rolled, she felt numb with relief. *The Unbearable Boredom of Being*, Nicky called it, filing out of the theater with his arm around her, periodically knuckling her head like when they were kids. "Those chicks weren't even hot," he said, "That one was old and the other had no tits. You put them to shame—why do you always wanna be somebody else?" It was the first time Annette ever felt embarrassed in front of Nicky, like he'd figured out something weak about her that she hadn't even known herself.

Afterwards, though, clips from the film began playing in her sexual fantasies. She went out and bought the novel, by a strange Czech dissident whose jacket photo looked aggressive, angry, potentially violent. In the book, the Tomas character was supposed to be a much older man than scrumptious Daniel Day Lewis—probably near fifty. The author used simple words, but his train of thought was confusing, preoccupied with classical music and philosophies with which Annette was unfamiliar. While she could sense the same erotic current of the film swimming just beneath so many inaccessible ideas, she ultimately tossed the novel aside and allowed Day Lewis and his voluptuous on-screen lover, Lena Olin of the sultry bowler hat, to claim space in her head again, dismissing the book on which their roles had been based as part of a giant heap of things in life entitled OVER MY HEAD.

Whenever they were bored and trying to figure out what to do, Nicky would quip, "Hey Netty, why don't you pick out a movie for us to see," and crack up. Sometimes she even scanned the paper for the dullest possible titles to throw his way deadpan—*Babette's Feast*; *The Belly of An Architect*—he got a real kick out of that.

Every week, she waits. The trick is enticing Brent into remaining with her past 8am Friday mornings. She calculates that it was 10:15 the first time she saw the window-washer, and she isn't quite certain why Brent was running so late, or rather why he wanted to screw instead of walking out the door at his usual time. If only she hadn't been so abysmal in bed that morning—damn Nicky, distracting her on her birthday—now there is probably no hope of getting Brent to sleep in again on a Friday morning so the window-washer can watch them fuck. The first Thursday after the flashing, Annette is so desperate that she just turns off Brent's alarm clock once he is asleep, although of course when he wakes, an hour late, he is frantic and rushing and would not touch her if he were off to spend a *month* in South Haven, and his wife was the only woman in the town.

It turns out not to matter because the window-washer does not show up anyway. The second week, Annette hits a grand slam by waking up and announcing she just had an orgasm in her sleep while dreaming about anal sex—that garners her so many points that she is even able to lure him out into the living room to do it on the floor only a foot away from the last window-washer sighting. But again, the Czech-jawed boy does not arrive. The third week, Annette feels depressed and gives no effort at all; she refuses his advances at 7am since his timing is all wrong—no way can he last three hours. She claims she has to meet her mother at the hospital for an early morning colonoscopy Ma is afraid to have, and scurries out, then regrets not even being able to verify the window-washer's absence. So the fourth week, hope renews: once a month, that would make sense. Thursday night she stretches in the crook of Brent's arm and says, "I never cook for you. I wish I could cook you breakfast tomorrow, before you leave for the weekend. Do you have any important meetings in the morning?"

Remarkably, the answer comes back, "Nothing I can't change."

The stage is set.

What she hopes: the window washer will imagine she's in trouble. He will think Brent is exploiting her—even heroes in movies fall in love with whores if they belong to powerful men. Her Tomas will be an honest, hard-working, blue collar laborer. He will be the kind of man she would have met in her old neighborhood—the kind of man her mother met—if she had not spent so much time chasing Nicky's drug-induced dreams of glamour and power and money. Nicky left her at the precipice between two worlds, where it was impossible anymore to be a normal neighborhood girl and get a job at the deli counter of Dominick's and marry the night manager and buy a characterless new construction home in the cultural wasteland of the far southwest suburbs. But she could never be *more* either—never move among wives who summer in South Haven, or Gold Coast career women with their law degrees and androgynously beige Todd flats. She is a mistress out on the ledge of wealth and privilege, constantly in danger of falling, and she needs someone—a working class hero without a fear of heights—to throw her a rope. They could marry. She is only twenty-seven. She would bear him strong sons. Daughters are just too hard to raise.

If this were a film, the past three weeks would end up on the cutting-room floor. Jump from Scene 1: *Annette sitting weeping on Brent's bathroom floor, cowering in his robe after having been (certainly, if it were Hollywood) seen naked by a roguishly handsome, young, foreign window-washer* to Scene 2: *Annette and Brent at dining room table, a distance from but still visible to the picture window where said washer first made his appearance. Brent's back faces window, since that is the chair where Annette set his mimosa (and the view is commonplace to him); Annette, at his right, has eye on window. Washer appears—it is nearly 10 a.m. on the dot, it is like fucking clockwork, it is symbolism of some kind that the audience will be left to decipher later. Annette loosens Brent's robe.*

The washer is not alone this time. (Did he have a partner last time too, and Annette was just in too much of a tizzy to notice?) He and the other man, also young, probably Mexican, halt laughing, stare as Annette, who has been serving breakfast in the nude, undoes her lover's robe and sinks to her knees.

Head is a sure way to make certain a man has absolutely no desire to turn around and look out the window behind him.

This other guy, not at all good looking, with a shadow of pubescent acne, unnerves her, but she has come too far. He will be edited out for the movie's release. No, he definitely wasn't here last time; he couldn't have been. *Her* window-washer will remember her, remember what he saw last time. Will know this is for him.

Between Brent's flapping robe and the fact that she must kneel directly in front of him if she means to keep his back fully to the window, Annette is unable to meet her window-washer's eyes.

Annette had just turned twenty-one the summer Nicky saved that woman.

The crime bosses with whom he was loosely affiliated were also heavily into construction, so since bouncing only took a few hours in the evenings, Nicky was a laborer by day. His buddies on the site mocked him when he shouted them over, "Look at that dude, shit, he's gonna kill that woman!" "Yeah, it's fucking *Rear Window*," one of the older men scoffed, but Nicky was already racing for the lift. They hummed bars of the Superman theme song as he rode down to the ground, sped up God only remembered how many flights of stairs in the building across the way. Nobody followed him. Sure, "everyone" had seen "that spade smacking around his old lady," several told the police later, but it'd looked like she was getting in his face pretty good—it didn't look like anything serious. Nobody, Annette least of all, could guess how Nicky knew.

By the time he got there, the woman was unconscious. Though not yet showing, she was four months pregnant.

Nicky ran right in through their unlocked door ("he wrestled the gun from that crazy sonofabitch's hand," said one of the witnesses at the construction site who'd watched it all through the apartment's window), but the assault victim still miscarried. Nicky mourned the death of the child—the fetus. Publicly. On the news, over and over, while interviewed about his heroic rescue. On local talk shows; NPR. On camera for Channel 7, he cried.

The baby-killer was strung out on crack, which he had not purchased from any of the numerous construction site dealers, having connections of his own. After that, Nicky wouldn't touch drugs. Mere weed was repellent to him. He put in his time at the site, but he wouldn't deal anymore. Even his ex-bosses approved. He was their resident hero, their local boy made good. They crowed when he joined the Army. His soldier's patriotism would atone for all their sins.

All at once it is clear: the first Friday of every month, Brent's building's window washers clean his windows. Though their staff of cleaners may be quite large, *her* window-washer is most frequently assigned to Brent's windows—though not always. Once, two completely other men appeared outside, and Annette calmly walked into the bedroom, dressed and went back to her own apartment to find her mailbox empty, then spent the day trying to find something clever to say to Nicky in a letter, but she suspected her grammar was faulty, her spelling childish, and that her life would depress him.

In *The Unbearable Lightness of Being*, the Communist official's wife opened her window and Tomas climbed right in, but the picture windows of Chicago high rises do not open. In order to reach her, the washer would have to go past the doorman, through the lobby, up the elevator. She would have to mouth the apartment number through the glass—she imagines their hands meeting on opposite ends of the pane, like prisoners and their wives on visitation day.

Except that here, she is the prisoner, by choice, in a very expensive cage.

He probably thinks she is a prostitute. He must figure Brent for some kind of exhibitionist homosexual who pays a beautiful woman to come to his apartment and put on a show for the young hotties who do physical labor at his building. What *woman*, after all, would voluntarily spend the first Friday of every month performing sexual acts in front of a stranger outside the window—sometimes more than one stranger? He probably thinks, on the mornings she has been unable to get Brent to stay put and put out (so she masturbates alone with her eyes clamped shut), that her john is lurking somewhere just out of eyesight, surveying his whore's performance from the other side of the wall.

Nicky stood on her parents' front porch waiting for her to come out and say good-bye. It was August then like now. She emerged with cotton stuffed between bare toes, nails glimmering with purple polish. He held out a can of MGD and Annette took a big swig, lipstick leaving a waxy lavender smudge. They stood swallowing hard like small town teens on a first date.

"They'll make you cut your hair," Annette said. His hair was not inordinately long. He stared at her, his expression vague, grasping.

"You'll be cool, Netty. You've got a job, a diploma—shit, your dad's right inside that door eating dinner with your ma, not rotting in jail like my old man. You've got everything going for you, babe. You don't need me."

She'd scraped her wet toenail against the tiny rocks embedded in the cement of her front steps, ruined all her hard work. "I never said I did."

"Yeah, see," he punched her in the arm, "you're tough." Then, like he couldn't make up his mind: "Don't be that way."

He was right. His control over her life had always been conceptual, not actual. Sweat drizzled the bones of her chest, bare above an old terrycloth tube top she'd had since eighth grade. He was right. No point in even bringing up the three abortions she'd had over the past seven years at his counsel, or the fact that only the first guy to knock her up even merited a punch, while the other two were in his inner circle, entitled to plant their seed even if they did not want to raise it. No point in asking why he'd never shed any tears for her dead children, *his* thick blood, even when Channel 7 panned in for a close-up of his dramatically rolling tear over the probably-brain-damaged product of junkie parents. Annette's nose membranes were so abused they both knew hers would have been brain damaged too.

He leaned in to kiss her cheek, some kid sister too young to care that he was heading off to college. She turned abruptly so he got her lips instead. He jerked back and she glowed, triumphant, but then his hand reached out just as quick, so fast she feared he might belt her. Instead his fingers grazed lightly, almost lazily over her collar bones, downward, wiping away perspiration. She jumped, bumped her hip against the door frame. He grinned, and all at once it was a smile of everything, a smile of *I could've had you if I wanted to*, a smile of *See, I did the right thing there too*. She sensed he wanted her to be grateful somehow, for leaving her intact. She felt abject, insignificant, naked. Nothing like gratitude.

But he was backing down the stairs, hands spread between a wave, an apology, an offering. Her lips parted to speak: nothing else. His eyes were over her already, busy doing his bad-boy-poet thing, dreaming of the stars.

This is how a hero is fashioned: like everyone else who knew him, the Army was impressed by Nicky. With the earnestness of a new convert, he set about devouring every education they could offer. In the span of four year's time, he finagled not only a GED, but a BA in computer science, then hurled with all his might towards the Peace Corps. To Ghana, where fellow aid workers muttered how he'd "gone native"—that he failed to exhibit the proper alarm when flies congregated on an open sore. He wrote these things in letters at first; he wanted to impress her, maybe. He preached of his determination to drag his corner of the Third World into a technological age that, here in Chicago, still baffled Annette. Words like *archaic* rolled off his pen. He learned to see art in the dusty dirt powdering a young African girl's night-black skin. He forgot the audience of his letters home, then forgot to write letters home altogether. He *was* home.

"Are you leaving early this morning?" she asks Brent when he slings his suit jacket over his arm: another man with a mission.

"Early for what?" he asks. "I was supposed to be at the office five minutes ago."

She has no answer. She has long suspected he is secretly aware of her games with the window-washer—that he allows himself to be detained in order to play along. But no, Brent is a shy man really. He once told her a story about going to a nude beach with friends and pleading with his wife

111

not to take her suit off so that he would not be the only one who refused to undress. His wife laughed at him and flung off her bikini—Annette has seen photos of her (clothed) and she is overweight, very Tipper Gore. Brent has a nice body, swimmer's shoulders and no spare tire to speak of. The story surprised her—made her wonder for the first time if his wife might have a lover too. If she might not consider Brent any great loss.

She re-dresses in the lingerie she wore last night, it having spent only five minutes on her body before Brent peeled it off. Patiently, she reclines on the leather sofa—but it is only 8:15 and she will have a long wait. She stands and paces the room, restless in luxurious captivity, touching everything she passes, leaving her scent. Brent's bookshelves bear titles too divergent to reflect the mind of a man she has never seen reading anything but the *Wall Street Journal*: from self-help for golfers to volumes on the Ming Dynasty to Stephen King to *Men Are From Mars, Women Are From Venus*. Although the city apartment is mostly his, perhaps some of these belong to his nudist wife. That she is utterly uncertain which—cannot differentiate her lover's taste from that of a woman she has never met—saddens her only vaguely. Among the closely packed book spines, she recognizes the name of the same angry Czech who wrote *The Unbearable Lightness of Being*. Has this always been here? It is a short story collection: *Laughable Loves*. A less imposing title, surely. She extracts it carefully, memorizing the books on either side, brings it back to the couch.

Annette's course without Nicky was a smooth ascent among married men. From hostessing at *restaurantes* run by whichever of Nicky's friends she was currently banging, to affairs with coke-loving options traders who frequented these establishments, and finally to the fortysomething head of a prestigious, privately-owned trading firm. Once she met Brent, being a "restaurant girl" didn't fit anymore—didn't leave her evenings free enough to accommodate a busy lover; made her too visible, exposed her to the eyes of too many men. Her breakfast of coke, snacks of speed, and bedtime milk-and-cookies of Flexiril compromised her looks, her ability to say the right thing at all times, so she quit cold: her own choice. She learned never to wear eyeliner on the inside of her lower eyelid—to wear just enough makeup to look like she didn't need makeup. To wear very high heels, but not too-tight clothes. She keeps her nails short and square.

Yet here she is. She cannot understand *The Unbearable Lightness of Being*. She does not even have a job. Her apartment is a shithole because she spends all her money on the maintenance of beauty, and Brent will *help*—as they all have—but not so much that she might feel she has enough and want to leave. Not so much that someone better might mistake her for being in their league. Her haircut is more flattering now; her life has been prolonged by getting off drugs; a rendez-vous in Paris with a lover who speaks French beats those old weekends in Vegas hands down—obviously. Annette *knows* that Nicky saved his own life when he saved a stranger from a man just like him.

But what is that woman doing now, with her miscarried pregnancy and husband in prison? Is she in Ghana too? Or is she letting some other jag-off pistol whip her and hoping he gets it right this time without some freak playing Superman barging in?

Why couldn't Nicky have just let that stupid woman die?

This Doctor Havel, who stars in two stories, might as well be Tomas. The plots are different, but the same things *happen* here, really. It's simple: Big-Brotherish political backdrops, women reluctantly experiencing sexual pleasure divorced from love, *succumbing* to freedom. Annette is reminded of Tomas' wife, Teresa, and her adulterous jaunt with the architect who may or may not be a Communist spy. Kundera's women are so often devastated that bodies have wills of their own— Annette feels for them even though the only man she has ever loved is the one she never fucked. Still she recognizes herself here—a roving shame turned into language—as surely as if she were forced to read a million books (imagine reading a million books!) and told none of the authors, she would know these words as Kundera's. The restrained violence of his jaw and his personal demons are smeared all over the pages. This time, she finds herself scanning stories almost hoping to find obscure musical bars transposed onto the page, obtuse references to composers and philosophers of whom she's never heard—she longs to greet her own confusion like running into an old friend after many years and recognizing his befuddling traits and viewpoints as familiar and comforting. Rage boils, obliterating her desire to reach into the pages and grab Kundera's hand—if this writer who makes his living adopting masks cannot hide his own soul behind the words, then how then can *Nicky*, who had scarcely ever written more than his name before he left her? Did even the fingerprints on his Army gun become different than on the one he carried in Chicago? How can the boy she loved shield and remake his identity so completely to shut her out?

Knocking, *rap rap rap*: where is it coming from? Annette jerks, bolts upright from where she has been curled over her book, whips her neck around to survey the room. Then she sees him: the Mexican window washer thumping Brent's window with his wiper—has he already tried his own stocky hand and found the thick glass muffled all sound? She looks up and meets his eyes square on. He smirks at her expectantly, raises his eyebrows in question: *Where's the show?*

She lowers her head again, searches for words on the page, a soul to recognize.

But the noise continues. Staccato, persistent, so she stands. Outside the window, the boy grabs his crotch, motions down—she thinks at first he's suggesting she grab *her* crotch too—but no, he is pointing at the ground. Gestures his watch, holds up all five fingers spread wide and mouths *five* since her track record of behavior surely necessitates stupidity. Her feet move.

It takes only moments to dress and make her way through the lobby to the wall of hot wet air waiting outside. Once out in the open, she nearly scurries to hail a cab instead, then stops, marches to the side of the building where she has seen trucks pull up—where workmen sometimes congregate. In the distance, that monstrous ferris wheel watches over the city from Navy Pier, the pier itself remade from merely the ship's port of her childhood into a tourists' amusement park full of bells, whistles and glitz. Annette's legs plant strong on the pavement, waiting, her blood simmering a witches' brew of shame and hope.

Then *he* is there. Walking with a cluster of six other men: the men who share his days, mock his frailties. Men he may someday surprise by saving a woman he does not know from a danger that does not quite have a name. He walks as though one leg is slightly shorter than the other; his jeans are too big. His hair, dark brown, looks dusty, and Annette thinks: *I could find poetry here too. I could see like Nicky sees.* They approach, so close she can almost feel the steam of their cluster. They are a tangle of accents, but everyone is speaking English. Relief floods her—he will understand. Then terror. Understand what? Why is she here? He moves on, cloistered in his herd of men.

Her secret Tomas has passed. She stands, decked out in her filmy Gucci dress, hair slicked back tight from her face and suddenly pinching her scalp. Among the men he was with, two others have seen her naked. She turns to leave.

Their bodies collide—Annette stumbles. Inches from her body, spewing apologetic murmurs for his clumsiness, is, finally, the Mexican. He looks at her and, like a character in a soap opera or Shakespeare, blinks hard as though she is unrecognizable to him under the disguise of her expensive clothing. Where is his crotch grabbing now?

"You're awfully shy," she drawls—she wants to scare him, to be a scary, inappropriate woman; she does not know why. "For somebody who's seen me give my boyfriend head in his dining room."

"Shi-it," the boy drawls, laughing. Then: "At first I thought you couldn't see us, but I hear you do that all the time, huh? Put on a show for Canji. Hey, I would too if I were fine like you—you look pretty good even in them clothes. We see some weird-ass shit in this line of work, lemme tell you, but ain't half of it fine like you—"

"Canji—is that the other guy?" she bursts. "Good-looking, maybe Eastern European—"

"Damn straight, mama, he goes for your show every time. Personally, I think a person ought to share, but the boss man heard about you and he don't like no trouble. Guess he wants to keep you from wolves like the rest of us." He howls: "*Ahhoouu!*"

"Does he just?" Sweat stains must be visible. Now *that* is what the rich really should invent: clothing that under no circumstances shows moisture—that lets you truly look like a different breed. "So Canji's supposed to protect me, huh?"

"Naw, man." The boy cannot stop laughing—Annette is not sure whether she makes him nervous, or if he is simply giddy at his good fortune to be talking to the building's stripper right out in broad daylight. Sing-song: "It ain't like that—*he-be-likin'-the-boys.* He'd rather be watching, like, Broadway, eh? It's an offense, for real, I'm telling you. I didn't sign on for this kind of work thinking I'd have to be up on a ledge alone with a faggot. I'm scared for my life, if you know what I mean!"

Annette's mouth has gone dry. "You're lying," she tries. "You're telling me he's gay because you know I like him."

"Sheee-eet! Naw, I would not a guessed that one, no m'am. I 'aint shitting you, I swear on *mi abuela's* soul, no bull. You can ask anyone. You want me to call one of the guys right now, hey, I can do it, I got my cell—"

"That won't be necessary." Annette's hand flutters to the gap in her suit jacket; the flesh stretched across her breastbones suddenly feels indecent. "I've got to go."

"Hey, naw, don't leave—!" His voice, so loud—can the others hear him?—chases her through the tunnel of her own humiliation, her heels clicking on hot concrete. The air itself seems far away. She is heading the wrong way to best hail a cab.

"I'm no faggot!" the boy calls. "We don't got no other faggots on our crew. If you're lookin' for a date, you look me up, my name's Angel, remember, like I-will-be-your-Angel-of-Love. Uh-huh, girl, I'll give you a real man, you come asking for me . . ."

Annette gathers the suit jacket tighter together until it skims her throat. Her heart, thrashing so loud in her ears, pounds like heavy running on the ground behind her—like the whole crew in hot pursuit. When she looks, though—once, twice—there is no one. She can no longer hear the boy's voice, taunting. Inviting. She stands in the middle of Olive Park, in the shade of trees, the deceptive bliss of green sanctuary amidst urban sprawl, body trembling. Is Canji really gay? And if it were a lie, then what? Did she expect him to arrive at her door with flowers, open the passenger's door of his battered car, kiss her close-mouthed at the drive-in and ask her father for her hand? What made her think she could go backwards? What, exactly, made her think it would be less stifling this time around than when she and Nicky were so hot to court death just to get out?

A man can join the army. A man can save one woman and make up for the trail of female bodies strewn behind him just like that. Presto, chango, instant hero, the world at his feet.

A woman can clamp her legs shut tight, declare *No more*, and watch herself become even more invisible—give up what little of the world she has.

Annette gropes through her Louis Vuitton tote for a tissue; her fingers brush her Tiffany's keychain. Her mail key, Brent's key, the key to an apartment she despises. Then: the slightly ragged paperback cover of *Laughable Loves*. She didn't even realize, in her haste, that she'd taken it. Her fingers plunge deep inside the pages like a bucket of ice or a Bible: some chilling relief. The sun scorches, a mere sliver of the heat of Ghana, this thin book under her hand slim substitution for the redemption Nicky found under the African sun. There had to be a way he could have taken her with, like he planned when he was going to be a wise guy and shoot them to the moon. She was good enough to ruin, not good enough to save. But no, Nicky hadn't ruined her fully either—he'd made sure she knew that, knew it was his choice. A hero would have let her believe in her own decency, her own importance— would have allowed her one small moment of triumph on that porch. O.K., maybe she *was* merely beautiful, not entitled to transcendence, even in the anonymity of a movie theater, the pages of a book. But what more right had Nicky to the transformational, sun-parched, ugly beauty of this wide world than she?

"Hey!" she shouts out in the direction of the Mexican boy, though she can no longer see him. "Angel . . . !" He could have taught her Spanish. Something she would carry inside that nobody could take away. Light breeze answers. *He was only a child.* Besides, what would her end of the transaction have been but the same?

Annette's tote is heavy. Holding her breath, she shoves the stolen book under a damp armpit, palms only the key to her apartment and stuffs the tote and its remaining contents under a tree. Less an offering of peace than a sacrifice she prays will be miraculously ignited by the heat should she panic and rush back. Her wallet, spread open on top, should help in case the elements alone will not assist her. At last sucking air in, fast and thick, deliciously anonymous and far from dead, she slips out of her high-heeled mules, steps out of the comfort of shade, and begins to walk.

Building Tall
Siân Griffiths

I measured the garage in Megans, an inchworm kind of measuring. I figured it would take about three little sisters to be building-tall. "Yeah, you can do it," I'd said, confident. "It's safe."

"Are you sure?" She squinted at me, small and brown in the sun. I was almost six years old. I would know. "Definitely." I looked back at the garage. "Use the umbrella, though, just to be sure. Like a parachute."

She hesitated a moment, looked at our friend Kim who stared wide-eyed at the garage. Megan smiled, turned, flew over the gravel and up the steps in her orthopedic shoes. For a moment, she disappeared. Reappeared, on the roof, giggling.

"Come on," I said.

She popped her red umbrella open. Her legs still pale on the sides from metal braces. Kim said, "I can't watch, I can't watch." Megan didn't wait for Kim to turn her head.

I had thought she would float to the ground like Mary Poppins, but she came fast. The umbrella inside-outed itself.

When her shoes hit the gravel, they sounded like triumph.

d(ANGER)
Megan Jones

"We are in the trouble of a sleep we did not dream"
- Brigit Pegeen Kelly

I. we are a people raised
                        on the taste of shifting
                truths, that is to say,
                        lies
                and too stubborn to admit that
                kings are
        not born but created
                        blow by blow
        we return,
                        itching the same
                                ache
                hanging on for
                        shame's sake because
        nothing remains save
                        the sum of our discontent

II. two elections running
                        the hoi-polloi are divided
        down   the   middle on the big one
                        one state – panic - decides

                              a party for color
                        a party for gender
and let's just leave
                  the hippies to grow their soul
          patches a little longer and
                              imagine sighting a
bohemian Jesus in the mirror
          sprinting behind the juggernaut

III.   madness is
such a supple thing
                        but even so
          there is a limit to
                  what we can take
do you remember when we passed it?

          and if we're not going to
plunge madly through
                        the smokescreen or
          force that newspaper to fold
against the lines it
                  may be prudent to admit this
experiment of violent truces
          has failed miserably
                        and permanently
          and perhaps
                  now would be a good time
to file this baby under
          democracy,
                        end of

IV. how many times can you
                        reset a break and
          how many ways?

          mouthing the sacred shibboleths
                  each election, i know some answers
extend the rhetoric of truth
          while others just
                        extend

but we must claim the ideal
as our own
and say it until
it gets said right for in
broken times
mere silence is a lie

and i may choose to hold
my tongue
feeling the small pellet of
anger
placed just so
underneath

i may take an oath of
silence, hold my patience
and   finally
call for mercykill

or i may
touch the fading scar
beneath my tongue and know
it still holds
words

Rejection Letters
Edited by Trevor Dodge

This section of CLR collects a series of rejection letters---some real and some imagined---running the gamut from fanciful to angry, enlightened to enraged. The writers here are smarmy, sweet and brave.

As, of course, are you. And we thank you for your consideration. But for now, we're going to pass. Please send more when you can. Especially the kind like that one, you know?

Of course you do.

--eds.

April 26, 2006

Clackamas Literary Review
19600 S. Molalla Avenue
Oregon City, OR 97045

Dear Clackamas Literary Review;

Please find the enclosed submission, "7000 Winterized Monkeys can't be Wrong, or, Coal-Pappy's a comin' down to Frisco Bay (for a Whoopin)," for consideration by Clackamas Literary Review. Right off, let me tell you that I have written many stories in the past few months concerning a band of winterized monkeys who survive a deep freeze at the end of the next ice age (that's right—watch the horizon!). In this piece, with the help of a wizened (yes, shriveled) elf-orc-wizard called "Coal Pappy" (birthed from the fiery canal of distant constellation [Rigel Kent, in this case]), the winterized monkeys fight to unfreeze the planet before they evolve into "higher" life forms, who, instead of seeking an eternal return to the bucolic pre-frozen pastoral of enormous guava melons, would simply adapt—by building crude shelters and gas-guzzling Hummers to make them forget entirely about their crass simian origins.

Think on it for a moment; the enemy here is not some "abstract" and "unbelievable" threat from a warring tribe or significantly divergent genetic offshoot of winterized monkey, but an enemy from the future—an enemy that is you. Imagine if your purring little house cat, lying quietly on the divan right now and (perhaps) choking up tiny bones from the $.39 can of generic wet-food meat-like amalgamate were to suddenly stop curling on your lap as you frantically type for a few minutes each morning, and began to keep to herself—suspiciously rejecting the rainbow-colored ribbons that you bandy about her face like slow-motion fireworks unfurling against a jet-black sky. You would, of course, be shocked by such a change, but would probably never think, even for a second, that the cat was attempting to defeat a future version of herself before her time is up—something vaguely feline but much more advanced, with poly-digital claws slowly becoming opposable thumbs, ad infinitum...

Hence, your position as a reader in relation to the winterized monkeys, as the aforementioned simians—if successful in the quest to put the kibosh on the wrong type of evolution— will slowly begin to write their own stories. My dream, no, my horrific vision, that I both fear and anticipate, is for these monkeys to eventually write and edit their own sage tales. Just between us, I think they will soon pick up the necessary skill sets.

Other stories from this series include, "Blister Popping Renegades: Monkeys go Apeshit on the Intergalactic Tarmac" and "Smell No Evil, Touch No Evil, Sixth-Sense No evil—De Verbo Magnificum." [I realize these are funny titles, but you wouldn't laugh after reading them, because by then, the post-structuralist elision of the phallocentric order would clearly be applied to a forced, or "compulsory" heterosexuality, which revises the "essential" bisexuality of all subjects and presupposes an gynocentric matriarchy predicated on the defeat of the transcendental signifier that powers the illusion of an essential biological "sex" to begin with!)

And so, my bio:

Henry Mescaline is a pseudonym that I adopted upon first submitting a set of poem about garbage cans, animatronic dildos, and my high-school girlfriend, to one of those anthologies that ends up accepting everything submitted, and makes its money by charging 60 bucks a copy for each print-on-demand volume of its finely-crafted collection. And so, yes, maybe not too many people ordered this book, called Clouds and Sunspots: The New Poets, compared to the circulation numbers of your so-called respectable literary journal, but really, have you conducted any research on how many of your so-called subscribers actually do any so-called reading of your so-called contents? Maybe some university libraries purchase their requisite copies—but let's come clean, shall we? Those things may as well be dust-collecting relics from the next ice age. And for those copies which actually arrive in the mailbox of subscribers and contributors—most people either toss that thing on the coffee table after mindlessly thumbing through a piece or two, content that they are supporting the "small" magazines up against the hegemonic juggernaut of the mainstream New York houses and cash-money journals such as Poetry, or, if they have a piece printed in the current issue, they scan their own words for about twenty seconds, hungrily looking for either typos of that satisfying dopamine rush of seeing their work in print—before the whole perfect-bound pamphlet ends up on the bathroom floor next to the toilet, on top of the flyer detailing the "threat" of genetically-altered crops and so-called "frankenfoods," a dog-eared copy of The Onion, and some half-assed solicitation letter from a local politician….so if you think that Henry Mescaline is ashamed of being printed in one of those scam poetry publications, think again, motherfucker! I'm proud that I have at least as many readers from that thing as any average copy of your journal. In my case, the other contributors were more likely to read my work, since together, through a real esprit de corps, we were all there at once in naïveté—the "new poets" triumphant!

So maybe what I'm trying to do for you with this ramble is to precisely sketch the type of manufactured camaraderie that my winterized monkeys are up against. It's no wonder that they remain in a sort of limbo now, planning for a way to be released into the water supply—dissolvable little memes of cultural ennui that you can suck down your gullet and absorb onto the tip of you hang-dog tongue.

This manuscript may indeed be disposable, and I have included a SASE for reply. But will you be the one to tell the monkeys "no"—will you be the one to condemn them to an eternal evolutionary drift that can only end with the eventual darkness of the sun blazing out everything—including the Clackamas Literary Review—from our broken post-industrial sky?

Thank you for your time and consideration, should you even give us any. For god sakes, before you toss my work in the trash and put that half-sheet of paper rejection notice in my envelope—think long and hard on the position of the winterized monkeys, and wonder if they will show you the same courtesy once the positions eventually become reversed.

Yours, on hind legs,
Henri Mescaline
Auteur-in-exile

Fuckface Books
69 Eat My Ass Circle
You Think You Are Better Than Me, NY

Dear Fucko,

Remember when you heard your doorbell ring last month and went outside to see who it was and found a flaming, steaming bag of dog shit on your porch and had to stomp it out before your bonsai tree caught fire which caused you to slip and fall onto the concrete and dislocate your shoulder and have to wait three hours for your wife to come home from yoga while your knees bled onto your porch steps and you howled in excruciating pain and how bumpy the long ride to the hospital was from your fabulous country estate and then the doctor had to admit you because you had lost so much blood and then you got that flower delivery which caused you to have a hideous allergy attack and made you sneeze so hard you threw your back out and had to be put in traction and cancel your trip to the Bahamas and your wife got pissed and took your brother instead and then served you with divorce papers while you were still laid up in the hospital and how she got full custody of your kids and a new set of tits that you have to pay for but will never enjoy and then your depression spiraled out of control and you lost the will to live and the only thing keeping you going was knowing that your fancy publishing job would be waiting for you when the nightmare ended and then the day you were discharged from the hospital your wife had packed your clothes and left them in your room and you had to drag everything with you to your office on your first day back to work and then when you got there you found out that the building had burned to the ground?

That was me.

Sincerely,

Ritah Parrish

PS – Thank you for your thoughtful consideration of my manuscript.

Dear Retards:

No.

Dear Madam/Sir:

My name is Ben Slotky. I live in Bloomington, Illinois and am a writer.
Recently, I sent you a copy of a story I had written. I sent it to you so you could publish it. It was a good story, called Red Hot Dogs, White Gravy: A Play In One Act.
I call it a play even though it isn't. This is a large part of its appeal, its not being a play.
Anyway, I just got your letter and it looks like you may not publish it. In fact, I'm pretty sure you aren't.
By *pretty sure* , I mean positive.
In your letter to me, in the letter you wrote to me that I have in my hand right now, you call my story Not Particulary Funny and A Little Disturbing. I'm not sure what you mean by this. It is funny, particularly funny; have you read the title? I'm laughing just thinking about it. And it's supposed to be disturbing. It's disturbing because Life Can Be Disturbing is what I would say.
I don't care that you're not publishing Red Hot Dogs, White Gravy. I'm sure somebody will; that's not why I'm writing.
I'm writing to say I'm sorry. I'm so sorry I didn't write some story with lots of Emotion or Description or Character Development or something.
Just so you know, I'm sitting in my basement reading this out loud right now and when I say the words Emotion and Description or Character Development, I'm saying them like Eeeemowshun and Deskwipshun and Chawactuh Deevewopment like a stupid fucking baby because I think you're a bunch of stupid fucking babies.
I have looked up the word Besmirched. Recently. That is what you have done to me, to my name. You've besmirched me. Have you ever heard of the Santa Monica Review? Have you? They publish hip writers, hip fucking writers who probably think your magazine is stupid and weak and just so Not LA. Well let me tell you something, I'm huge in LA, even though I've never

been there ever and live in *Illinois* for fucking christ's sake. But you don't like me.
Huh.
Shot of me nodding my head slowly, up and down, real qucik
Your shitty stupid fucking baby mag doesn't like me.
Shot of my literal tougue in my literal cheekc
Go Figure is what I say.
Go Figger is what I say.
You besmirched me. You retards have besmirched me. Everywhere I've sent stories to, and by *everywhere* , I mean every fucking where, they've published it, both times, and here you come along with your bullshit and your letters and your No I Don't Think So Ben.
Well, Fucking Shit is what I say to that.
Because that story's fucking something, you know. All one shot, the way everything is, the way everything should be. No revision. No weevishuhn. Revising's for cripples and little girls who play with their flauw-flauws.
I talked to my friend about it and we think we know why you didn't like my story. I think maybe you were reading it and something happened, like maybe a bear. We think it might've been a bear. You were sitting there in your office in wherever your office is and in your hands was my copy of Red Hot Dogs, White Gravy. My story was in your hands and on your hands, on your fingers, were maybe rings. Maybe you were holding my story with hands that had fingers that had rings and then maybe a bear came in and scared you and frightened you made you pee in your shiny pants.

129

We think that might be it, my friend and I do.
My friend thinks I could be right about this. About my story, and your rings, and that bear. My friend who looks a little like Darlene from *Roseanne,* one time gave me a bite of a sandwich that was the biggest sandwich I'd ever seen and yeah, he talked about shit like this alot, but that doesn't mean anything about him or me being right or wrong. Maybe you ought to read it again. Maybe you should read my story again when there's not a bear around is what me and my friend think.
Here's what you think.
Maybe you think Red Hot Dogs White Gravy isn't funny but is disturbing because you don't understand it. To understand it you'd have to understand just what the fuck is going on here,

which is something I don't think you do. I'm into ass kicking fiction.

I know what you're thinking.

You're all like Ben, Aren't You Into Bear Fiction.

And yes, I'm still into Bear Fiction, just now I'm into more of the Ass Kicking kind of Bear Fiction. Is that what this is about? Me not being into Bear Fiction? That's so gay. So I'm into Ass Kicking Fiction, into Bear Fiction, into Two-Man-Enter-One-Man-Leave Fiction and maybe you aren't. Maybe you aren't, maybe you're not. I don't know and I'm not saying that. What I am saying is that I'm mad.

You're going to miss out then, on not only Red Hot Dogs White Gravy but on everything else, because I'm not sending anything to you anymore.

Thank you for your time,

Ben Slotky

Prairie Schooner
P. O. Box 880334, University of Nebraska
Lincoln, NE 68588-0334

We thank you for submitting the enclosed
manuscript for our consideration. We regret that
we are unable to accept it for publication.

Hilda Raz, Editor   02-10-01

▲▲

hilda + me ①   hilda + me ②

February 11, 2001

Dear Hilda:
We thank you for your royal **rejection of my poems**. We hope our
split personalities will meet your split personalities someday and
go out on a double date. Dutch, of course. We are poor.

Jirí Cêch, Good Poet
Jirí Cêch, Evil Poet

3-5-01

the washington review
p.o. box 50132
washington dc 20091

Thank you for your recent submission. We regret that it does not meet our needs. Please note that the *review*'s literary division is increasingly focusing primarily on DC-area based avant-garde and experimental writers.

Sincerely,
The Editorial Board

132

March 6, 2001

Dear Editorial Board,
That makes **PI**rfect**S**en**S**e. A magazine in our nation's capitol and it's got to be a BOaR(E)D **rejecting my poems**. Of course, I know this is just a ploy to get all **edrag-tnava** *[please use mirror to decipher this message]* and **EXPER**imen**T**al poets to move to Washington, DC where Re**PUBLIC**an politicians from formerly Confederate states will herd them all into a concrete cell and sh**OW**[!]er them with Zyklon-B.

Jirí Cêch-Your-I.N.S.-Records

Thomas Ryan Singleton
137 S Woodward
Beaverton, OR 97005

Mister,
How can you say you do not see the sense of my character
and the demise he brings? When have you ever smelt a dead
woman's sad perfume? Say I told you that I saw this story on
the news. You couldn't tell me it was not real. I did not see
such a thing on the news thouh.

I want you to suspend your belief and that is why I named the
killer Norm Cook. To make him seem ordinery. Like "normal
cook." That's why he works at Red Lobster.
You also say that the action in the story is akward and stunted.   133
Do you think a woman dies smoothly?
She does not.

Think of it this way: You are at the underwear store where the
pretty mall ladies shop. You want to buy something nice for
your wife or brother's wife. Or your mother or what have you.
The flower-scented saleslady asks what size she is and you
motion a space between your hands, just wider than your own
waist. She curls her lips and blows air between her teeth. You
could be tempted to snuff her out right there. She would be
easy to pick up off the ground. See her little shoes fall off. See
her feet kick the air. Those girls always look small but dont be
fooled. You almost need to wear a helmet because she'll claw
your eyes out.

Things happen like that all the time.
You don't believe me?
Open your paper tomorrow.

I read stories about people getting killed all the time and I never
beleive them. I showed the story to my friend downstairs and

she said it seemed real. She said it felt like it was happ;ening to her. And she reads alot. I know you read alot too but if you haven't seen a person die before, I don't think you can judge my writing.

Lastly, I want to reply to your comment that the use of gloves was like a cliche'. But would I want to feel a kill with my bare hands. Its not fun with bare hands. I mean those that kill with there bare hands are more like animals. But we as humans dont want to kill even when we do. Gloves are ALWAYS USED because you do not want that feeling stuck in your fingers. It's like mud under your fingernails. Thats why there are gloves. Killers aren't stupid. And they are not NOT human. To kill is to feel. And sometimes the people who die are already dead inside anyway.

I guess I'll say thank you for reading my story though and I hope our exchanges can grow into a writerly friendhsip.

Good luck,
Thomas Ryan Singleton

Excerpts from My Rejection Diary
By Jay Ponteri

January 2, 2005
At home, in the mailbox, another rejection (count: 659). Says
my story's central theme (death) is cliché, says he quit reading
halfway through page 1, says, *don't send us any more stories
for a while.* I imagine us sitting across a table from each other.
Like a butler carefully arranging tea and biscuits on a silver
tray for his master (OK I admit, I'm thinking of Stevens, the
narrator in Ishiguro's *Remains of the Day*), I'm preparing a
single, thoughtful response for each criticism. Everybody dies.
Not using paragraph breaks suggests the narrator's crowded
consciousness. I cannot stop thinking about his words. Feel
sick with them, like I'm locked up inside a small, poorly lit room
in which his words repeat themselves and everything that
matters in my life (my son and wiffy, my books, my writing)
dissolves and I become the room itself, four bare walls, ceiling
and floor closing inwards; in this shrinking space those words
echo and I become the rejection being mailed to myself.

February 5, 2005
Hated words: cubicle, cube. Suggest something enclosed,
toy-like, miniature, a decorative container in which a useless
object is stored. A box of drinking straws, a paper weight, a
picture frame, a letter opener, a book of inspirational quotes.
I prefer to use the word *space*. My space is small, yes, but
circular and open and clean. It does not contain me, it enables
me. We exist together, we are enmeshed. Like liquid poured

over ice. Our fine corporation believes in low walls. Visitors comment on how our privacy must be compromised, but experience suggests that high walls merely offer illusions of privacy and entitlement. Our corporation is, in this way, honest. Any phone call we have, any Web sites we peruse, any e-mails we write belong to the corporation. We are on display. Walk up on Floor 30 and you will find me. —Like words scribbled on a postcard we exist in the public domain, I often say to visitors. Something I keep to myself: it's lovely to see a field of heads, widened and tired eyes split with blood vessels from staring too long at monitors floating in blue-gray office space.

April 11, 2005
A complete stranger stopped at my space, set down on my shelf a Starbucks coffee cup and a wadded Kleenex, and said, —Can you throw these away for me? He walked on before I could say, Yes.

May 1, 2005
Count: 698.

May 12, 2005
Memory of a crybaby. I watch North Carolina State play the University of Houston in the NCAA championship game. The year: 1983. I'm surrounded by the males of my family. In the final seconds, the underdog NC State wins on a tip-in and their players and coaches jump all over each other. Fans rush the court. My older brothers and father and grandfather jump up and down in ecstasy (coffee table shaking) because the Cinderella team, the team everybody has predicted to lose, has won. I'm taken by the losers. The University of Houston players (among them, Clyde Drexler and Akeem Olajawan) have collapsed onto the court, crying, slamming fists against the wood floor. The Houston coach bends down to console his player, bracing his player's shoulder, and the player, his face awash in tears, shakes his head incredulously. I cry too. I cry because loss feels good to me, familiar. The loss engages the sadness I already feel. I like how the coach consoles the player, like the idea of somebody not pitying me but acknowledging that I'm a lost little boy. Two years later I'm a catcher on my little league team, in the final inning of the

championship game. There are two outs, and an opposing player, the winning run, sprints towards home plate, and as the ball whizzes through the air, I conjure up the image of the loser and the consoling coach and this slight distraction causes me to take my eye off the ball so that it ricochets off my catcher's mitt as the player slides safely across home plate and I become the loser, my knees splayed across the dirt, my head in the cup of my hands, tears dripping down my dirty cheeks. I believe with certainty that I lost the game for us, and father, our team's head coach, tries to console me by picking me up off the dirt and wiping my tears away, but his face with its straight lips and squinted eyes and ghostly pallor is not consoling as much as worried, scared even, for he cannot understand from where all of this misery comes. I am not sophisticated enough to tell father that, simply enough, it comes from inside of me.

July 14, 2005
Another e-mail from a friend saying she sold her book of stories to _____ Press. I send back my usual reply of congratulations, and yes, I am happy for this friend, happy that ·her hard efforts are being rewarded with publication. Envious too because this is another book launch I will attend that is not my book launch. Envious because people will read her stories and be (or not be) touched by its emotional tissue. Envious because readers will say to said friend, —Good work. You're a fine writer. A talented writer! Or —When will you write again? —When will your novel appear? Do I think this friend's book is better than mine? If it *is* better, it's not that much better. It's just that the editors for _____ Press don't like my work. A published book by a friend reminds me of my unpublished manuscript: nestled in a pile of other unpublished manuscripts. Unread words.

July 15, 2005
Feeling better. Stevens' resolve, his attention to detail always soothes the pain. When Mr. Farraday, the new proprietor of Darlington Hall, asks Stevens to make do with a staff of four, Stevens without complaint makes a plan. *Almost all of the attractive parts of the house could remain operative: the extensive servants' quarters—including the back corridor, the two still rooms and the old laundry—and the guest corridor*

up on the second floor would be dust-sheeted, leaving all the main ground-floor rooms. So sadly acquiescent, so task-minded. In the consciousness of fastidious Stevens, the noun *dust sheet* becomes an action verb: *dust-sheeted.* Such a quiet, lonely image. Beautiful too. Empty rooms of furniture that go months, possibly years, without inhabitants.

September 26, 2005
Our company has two other male secretaries. BT works in facilities. *He's gay.* SW supports Accounts Payable. *He's black. And gay.* So what's my excuse? How do others explain to themselves why I, an educated male, refuse to step on the first rung and begin climbing? Why am I seemingly comfortable in a position that only rewards selflessness and subservience? I am our resident artist, our fledgling writer. People walk by my space or they see me in the elevator, and ask, —How's the great American novel coming? In their tone, a hint of condescension, as if they know, sadly enough, the answer is that I'll never sell my work, that I will, five years from now (ten years from now), sit in this very space, my fingers quietly tapping away at my ergonomically friendly keyboard. I don't say, —Horrible, considering I can't even find a agent to read the first 20 pages, or —It's not a novel. Instead I say, — Fine. It goes fine. BT and SW never ask me about my writing. We talk shop: office supplies, catering issues, best practices. Sometimes we don't talk at all. We say hearty hellos, we clap one another's thin shoulders. We are colleagues.

October 10, 2005
I put the manuscript inside my bottom desk drawer, amidst other important documents (to keep stored) like insurance records and tax returns and passports. I know I'm not alone, that there are a couple thousand people like me, at any given moment, trying to peddle short story collections. —Enter your book into a contest, one of my former teachers says, —Contests are great. Ok, take the _____ Press contest. Six preliminary readers together sort through 1,200 entries. Each reader hands their favorite ten manuscripts to the actual contest judge, and from these 60 finalists, the judge picks a single winner. Don't take my cynicism as bitterness. I am grateful to all the readers and contest judges, grateful that one of my fellow apprentices earns publication, but admittedly

I have a better chance of winning enough cash in the lottery to fund a small press of my own. Another teacher pulled me aside at graduation and said, —The secret is to keep at it. I agree: that is to say, if you want to be a writer, then write five days a week, write in the face of rejection. Like Merwin says in his poem, _Berryman_: *paper the walls with rejection slips.* But how can I live? How can I feed my family on rejection slips? What if I write book after book after book after book and not one gets published and with each one I grow to be an angrier person and this anger permeates my consciousness and, in turn, spreads outwards to anybody in near vicinity: Wiffy, my boy, my colleagues, father and my brothers (who never fail to ask, over the phone or via e-mail, —Have you found an agent?)? Maybe I should give up trying to publish. I mean, would I rather open my mailbox without the possibility of receiving a rejection letter (thus without the possibility of publication) or would I rather find, tucked between the bills and a *VIA* magazine, two or three white envelopes I've addressed to myself?

October 20, 2005
Count: 757.

October 21, 2005
Memory: I'm six, my brother, Chris, 11. In the basement we toss a hardball back and forth, catching it with plastic lacrosse sticks. My throw is wild and too hard. It misses Chris's basket and smacks into the Calder print, shattering its glass frame, spraying shards into the thick carpet pile. Slamming feet thud the papery ceiling. Dad screams, his voice booming like those awful gunshots at track meets that make my organs leap into my throat (too scared to cover my ears, for somebody to see I'm scared). His voice's echo swirls around the basement ceiling, rebuking me, *I am bad, I am bad.* He pounds down carpeted steps. His pinched face, his mouth ajar in a furious scold. Fast forward one year: 1979. My parents are at a Notre Dame football game. In the basement my best friend, Scott Johnson, and I play pitcher-catcher. Scott pitches, I catch. Never the other way around. I don my older brother's equipment: mask, shin guards, chest protector, Rawlings catcher's mitt signed by Gary Carter. Without the equipment, without the shared dream the equipment helps to conjure, the

game is not worth our time. Scott muscles one high and wide and a second or two before the ball plunks into the Calder print I see the whole scenario unfold before me: glass everywhere, my dad's clenched fist pummeling his dresser top. I wail, I cry. What happens to Scott? Does he decide to leave the moment he witnesses my babyish behavior? I do not recall. I hide underneath my brother's bed and cry and mew and wimper. It's not that I actually think my parents won't find me, they will. It's that I want to punish myself before they punish me: I want them to see how miserable I am. I want them to see I agree with them.

November 22, 2005
This is a diary. Yes, it contains some intimate, even secret thoughts. Like: *Sex I imagine during masturbation is more gratifying than sex Wiffy and I have.* Like: *I take pleasure when others look down on me.* Like: *I will do anything to please a stranger.* Like: *I'm a mediocre writer.* Like: *I'm one of the Great Executive Secretaries.* I would by lying if I said I was writing this for myself, if, as I scribbled these very words, I didn't envision a large readership: multitudes.

November 22 , 2005
Can't sleep. Imagining editor of press who rejected my manuscript, seeing me from across the room, years from now, at a reading, saying to an acquaintance, —I knew he wouldn't find a publisher for his manuscript.

November 24, 2005
Lashed out at Wiffy again. Every time she calls at work she wants me to do something. Her requests are reasonable enough (pick up dinner, call the phone company) and I obviously have the time, but her eager tone makes me gnash my teeth. I told her to stop calling me at work and I hung up. I know I'm mean to her, know that her simple beauty, her exuberance for the present moment, for the moments to come, incenses me. I am an angry person, I admit this. I sometimes tell our dog to shut the fuck up. If either the dog or Wiffy interrupts a writing or reading session, I flip. A pool of dark blue anger opens inside of me, its frosty waves prickle my skin. In my mind I promise to be nicer, to treat Wiffy with the compassion she deserves and that lasts a few days but then she dials me up at work or she buys cereal with raisins or she puts away something of mine

(my work badge, a pen) I want left out or she makes weekend dinner plans without consulting me and I lash out at her. I am afraid for my son.

December 1, 2005
Your manuscript does not fit our needs at this time. The Editors. [Unsigned.] The phrase *does not fit our needs* implies the editors need something other than what my manuscript offers. What do they need? Different story material? Do you have a story about your grandparent's (or parent's) struggles upon immigrating to this country? About S & M? About your travels to India or Eastern Europe or Russia or China? Maybe the editors *need* a better executed story. Can you use more paragraph and space breaks? This story feels like a character sketch; I'm not sure how the narrator changes at the end. Or the editors need a story written by a writer whose name suggests accolades and success, a name that can sell copies. I'm struck by the modifying prepositional phrase *at this time*, as if to say, no, we do like this story, could even envision publishing it, but not right now; maybe in nine months, yes, keep sending us your work just in case you happen to become a better writer or write that immigrant or S & M story we like or in case your name does, one day, garner national recognition. The best is the sentence's subject: *your manuscript.* You, you who writes this story, you who sits alone in your garage-studio ten hours a week, you are the subject, the captain, you are driving this rejected boat. *Unsigned* means that my manuscript didn't even raise an eye brow. The reader didn't get past page one.

December 15, 2005
Went to bakery and bought 350 chocolate chip cookies for our corporation's Holiday Executive Open House. Worker bees ride up the elevators to the executive floor (Floor 30) not so much to eat the cookies or to drink free hot apple cider, not because these plebeians enjoy mingling with our company's executives (usually the executives stay to themselves or converse with their assistants), but because they are afraid if they don't show, someone higher up will take note of their absence. As if.

January 16, 2006
When you reject, you say, *please separate yourself from my existence.* Your words do not belong here. Your words are

simply unacceptable to me. Your story, your characters, your sentences which evoke actions and speech and mind-states need to get the hell out of here. Clear your desk, leave immediately or you will be escorted off the premises.

February 17, 2006
Count: 800.

February 28, 2006
Sometimes a rejection just isn't punishing enough. *Your manuscript doesn't fit our needs at this time.* Is that all you got for me? I want more of a rebuke, a slap to the cheek. When I begin my literary magazine (title: *HammerToe*), I intend to hand-deliver my rejections. Example: I knock on the rejectee's door till the coward shows her timorous face. I say, —Are you so-and-so who wrote so-and-so story? —Why yes I am, did you like my story? —No, In fact, please remove your right shoe and sock. Then I take a hammer out of my pocket and crush her big toe so that the pain she feels renders her properly punished. —Please feel free to submit to *HammerToe* again, I say.

March 29, 2006
Dream: I drive to Idaho, past this house which houses the small press to which I've sent my manuscript. Above the garage hangs a neon sign, big pink cursive letters spell out, _____ Press. I think, I can stop by, can ask them, —Do you have my manuscript?   —Do you like my work? I ring the doorbell but then notice a sign in the front picture window that reads, *On Vacation, Back in Ten Days.* I will not be here in ten days, I am here now. Worse: my manuscript sits in this uninhabited house.

March 29, 2006
Am I feeling sorry for myself? Yes. Writers work alone. Period. In an interview, I asked short story writer David Means about the distraction of getting work out there and publicizing oneself; his response: "I'm not an actor. I'm a writer. Writers, for the most part, like to be alone. Should be alone. That's why they do what they do." So it makes sense that my reaction to rejection is self-pity. I don't ask my fellow writers to feel sorry for me; I ask that of myself. I see it as a way of caring for

myself, an acknowledgement to myself that the world is not so much against me but that I exercise little control over it. Poor Stevens: if he only he could care for himself a little more.

March 30, 2006
Even my friends who get their stories and books published still deal with (and write in the face of) other forms of rejection. Negative reviews or worse, no reviews at all. Friends and family buy copies but then offer no feedback. An e-mail from your editor that book sales are very poor (*By the way, how's the novel coming along?*). Bookstore reading events where three people show up and two of them (never read a short story in their life, bored) accidentally wondered in from the Self-Help section.

April 1, 2006
Happy April Fool's Day! On the coffee table lies an SASE. Inside: nothing. Not even the tiny standard rejection slip. Rain has smudged the ink of the postmark making it illegible. Its blankness speaks clearly, concisely, it achieves real beauty my work does not.

143

July 1, 2006
The last male assistant (besides me) SW left the company today. He's starting his own business. A café. The usual ceremony: a good-bye lunch at Red Robin's (unlimited soda refills); co-workers, strangers to one another, struggle over small talk (topics: weather, e-mail etiquette, babies, books and movies I will never read or see, wine I don't drink); SW opens goofy cards. One, once opened, sings, *Take this job and Shove It, I ain't workin here no more.* SW's face shines with liberation, for he no longer has to endure his executive boss flinging a fifty dollar bill onto his keyboard and saying, —Vente Mocha Decaf with skim. No longer has to facilitate a video conference or add paper to the copy machine, no longer has to experience language wholly devoid of meaning, e.g., *out of the box, working in silos, drilling down, going forward, talking points.* I dream of my own exodus: canceling my purchase card and notifying accounts payable they no longer will receive my check requests. Cleaning out my desk drawers and filling a recycling bin with dumb papers. In this dream, I wonder, where am I going? What else (besides

writing) can I do besides assist my fellow ladder climbers? In my acquiescence, I bring them comfort. I do not remind them of their own greediness, their impetuous power grab. I do not pose a threat to their success. For them I hold open the door. For them I organize their precious slots of time. For them I refill their coffee mugs. But I still dream of that day I can leave, dream that my boss walks me to the lobby, carrying for me my box of belongings (post cards, CDs), calling the elevator, hugging me before I go, waving me off as I step inside the elevator and there, a stranger, a co-worker from the other side of the floor rides the elevator down to plug another five hours worth of quarters into the parking meter, looking at me with a weary kindness, understanding that I am moving on and that I am well-liked, admired, that I am entirely replaceable. We all are. We ride together with this understanding, the elevator beeping as it drops through the building's spine, floor after floor, five, four, three, two, one and the doors slide open like a window on a breezy summer day and out we walk together into the lobby with its industrial brown carpet and fake plants and corporate-art landscape paintings and bored, ambling security guards. We are strangers together. What lies ahead is not happiness but it's something.

For DB at Spork

The Milky Way
Paulann Petersen

ö
My thumbnail severs
the lettuce plant's stalk,
its acrid milk flung in a path
of shining drops across
dark soil as I carry the leaves
off to be washed, chilled,
torn and eaten.

ö
The Virgin Mother uncovers
one breast so a master painter
can depict this world—
how milch-stars spray
light from her nipple.

ö
Night lets down the galaxy,
a nacre-white stream.
On a map's *You are here*, the *here*
is less than a speck in the swath
made from dying or forming suns,
gasses, and dust—
what seems to lie far beyond,
but cradles us.

ö

My breasts, slack.
Decades ago, hungry for
whatever thin, bluish food
they could suck from me,
my children sloughed off
then replaced each of their
own cells. My babies nursed
and became something else,
themselves anew.
The way of milk.

To the Coffin Maker
Paulann Petersen

Make me a wooden coffin,
one to house my body above ground
on a far-flung, wind-scoured place.
Use boards already weathered,
wide and old. Pine. Dimension lumber
you're not likely to find in the fresh stacks
of some resin-scented yard.
Raised grain, warps,
a popped knot or two: all OK,
as long as it has that silver, water-rubbed
finish of age. Shape the box itself
as you like. Just remember: 5' 8,"
wide shoulders, long-toed feet.

I want two uprights
bolted to the coffin's sides—
one to the right, one to the left,
aligned with a line
that would pass through my heart.
These are perches, for birds you'll make.
Two pine birds of a type
that might nest in the pines.
Carved feathers, carved claws.
No paint or stain.
Make the first with its beak
open. The other, shut.
One for song,
one for the quiet after.

The Parable of the Gun
Stephen Graham Jones

We locked him in the old fitting rooms because he said he was Jesus. And because it was the end of our shift.

"Save *them*," Marco said to him through the louvered doors, and swept his hands to all the naked mannequins the fitting rooms were already storing, their arms in every posture of worship.

Jesus pulled his face over the top of the door, rested his bearded chin on the backs of his fingers, and watched us. He wasn't even mad about the way we'd tackled him off the cosmetics display pad. How the customers had laughed and clapped and then turned away, embarrassed. What Marco had threatened to do to all that long hair. What I had done with the leather sandal that had been left on the display pad, as if Jesus had just been transubstantiated up to the second floor. Lingerie, probably.

It was as close as there was to heaven at Dunlap's.

In the security booth we spent the rest of our shift with sticky notes, putting one on each monitor, telling Jarret and Kale, the night shift, that Jesus was their problem now. Through the walkie-talkie Marco had left keyed open by the fitting rooms, we could hear Jesus humming. It wasn't even a hymn, just a song from the radio.

"We should throw him to the lions," Marco said, smiling to himself, wheels turning in his head that hadn't turned in a long time.

"You mean Delaney and Gale?" I said, after checking behind me.

Delaney and Gale were the area coordinators, the bosses when the manager wasn't on the floor. They took it very seriously. Marco hissed through his teeth, dotted an *i* on some complicated insult he'd been writing to Jarret and Kale then fixed it on the last empty screen. He nodded to himself, satisfied with his work, and leaned back in the ergonomic chair we'd had to make special requests for.

Jesus still humming, the dial tone of his voice starting to break into words in places. The lyrics would be next.

"He didn't have headphones, did he?" Marco said.

"Gale's going to hear him," I said back, nowhere to put my eyes now that all the monitors were covered.

Marco focused his attention on the walkie-talkie again.

"Watch this," he said, and palmed it, thumbed the line open. Said in his deepest, most resounding voice, "Son, this is God, your father. Don't make me come down there again."

The humming trailed off, got swallowed.

I shook my head, looked out the small, wire-mesh glass window set in the steel door of our security booth.

"We're going to hell now," I said to Marco. "You know that, right?"

Marco laughed, stood. Said, "This place isn't hell, I don't want to see it, man," then started unpacking his belt into his locker, shouldering into his jacket. I fell in, standing my pepper spray on the top shelf of my locker, hanging my stick from the hook. Charging the batteries on my hand-held. The one we'd left by the fitting rooms with Jesus was Jarret and Kale's problem, now. Let them charge it.

Walking out, my foot stopping the door for Marco to ease through, I almost saw something on the monitors, I thought. All the sticky notes, though. I couldn't be sure.

"What?" Marco said.

"Goodnight," Jesus said, clearly, though the walkie-talkie. As if his beard were right up to it, rustling into the receiver holes.

"Shit," Marco said, drawing his lips up from his teeth. "I see a donkey in the parking lot, my dumb ass is calling in tomorrow."

I pulled the door locked behind us.

Jesus was Jarret and Kale's problem now.

Part of the end of rounds—what the OP called it when security was clocking out—was making a final circuit of the store, to be

149

sure what you were handing off to the next shift was as safe and secure as you could make it. It was a useless procedure, of course: on the way to the timeclock, not only were we in our civvies, but our spray and sticks and walkie-talkies were back in the box. It kind of made any kind of walk-through useless. Except for Jeanine, of course, the built-for-sin holy roller in Misses, who for some reason thought we were real cops, or cops in training, or something. It didn't matter. If we got there at 8:45, she'd already be zoning her area, squaring all the shirts onto their aisle displays, fluffing collars, refolding pants. To one degree or another, of course—because of Delaney and Gale—everybody at least went through the motions of zoning. Not everybody wore blouses as loose and lowcut as Jeanine, though. All you had to do while she folded was stand there, and, bam, suddenly the last eight hours had been worth it.

"Guess you heard we caught your boy today," Marco said to her, his right arm cocked up on a rounder, "Jesus I mean."

Jeanine looked up to him, then me.

I nodded, said, "The real one."

She shook her head, smiled, and said we must be real Philistines then, right?

Over her shoulder, Marco bored his eyes into me, waiting for a signal, to know if being a Philistine was good or bad.

"That a commandment?" I said to Jeanine.

In reply she hit me lightly on the shoulder and I acted like it was a roundhouse, folded over the register in fake pain, then, walking through Housewares minutes later, realized that I should have played along, gone farther, should have spun her around by the wrist, her arm behind her, as if I were apprehending her. It would have pulled her right up against me.

That's why I was working security at a department store, though: because my whole life had already been a series of not thinking of things in time, when they could have done some good.

At the end of the Housewares, the final stretch to the timeclock, me and Marco both saw the trenchcoat guy, already turning away from us, the tails of his black coat swirling around like the cape of a superhero.

Marco pretended just to be looking straight ahead.

"You care?" he said.

"Amateur," I said back, about the trenchcoat guy, and like that we let him slide, didn't want to do the paperwork he was obviously going to require. All he was stealing was plates or saucers or something anyway. For his grandmother, what? It didn't matter. Fine china wasn't why the store had gone full-time with security last year. There wasn't really a market for hot saucers, nice forks. What there was a market for, however, always, was electronics. It's why we kept them in a chain-link cage in back now, locked with a set of keycodes that the computer kept track of somehow. It didn't stop the handheld stuff from walking out of the store, but it did make it walk slower, anyway. Sometimes in our pockets even, which management had gone to special workshops about, learned to expect. The way they dealt with it was to try to buy our loyalty, show we were part of the family—that it was our stuff too. What they tried to buy our loyalty with was a twenty-percent discount on all electronics that weren't on clearance. To get that twenty percent though, we had to use a charge card. Which is to say the store owned us now, more or less. Had even cut off the ten percent discount all the floor employees got, for work clothes. Cut it off and still made us stick to their stupid-ass dress code: black slacks, shirts with at least three buttons, not counting the sleeves.

What we could have done with the trenchcoat guy, I guess, was lock him up with Jesus.

What we did instead was home in on that timeclock, lean against the wall around it with unlit cigarettes in our mouths, the third shift cleaning crew waiting there as well, to clock in.

"Say a prayer," Marco told me, lifting his chin to the timeclock that was taking hours, not minutes.

I looked at it hard, nodded, and said, "I wish I may, I wish I might—" and then didn't get to finish.

From the floor, a woman was screaming.

Marco closed his eyes, thinned his lips, and shook his head no, please, but it didn't matter: we were still clocked in.

Before following him back through Hardware, I balanced my cigarette on top of the timeclock, shook my head no to the custodial staff. That was my cigarette.

When I turned to take the impact of the aluminum doors Marco had left swinging though, my cigarette was already gone, the custodial staff all just standing there with their hands in their pockets, no eye contact.

Of course I didn't believe our guy in the old fitting rooms was really Jesus.

In my eight months at Dunlap's, the eight months since the other security crew had gone up on grand larceny charges, there'd been a total of two screaming women. Just absolutely hysterical I mean, unstoppable. If we could have restrained them, we would have, maybe. Instead, because the women had been screaming due to some bad or good news they'd just got on their phones—a death the first time, an engagement the second—we'd let the women on the floor talk them down. Sit with them until they were just sobbing, then lead them away. Knowing the girls on the floor, sell them something along the way.

This third screaming woman was a whole different scene.

It was Gale.

She was on her knees at the intersection of the two main aisles, where the tile was still rough from the watch stand that had been pulled up from there my first week on.

She was screaming because the man in the trench coat was standing behind her, a large chrome pistol held to the back of her head.

I slowed down my run.

"Do it!" the trenchcoat man called out across Misses, and I followed his voice to Delaney.

Her key was in the console that dropped the cages on all the exits.

She turned it, the ceiling shook, and the trenchcoat man smiled, and together we watched all the rounders move like savannah grass, when you know the small, tasty animals are moving away just beneath it.

In turn, one by one, the trenchcoat man waited for the shoppers to make their last scuttle from the make-up counter to the freedom of the mall, and lined up on them. It was fourteen feet, I knew. How far the sales people were supposed to keep their merchandise from the exit.

Because the trenchcoat man's pistol was a revolver, only had so many bullets, he just held it on each person who escaped and fake shot them, the barrel rising with the sound his mouth was making.

The last of the shoppers to slide under the door on their stomachs wasn't a shopper at all, either. It was Marco.

He splashed through the fountain, silver and copper rising behind him, and was gone.

Trenchcoat man came back to me, scratched his forehead with the sight of his pistol, and said, "You should have gone with him, yeah?"

Story of my life.

Six minutes later—I could tell because my ears were so tuned into the timeclock, which cut the hours into tenths, into six-minutes sections—the trenchcoat man had all of us down on our knees. Not in a single file line, but two single file lines, that crossed where the aisles crossed. From the top of the escalator, that's what we had to be, too: a cross.

It wasn't accidental.

When the bottom of the cross, the base where I was, had needed a little more length, the trenchcoat man had scared up two more bodies from Misses. One of them was Jeanine. Her fists were balled tight, her skin glistening.

I put my hand on her shoulder and the trenchcoat man smiled, nodded me on.

"Get some," he said. "It's the end of the world, man. For you I mean."

I lowered my hand.

When the trenchcoat man had passed, was inspecting his work, how even we were, how much like dominoes, Jeanine shook her head no to him. Said, "It doesn't matter what you do to us, y'know? It won't be as bad as what you'll have waiting for you."

The trenchcoat man nodded, smiled a gap-toothed smile at her, and produced a bible from his right pocket. Waggled it like a revival preacher.

"Talking about this?" he said, stepping in.

Jeanine just stared at him.

"Thou shalt not kill," she said, her voice so even now I thought maybe she was channeling or something. Possessed.

I could feel myself pulling away from her, from the line of fire.

The trenchcoat man leaned down to her, to her ear, his eyes locked on mine, to keep me in place.

"You're right about that, missy," he said. "But you forgot one, too."

She angled her body away enough to face him.

He nodded, opened the bible. Cut into the pages was a box. In the box was a small automatic pistol.

"Why are you doing this?" Jeanine said, shaking her head at him, in disgust.

"Me?" he said back, doing some fake-offended shuffle, then stopping, looking down the line at the rest of us. "More like you, I'd say."

Jeanine held his eyes for maybe three breaths, then turned forward as if he weren't there at all, and started praying.

The trenchcoat man nodded, fingered the gum from his mouth, and fell into Jeanine's prayer with her. Knew it as well as she did.

It shut her up.

He trailed off as well, then held the automatic in front of her, for all of us, and loaded a single shell in, pulled the slide back.

"Don't give it to me," Jeanine said. "I don't want to go to hell for shooting you."

The trenchcoat man shrugged, stared at her, then said, "You're part right, anyway."

It made Jeanine turn to him.

"You are going to hell," he clarified. "But not for me. No. Thou shalt not kill, right? But there's another one. Kind of an automatic deal, like. Don't pass go."

Jeanine smiled now, said it: "Suicide."

Yes.

She closed her eyes, opened them again. Said, "You mean, you're going to hold one gun *on* me, so I'll *shoot* myself? And your threat is that, if I don't shoot myself, then *you* go to hell?"

The trenchcoat man just stared at her.

Jeanine shrugged, held her hand out. Said, "So give it to me then."

This made the man smile, look down the line at the rest of us. To see if we were getting it, if we could see the joke here.

When we couldn't, he pulled the punchline out from behind the counter.

An eight year old boy. The pistol to his head.

"Now what do you say?" the trenchcoat man said, and slid the automatic over to Jeanine.

"You don't pick it up," he said, "bang, I go to hell, he goes the other direction. You point it at me . . . bang. Get it? Make sense?"

Behind us, Gale lost it again, started sobbing, having some sort of attack.

The trenchcoat man sneered at her, pushed the barrel of his chrome pistol deeper into the boy's blond hair.

Outside now, sirens. And Marco, probably still running.

Inside, us, on our knees, in the form of a cross.

It's the best way to be when Jesus comes down from Lingerie.

As you would expect, Jesus wasn't one of those people who walked down the already-moving escalator. Maybe because of his robes, or the sandals he had to have just lifted. It made him look like he was floating, anyway, the way he didn't use the rubber banister. His eyes locked on each of ours in turn, his face so—there's no other word—*serene.*

The trenchcoat man watched him descend too, swallowed whatever he'd had in his mouth.

From somewhere in Mens Casual, a man threw a package of dress socks up against the tile ceiling, to herald Jesus' arrival. The plastic of the sock bag clung to the rough ceiling for three impossible seconds, then the socks tumbled back down in what felt like slow motion, made no sound when they hit the carpet.

Jesus smiled about it, as if in thanks, then folded his arms the way people do in the bible: with his hands up his own wide sleeves.

The teeth at the bottom of the escalator were nothing to him. The whole world.

Instead of keeping to the wide aisle, he navigated through the rounders and t-bars, looking at each of them in turn, finally touching them as he passed, leaving the palm of his hand on them long enough that I knew they were holy now. Cured. Blessed.

I was crying maybe, I don't know.

Jesus fixed the trenchcoat man in his benevolent stare and held him there, turning the pages of his soul, reading the book of his life. When he was done, he nodded, looked down to us again, the corners of his mouth ghosting up a little at me, in recognition. And forgiveness. Then he came back to the trenchcoat man. Said, "You're sure you don't want to reconsider?"

The trenchcoat moved his mouth but didn't have any words.

Oblivious of the chrome pistol, Jesus stepped in, close to the trenchcoat man, then lowered himself to one knee. Not to wash the man's combat boots, but to pick up the cored bible.

"You know why they put my words in red in here?" he said, paging through, amused. He shrugged, looked up to the trenchcoat man. "Supposed to be like blood," he said. "As in, this is my body, this is my—?"

The trenchcoat man gave one nervous nod.

Jesus shut the bible. "I can see you believe," he said, tracing the cross we were all arranged in.

The trenchcoat man nodded again.

Jesus nodded with him, chewed his cheek some. Didn't need to have the ridiculous who-was-going-to-hell-for-what thing explained to him. The way the trenchcoat man was clinging to the eight year old boy, the whole scheme was obvious. Undeniable.

"Would you do it?" Jesus said then, focusing in on Jeanine suddenly, intensely. "Would you sacrifice your eternal soul to the save this boy you don't even know?"

Jeanine closed her eyes, nodded. Was crying now.

Jesus looked up to the trenchcoat man and smiled, satisfied. Did something vulgar with his eyebrows it seemed, then shrugged the temptation off. Raised his hand to his beard instead, a tic the bible never said anything about.

Finally, to the trenchcoat man, he said, "You were going to let her do it, too, am I right? Let her make that sacrifice?"

In reply, the trenchcoat man flared his eyes and his nostrils both, and took a long step back. Pushed the barrel of his pistol even harder against the side of the boy's head.

Jesus nodded as if to himself, didn't press the trenchcoat man about it anymore. Said instead, looking back across the store, as if savoring it, "Good thing I showed up then," then came back to the trenchcoat man all at once. "Sacrifice is kind of my thing, y'know?"

Somewhere in her sobs, Jeanine was laughing too now. With joy.

She couldn't see what I could, though: Jesus, lowering himself to the loaded automatic, weighing it in his hands.

"I'm here to take your place," he said to Jeanine, then, looking along the line, at each of us. "All of your places. This sin, what he's asking, it's . . . it's too much for you. And anyway"—winking once at the eight year old—"Jesus loves the little children, right?"

The boy nodded and Jesus liked it, bobbed his head forward as if it was time, now. No more stalling.

He raised the automatic to chest level, held it sideways to study it, the trenchcoat man stepping back again, into a rack of blouses, his eyes all over Jesus' automatic.

Jesus smiled.

"Don't worry," he said, and lifted his face as if hearing something, focused again over the tops of all the clothes, all the merchandise. At the cage bars over the mall entrance, it seemed.

He nodded, shrugged. Said it again, to himself now: " . . . if there were just one person, willing to take all that sin upon himself . . . "

He was talking himself into it.

I opened my mouth when I understood, turned all the way around to him, to Jesus, and was too late one more time: already, at the right arm of the cross, Jesus was lowering the small automatic to Gale's left temple.

He didn't close his eyes when he fired, then held the automatic there until Gale had slumped down.

"One," he said, holding his hand back to the trenchcoat man, for another shell. He thumbed it in like it was second nature.

Next was a shopper, still gripping her bag, then another shopper, then up the post part of the cross for Delaney. By this time I wasn't even hearing the small, wet popping sounds anymore. Just Jesus, killing us so we wouldn't have to kill ourselves. Saving our souls, becoming a murderer himself so we wouldn't have to.

Jeanine, singing quietly, perfectly. A hymn, it sounded like. I hummed along as best I could, felt the woman behind me lean forward into my back, dead weight, and closed my eyes for what was coming, what was here, even felt the hot barrel hiss into my hair, and then the shot, the sound, filling the store years before I was ready.

The automatic jerked down to my ear, then my neck, leaving burns in both places, and I turned to see: Jesus was still standing over me, but the center of his robe was red, and spreading.

Opposite his chest, a hundred and fifty feet away, was the mall entrance, the wall of aluminum bars. Resting at shoulder-level on one of those bars the thick barrel of a sniper rifle.

157

Before Jesus could even fall, the trenchcoat man was dead too, the eight-year old boy just standing there.

I started to stand, to help him, to shield him—I was *security*, for Chrissakes—but then Jesus was slumping over me, pushing me down, the smell of his hairspray harsh against the back of my throat, his blood washing over me.

From the second floor, Lingerie, we would have been the bottom of the cross, where it's buried in the ground.

I closed my eyes, saw the silk and satin of the teddies up there undulate away from something huge, moving among them. Saw them undulate away and then reach out, after it.

Four months later, I said my first cuss word since the shooting. It was *goddamn*. One of the bad ones.

"Lord's name in vain," Jeanine ticked off for me.

We were in the food court, trying to reclaim our lives.

I slung my finger back and forth where the napkin dispenser had snagged it, said it again: "God-*damn*it, I mean."

Jeanine leaned back in her waffle chair, raised the straw of her red ice drink to her lips. Didn't approve.

Because the sex we'd had two weeks after the shooting had been premarital, and kind of just compulsive, and had started with her explaining the bible to me anyway, she was pretending it had never happened. Repressing me. A mental virgin.

I didn't care.

She wasn't pregnant, I knew, but I was. Not just with the halfway disappointing memory of her breasts, but with something else, something not quite religion, or faith, but having to do with how Jesus' name turned out to be Harold Gaines. How, in those last moments before he started shooting, he, Harold Gaines, had looked across the store to the mall entrance, what was waiting for him, and then done it anyway, lowered the automatic to Gale's head.

How, because of that, I think, I had tried to stand, to save that eight year old boy.

How, eight months after signing on, I had become security.

Because Jeanine was still watching me, waiting for me to apologize for breaking the third commandment or eight amendment or whatever the hell it was, I looked away, over her shoulder. Focused on the shape walking up to our table from the pizza place after four months gone.

It was Marco.

For the briefest possible moment our eyes locked, and I read the pages of what he was here for—his old job, how I could get it for him, because I was a hero, how it would be just like old times—and then I lowered my face. For once in my life did something in the moment, instead of just after: stood, turned, and walked back to the store.

What I Told My Friend
Robert Parham

My friend said his life
was like a Russian novel,
or that he wanted it to be,
one or the other,

so I asked him if that meant
it was too long, after all,
I'd read Tolstoy right down
to the preachments

because if you don't like yourself
you have a tendency to drag it out,
make self-loathing an art,
make punishment anything but light.

What about you? he asked.
Whose books are you?

I thought, since his question
wasn't so much about fate
as it was about wishing,
of the way imagination shakes
the dog by its leash before letting go.

Drieser, I think I said,
all the rough edges that mean

nothing in the end because the fierce
appetite that was the truth
in the center, its magma,
its heart, came from the tiny god
who watched and watched
until, on those pages, he told
it, act by act, the way we're amazed,
licking an envelope, turning a page,
paper cuts, the thin line of what it's done
turning red while the pain, small at first,
swells until we tear, and sometimes cry.

The Death of Charlotte Brontë
Matt Briggs

An account of the awfully sudden death of Charlotte Brontë, a naughty child addicted to falsehood and deceit.

Let me ask: Who is Charlotte Brontë?
She is the parson's daughter.

She is the quiet, plain daughter of a parson raised in Haworth, a remote village in Yorkshire. In a rigid class system she and her three sisters have neither the income to have guests or to travel, nor the freedom to freely interact with the other citizens of Haworth, so she and her family live in relative isolation. Yet from this relatively unremarkable background, Charlotte becomes the author of *Jane Eyre,* and three other novels under the pseudonym Currer Bell. Her sisters Emily and Anne also write books as Ellis and Acton Bell; however, both die shortly after the publication of their works. Emily dies within the year. Its as if they are rare lichen that cannot withstand the direct light of public opinion. With the last Brontë death, hundreds of neighbors visit the parsonage where they were born, reared and died.

She is Currer Bell.

Mr. Bell has a modest income and enjoys spending his Sunday afternoons in reflection while ambulating through his rose garden and down the lane where the rustic country scenes provide many sources of unexpected delight. He frequently pauses to catch his breath because he enjoys his marbled beef and his port and because he slathers his potatoes in butter and will always ask the cook for a second helping of custard. He writes poetry for his own amusement. The dreamy angst of Bell's poetry is an expression of a misspent sense of humor. He lived his early days in India. He refers to this distant period of his life as the immoral adventures of his youth. He writes in the morning and then reads in the afternoon, carefully and unassumingly producing a thick tome every couple of years. Suddenly at the end of the 1840s, Mr. Bell finds all of these books printed under three different pseudonyms. He devised these names so as to confuse his friends and neighbors because they would view his silly novels with shock and disgust and failed to understand the amusement they had provided to Currer over the years.

I must mention his whiskers. His face is a botanical exhibit of whiskered growths, a mustache with exquisitely waxed and sculpted twists at each end, shaggy muttonchops, and a long, neatly trimmed goatee.

It is an unending source of pleasure that he can pass himself of as backward country girl from Yorkshire.

She is The Duke of Wellington.

Nemesis of Bonaparte, she began her military career in India in 1796 and was appointed the supreme commander in the Deccan in 1805. She fought in the Peninsular War and appointed Commander-in-Chief after the death of Sir John Moore. She liberated Spain and Portugal from French control and was created Duke in 1814 after defeating the French at Waterloo.

Charlotte says: Dirty Windows

I often imagine my sisters coming back to me. I watch for their black bonnets coming over the moors. Watching for them, today, I realized that the windows had not been washed for a long time. Droppings clotted with stray strands of feathers and small stones had dried to the window. In fact, all of the windows to the Parsonage were coated in filth, splattered insect bodies, cob webs, the dingy gray pills of gestating moths, and on one pane, I even found a patch of moss and a fully grown fern. The windows had turned fungus farms. "Tabby."

"Yes, ma'am."

I missed her calling me Miss. "The windows are filthy."

"Are they ma'am?"

"When do you think they will be cleaned?"

"I'll get to it as soon as I recover from the TB, ma'am. If you will recall, ma'am, I've just now gained the strength to crawl off my straw pallet and begin some of the housework that has stacked up while I was suffering a spell of the TB."

"The light can barely pass through the dirty window panes."

"Do you remember the view?"

"Yes, Tabby."

"Then, ma'am, you have better memory than that glass. The windows do not have a long memory of staying clean. They dirty themselves up. Don't care whether you see through them or not."

"They are windows," Mr. Nicholls, my dear husband, said. "Does this chair care if I am sitting on it?"

"It would if it knew how much you took it for granted, sir."

Emily had kept the windows so clear, I hadn't even realized they could become dirty. She kept the house cleaner than Martha and Tabby; Martha was careless because this was not her house and she was a young woman who was caring for a blind Parson, my father. His blindness provided for Mary an excuse for idleness. Tabby just could not manage the girl well enough to keep the glass clean.

Mr. Nicholls read the papers in the parlor while he drank his tea. He frowned as I returned from the kitchen with a pail of boiling water and ammonia. "You really should let the girl do that. Your hands are already raw from scrubbing the hallway last night." Emily's knuckle scabs lined the bridges of her fists like barnacles. The joints of her fingers had hardened. She gripped the pen with her fingers and made minute letters as she wrote in the booklets I made for her. I wiped down the surfaces of the glass. I wiped down each stile and then each pane and drew my nail along the molding between the glass and the stile sending a squall through the room. Mr. Nicholls did not say a word. He rattled his paper.

The majority of the soot had settled on the outside of the parsonage. I could not adequately clean the windows from indoors.

Rain drops clung to the blades of grass, but the rain had let up. The window was much higher than I anticipated. I needed the pruning stool from the shed. I rattled on the window to get Mr. Nicholls' attention. "Charlotte," he said. I watched him fold the paper and find his spectacles in his breast pocket. He wiped them clean and opened the window. "Yes?"

"I must have the pruning stool."

He looked up at the low clouds. "Perhaps you should come inside?"

With one look from me, he smiled and said, "Yes. I'll get the pruning stool. It is in the shed."

The stool was a gigantic artifact constructed decades ago out of hard wood. It had four iron wheels ostensibly to ease its transport from one end of the yard to the other, but one of the front wheels had rusted to its caster and dragged in the mud. Mr. Nicholls pushed and then dragged the stool across the lawn, grunting and sweating until he had it positioned. The Parsonage had fourteen windows.

By now, my pail of hot water had cooled and a spider had fallen into the bucket and floated like an octopus. I scooped him out in my hand and tossed him aside. I stood on the stool and rinsed down the window. Mr. Nicholls, my dear husband, shrieked. "Ah! A damn spider!" He adjusted his glasses. "Charlotte it is raining."

"I am washing the windows of the house, today."

"Come inside. Your constitution is not great enough to handle inclement weather."

"I am not the one shrieking at spiders," I said.

He stood erect in the middle of the lawn. He held his hand behind his back. I knew he could stand like this for hours. He stood with his back rigid and monitored my progress. Rain drops collected on his spectacles. The clouds rolled overhead, and everything darkened. A wind ruffled the leaves of the shrubs around the house. Small cold drops of heavy rain started to fall. My cherished husband, Mr. Nicholls, did not move. When I climbed down from the stool, he said, "Are you finished?"

"I have the rest of the windows to do. I need more warm water."

Tabby asked me what I was doing. She was in the kitchen cutting up a chicken and peeling vegetables. I'm not sure how she so thoroughly dissolved these seemingly wholesome ingredients into the thin greasy broth she pawned off to my father as soup. "What do you need a big pot of boiling water for, dear?"

"I am washing the outside of the house."

"I can get someone to do that. It is raining and Brontës can't take the cold. Come inside."

"I am washing the outside of the Parsonage."

"You can't see the outside of the Parsonage when you are inside."

"I want to see outside, Tabby."

"Charlotte, there is nothing for you to see out there anyway."

Mr. Nicholls stood silently in the place where I had left him. He did not offer to help me, except to shove the stool to the next window. "This is eccentric," he said.

"I am an author," I said.

"That is not an excuse."

"You say that to most people around these parts, and they would just nod their head and say yes, so she is, so she is, and let me go on my way and work on this thing. Wanting a clean house is more eccentric in their minds, I'd say."

I say: Glass Town Dope Epidemic

OKAY here's the situation. His parent's were not on a week's vacation, and Branwell was still in his room smoking opium. Maybe he shouldn't? Naw -- of course, he should.

Branwell at thirty years old sponged off his father while he got stumble down drunk. His father was a Parson; I might add. Maybe Branwell was thinking if Coleridge fried himself on half a bowl, Branwell would toast on an urn of assorted opiates and churn out an Illiad or two. It is all about dosage. Up until the time the Brontës were in their early twenties, Branwell had produced more work than his sisters would produce in the rest of their lives, combined. It was no worse than their writing of the same period, it was just when they began to get serious about writing, Branwell began to get serious about drinking.

Charlotte says: Yellow

We were used to smoke coming from Branwell's chamber, but before he set himself on fire, an incident occurred that should have warned us that Branwell had fallen into the final stage of dissipation. Yellow vapors escaped from his room. At first, this cloud had a somewhat pleasant odor but it gradually gained strength until the overpowering stench was obviously something toxic. How could he stand the reek within his room where it must be double-fold in intensity? I could barely stand the tearful stink at the foot of the stairs.

We gathered before his door holding napkins to our faces. "Branwell? What in God's name are you doing?" His door opened, and the stench became so thick it was a floating distortion of the atmosphere like the air above a boiling teapot; the lines of the hallway moldings distorted and twisted and snapped free. Everything seemed slower and blurred as water, tears, and sweat began to drip from our hair. "Branwell how do you live with that smell?" The stink at his door was the innards of the infected anthrax riddle sheep we saw slaughtered near Haworth, its thick black bile leaking like odoriferous mud from an incision in the poor creature's stomach. The yellow gas issued from Branwell's room leaving powder trails around the door frame. He finally opened his door completely, sending out a solid wall of brown smoke. We rushed down the hallway, gagging on our napkins while Branwell rubbed one hand over his swollen belly, distended and throbbing around his puckered belly button. He squinted at us through his bloated eyes. He leaned forward and held up a long glass cylinder discharging even more noxious vapor. He sucked on the fumes. "Sweetness," he said. "Can't you hear the summer sparrows, the hummingbirds, the marching of the ants?" The house shifted perceptibly in the rush of yellow gas as it sought to escape. It clotted in the cracks under the windows. It condensed on the walls, rolling down in a steady brown drool. Branwell burped a red belch of steam. Pom Pom Pom, he said. And, by the time we made it back down the stairs, our ears rang.

Tabby coughed and gagged, "What kind of spice is that Master Branwell?"

167

His arms seemed thinner and more emaciated than the thin glass cylinder he held to his mouth. He stuck his tongue down the shaft as he inhaled the burning clay. Pom Pom Pom, he said. "Chinese spice." He closed the door.

Tabby by this time had opened all of the doors and windows. Snow blew in. The white powder mixed with the yellow dust leaving a brown paste on the flagstones in the entryway. We set to work then rubbing every surface down with cloths and water and ammonia. A quiet feeling settled over us, a sort of laziness, until Emily said, "I want to show you something." In the front yard, we could see up to Branwell's room and his magic lantern revolved and cast red spheres of moons, triangles of white stars, and hoops of green Saturns onto his window pane. His window sparked and shifted. Emily was the first to do it. She lay in the powdered snow in the front yard and made an angel by flapping her arms. We all lay in the snow staring up toward the dark sky watching each fleck coming down. I don't know how long we lay there more pleased and distracted than anyone has any right to be because the cold snow felt soothing on our burning skin, and the flakes of snow floated out of the blackness and took so, so long to get down out of sight.

Emily leaned forward, her face blue from the cold. "I feel funny," she said. She was sick in the snow. We all were sick in the snow. I vomited a thick inky chowder. I was surprised out how hot and viscous this substance was coming out compared to the thin gruel that went in. I wondered what else came out with it, dissolved liver and kidney and bone? We crawled back inside across the icy flagstones and back into the parlor and sat beside the fire. The house was frozen now. It smelled like ammonia and our cleaning. The bare walls and the dark flagstones were desolate. The wind outside blew unrelenting against the house. The fire did nothing more than heat our clothes and skin but could do nothing to scour at the coldness in the pits of our empty stomachs.

Branwell was a constant danger to himself and others.

Shortly thereafter, he set himself on fire. This time the smoke was black, and the smell of burning clothes permeated the house. His bed burned and issued a slow and heavy smoke. His tobacco pipe had slipped free from his hands when he nodded off. When we noticed the smoke, we said, "Oh no, here it is again."

Tabby said, "Oh no, nothing. Not when I have to clean it up." She grabbed my washbasin. We followed her into his room, a jumble of newspaper, and crumpled balls of writing paper and crates and blankets. It looked like Branwell lay on a cloud, so much smoke came out of his bed. "Master Branwell, your bed is on fire," Tabby said.

He started to wake and then looked at us. "What are you doing in my room?"

"You are on fire you eejut." Tabby said and then doused Branwell and the bed with the basin. He didn't move, but lay in the soaked fabric, gray ash in his beard, stunned.

Branwell's handwriting failed over the years until he had distorted Glass Town's carefully formulated miniscule to a childlike block printing that he himself had trouble reading. He would sometimes demand that we read his latest composition, waving the piece of paper with the tiny marks from the top of the stairs. "This is a sonnet I wrote." He checked his pocket watch and then checked it again, "half an hour ago." He would try to read it and finally come down the stairs. "Charlotte, you are an excellent reader. Can you make this out?"

We sat with Branwell in his wrecked room. "Branwell, we are going to have to start some rules now."

He sat up. "About bloody time."

"You will have to follow these rules."

"I am a grown boy," he said. "A worthless sort, but grown damnit."

"Grown men don't urinate their pajamas," I said.

So he slept with Papa until he knew he would die. That last long month the house was quiet. We would visit him upstairs. He turned his head away from us. "I'm grown am I? I won't stand for you." Until finally when he wanted to stand, he could not even raise himself from the bed. "A cloud has crept into my vision, and it is making me dizzy. It is the color of a fawn, deep yellow with white spots." He could see it coming around the edge of his vision. "A rot," he said. He wanted to stand one last time to meet his death because "Let me face it sisters, I have been pretty damn lazy for a long time. I will stand before it comes. I will stand."

I say: Graphomania

The Brontës created the tiny size of their script to resemble the printed typeface for the books to be read by their toy soldiers, The Young Men, who lived in Branwell's toy city, Glass Town. This toy town persisted in the Brontë's life well beyond their adolescence. In fact, there was no real break between Branwell and Charlotte's Angrian writings and Emily and Anne's Gondall writings (the names of their respective childhood kingdoms) and the composition of their first mature works in the mid 1840's. The use of the minuscule script had become inseparable from the writing of fiction. The tiny script also conserved paper, which was not only expensive but difficult to obtain in Haworth.

Another effect of their tiny script was that it was very difficult to read for those not accustomed to it, and impossible to read by their father who suffered from very poor vision. For though they could be severely critical and sometimes poisonous in their sarcasm at each other's expense, to the world at large they presented a united and almost impenetrable front, which is a euphemistic way of saying they were quiet, shy, and unassuming, and who would guess that this plain woman hunched over a doll sized booklet was creating something like Heathcliff?

Emily says: Ellis

Sitting out on the moors in the dusk, I could smell the heather. The heather grew under the stones. The stones picked up the heat during the day. The heat that came down from the sun that kept hiding behind the clouds. The clouds that kept racing in the sky. I sat out with the stones, too, a dozen sheets of paper folded up in my pocket and my ink well and a pen and I listened to the wind come over the moors. The grass turned over and showed its silver undersides to the sky. I could see the wind coming from a long way off, a discoloration of the ground and then I leaned into the heavy stones like a warm brother out there in the middle of the sky and the hills, and the cold air brushed over me. The same air that carried the clouds to wherever they were going. I didn't like to write at home where Charlotte watched me. "What are you working on?"

"A letter."

"You must conserve yourself, Emily," she said. "You must conserve yourself for the writing session this evening. You do not want to be tired for the writing session this evening."

"I can rest between now and then. It is none of your business how I work."

So instead of fighting her, I walked out onto the moors and worked next to the large warm stones.

A stream ran down in the gully. I went down to get some water. Small flowers grew in the shrubs. The ruins of some dwelling that once stood in the hollow remained. Sometimes, if the wind were too strong, I sat next to it. This was my place. I hid my writing here. It sounds pitiable, the three of us sisters not even writing letters to distant people but writing to ourselves. This was the only constant company I knew these long years, myself. I read my former self and looked at the notes I left for myself, and I wondered how I would look back on this life here with my sisters and crippled father and dissipated brother years from now when I had gone on to find some respectable employment. Charlotte believed we would all be successful authors, but authors are not successful people to my understanding, as they all die poorly remembered, and it is a miracle we have their words at all. In this way, the words I wrote were a sad way to entertain myself.

I walked into Haworth sometimes to find company. I went to the stationary store and Robert Chambers smiled at me because I was there without Charlotte. He told me this. "When your sister comes, it means the next day I will have to make the trip into Keighley to purchase more paper. It is a wonder the quantity of paper your sisters and you use, Miss Brontë. You must write dozens of letters a week." I held my hand up to show him my callous, which I am very proud of because it is much larger even than Anne's and hers is larger than Charlotte's. Charlotte tells us that it is not an indication of anything except that we hold our pens too tightly, but I tell her the tightness of my pen is a matter of inspiration.

"I hardly think such a disfigurement merits anything except chastisement for a lack of disciplined penmanship," Charlotte said.

Sometimes when I come home early, I know she has gone through belongings looking for whatever I am writing.

That is how she found my poetry in the first place. Snooping about in my personal belongings. What is Charlotte's is hers and what is ours is Charlotte's. When Anne and I found a publisher for our first books and the publisher declined Charlotte's, she didn't seem angry even though Anne told me she expected Charlotte not to eat for a week. Instead Charlotte said, "The Brothers Bells have a publisher. I shall write another book to get Currer an even better one!"

Charlotte was cheerful. She said Ellis, and Action's books had finally been reviewed. When our books finally came out, riddled with errors, printer mistakes, and dutiful transcription of obvious verbal ticks, everyone assumed that the Brother's Bell were the work of a single man. Does it indeed take three women nowadays to make one man? Charlotte laughed as she read us the review. I asked not to hear it, as I did not feel well, but she read it anyway, and because Charlotte was in such good spirits, I thought it must be a good review.

> Acton, when left together to his own imagination, seems to take a morose satisfaction in developing a complete science of human brutality. In Wuthering Heights he has succeeded in reaching the summit of this laudable ambition. He details all the ingenuity of animal malignity, and exhausts the whole rhetoric of stupid blasphemy, in order that there may be no mistake as to the kind of person he intends to hold up to popular gaze. Nightmares and dreams, through which devils dance and wolves howl, make bad novels.

She said, "Isn't this delightful?"

I felt my face turn color. Tabby helped me up the stairs. Charlotte came to sit with me later. She didn't say anything, despite my pallor. I could see my reflection in the widow. When I coughed, she held a napkin to my mouth and concealed from me whatever I had coughed up.

Charlotte brushed my hand and then drew back. "You are so cold, Emily. It chills me to the bone just to touch you. You must be suffering horribly."

I nodded my head. "It is lovely weather for a walk."

"It is raining."

"I enjoy the rain."

"No wonder you are so ill."

The washing pitcher was too heavy for me to lift. I tipped it and poured a little water onto a cloth. I wiped the cloth over my skin. I dressed in clothes Anne had aired outside. I was not allowed outside anymore. When I smelled the fabric, I could smell the air and the wind and distant heather and I felt as close as I was likely to, to roaming across the grass and up to the lip of the hill where I could see everything. My legs ached from missed walks. Once I was dressed, I walked down the stairs and I was exhausted. It had been raining for over a month, and my lungs felt heavy. Out on the moors, the letters to myself were rotting, I was certain, turning into a fold of mushrooms and algae and moss. I had to stay up and moving because I did not want to go back to sleep and lose this day. Nothing was happening on this day. But dead, even nothing was something. So many days passed. I sat up in bed. The light came through my window, and I thought I should get someone to go get those letters and I could read them before I was gone because they were meant for me.

Charlotte says: Papa - I am the bestselling author Currer Bell

When demand for the work had assured me of the success of Jane Eyre, Emily and Anne urged me to tell Papa of its publication. I went to his study one afternoon after his early dinner, carrying with me a copy of the book with two reviews, taking care to include notices adverse to it.

"Papa, I've been writing a book."

"Have you, my dear?"

"Yes, and I want you to read it."

"I am afraid it will try my eyes too much."

"But it is not in manuscript. It is printed."

"My dear! You've never thought of the expense it will be! It will almost be sure to be a loss, for how can you get a book sold? No one knows you or your name."

"But Papa, I don't think it will be a loss; no more will you, if you will let me read a review or two, and tell you more about it."

I sat down and read some of the reviews to Papa. I gave him a copy of Jane Eyre and left him to read it.

When I came into the parlor, Emily and Anne asked me, "Did you tell him?"

"I did."

"What did you say to him?"

"I told him Jane Eyre had been published and well received."

"Is that all you said to him?"

"I told him all there was to tell. It just remains for him to read my book."

When he came to tea later, papa said, "Girls, do you know Charlotte has been writing a book? And it is much better than likely?"

"Papa," Emily exclaimed, "Anne and I have also published books."

"Indeed. Indeed. I shall go blind reading all of the books my girls are writing. Have you sold as many copies as Charlotte? She has developed quite a following."

"No, Papa," Emily said. Anne folded her napkin.

Anne says: [CENSORED]

"Words suppressed for your protection" -- Charlotte Brontë. Please refer to the authorized edition of The Life of Charlotte Brontë by Elizabeth Gaskell.

Charlotte says: Nine o' clock writing - alone

After I finished my indoor chores at nine o'clock, Mr. Nicholls returned and went upstairs to his room. He said he felt awkward sitting in the parlor to witness my nightly ritual of composition. Ever since the three of us sisters had been very young, at nine o'clock we put away our housework and sat down to write. Father even forbad there to be curtains in the parlor because we burned so many candles working. At nine o' clock, he locked the front door and put out the lights and kissed me on my forehead.

"That was a stubborn thing you did today exposing yourself to the elements."

"The windows are washed now."

"But they will get dirty again this week and if you die of exposure, you will be dead forever."

I didn't matter. Just as my sisters didn't matter. We were alone except for our family in this world, and our presence mattered only in our own limited sphere. I worked at the table on my writing. My manner of composition, I should note; I have found slightly different than other writers. My works accumulate, each sentence fully cast, and then evaluated in the context of the whole. I throw down a sentence I think will advance the work and consider it and then strike it out, or more often than not go to the next as yet unwritten sentence. Sometimes these sentences are as difficult to cast as passing a kidney stone, and I wander around the table in a circle where years ago my two other dear sisters also wandered. We bumped into each other as we struggled with these thoughts, and the mutual struggle of us three helped us along. I could ask Emily a question, and she would be grateful for the escape from her labors, or I would listen to her explain her problem, often finding that in removing the weight of all the words I had accumulated that the solution would present itself to me. In this way, each step forward became more and more difficult until I reached the end.

I felt a little feverish before going to bed. I climbed the stairs, washed myself, and finally lay down. I listened to my father snoring in the other room. Mr. Nicholls' light was still on. When he heard me lay down in bed, he knocked. "Hello," he said.

"Hello," I said.

"How are you feeling?"

"I am feeling," I said, "A little tired."

I say: Words are the slime trails of the living

Charlotte writes down Emily's last words in her journal and writes down Anne's last words in her journal and rewrites them for posterity.

Charlotte says: The Dead can aspire to be perfect; we can rewrite them.

The living are a bottle neck to the memory of the dead. The dead remain with us in memory but we are faulty reservoirs for remembering how things were because we are subject to petty grievances, annoyances, and prejudices. I felt a chill setting inside my bones, an ice that would not melt in the boiling water Tabby poured over my skin. "You know better than to tempt, fate, dear," she scolded. "What with me recovering from the TB." The living themselves do not have a long memory of the dead as they also pass along, leaving behind them notes and novels and heaps of trash. Yet, these words do not measure Emily or Anne or Branwell or myself.

I have burnt my tracks and die unknown. I watched Tabby in the reflection of the window as she folded up her clothes and lugged the pail of water into the hallway. At night, the windows are mirrors. During the day, I can look out and at night the outside can look in on me.

My Brother Enters Enchantment
                              Victoria Wyttenberg

At dusk, deer emerge and graze on acorns,
beechnuts, twigs and buds of viburnum and maple.
Like my brother in his younger days,

they don't bed down till dawn.
My brother rises from his comfortable chair
by the fire, puts on his sweater, walks away

from bluster and porch light and enters their world
of shyness. At first they stare at him from trees
along the river, grey brown coats and white patches

blending in with the birches, then they appear
from the foliage, one doe with her twins
and several yearlings. My brother offers apples

cut in quarters, carrots, lettuce, potato peelings,
ripe bananas, molasses, then lays down
the bowl and backs away.

Their large ears, supple movements and wildness
entice him but he stands perfectly, calling to them
in whispers. They gaze at him with clear eyes

as they stand together in star silence.
Memory and time rise from the damp earth

as breath rises white in the cold air,
as the moon rises. Leaving hoofprints
like split hearts, the deer come closer
on jointy knees and graceful bodies

and eat. For this tenderness
I am grateful, my brother, with his good heart
in the low fog of twilight, feeding the deer.

Bell Tower in Jerusalem
Kelly Terwilliger

So much begins among carvings
of camels, and crosses and small oil lamps.
Banners of mirrors wink in the sun
and toss their reflected confetti--
each gust of wind a patter
of pieced and shattered light.

To ascend one must submit
to being swallowed by stone,
climbing the winding throat of stairs
coiled upon themselves:
light and dark blink up
and up past the silence of bells
that wait for someone to sound them.

At the top a room opens,
a room that seems to see in all directions
domes, towers, walls,
and hills heavy with olives and gravestones.
Closer lie rooftops, a tree
of drying socks, tables laid for lunch, a cluster

of soldiers visible
on this skin of city, the last layer feet can tranverse
while pigeons veer from the shadows
of falcons, all wings perfect and taut
as the cupped shells of satellite dishes
staring past the ceiling of sky.

The Game
Kelly Terwilliger

She sits at the kitchen table
with the radio turned up high. She watches
her son's new bride:
the neat aproned dress, dishgloves up
to rolled sleeves, and the sink
a pillow of foam. Dishes clink
beneath the roar of Fenway Park,
the announcer's voice flying hard and white
through the wild nothing of sunlit sky,
high, higher until it is lost
in the screams of unseen crowds.

Suds ease
down the back of a plate
as the daughter-in-law sets it
in the rack to dry. A fork glints, a row of glasses
gleams with the iridescent kiss
of soap. She slides a glance to the table;
the game is nearly over. The mother-in-law rises,
clicks off the sound, then flicks
the ash of her cigarette
into the steaming sink.

Every Good Girl
Becky Aldridge

I smoke too much, but I like cigarettes because unlike men, they don't kiss back, and when I'm through with one I can toss it carelessly, stomp on it, grind it into the ground, and never look back.

You might think I have a heart like the Grinch, three sizes too small, but that's not true. I've been known to help blue-haired ladies with walkers cross the street. I even nursed a bird with a broken wing back to health.

But most people aren't little old ladies or fine-feathered friends, and men are a completely different ilk. *Flashback. The bruise on my face is so big it looks like someone has started drawing a map of America on the left side of my mouth. It hurts to talk. It hurts more to still want him.*

I've slept with 97 men. I keep track of all their first names but not their last names, and I rate them on a scale of 0 to 11. I like 11 better than 10, the zero in ten gives me pause. How could anything perfect be partly a zero? No man has ever gotten an 11, let alone a 10; 23 have received a big zero—couldn't even make it to one—flat as a flapjack. You may think that means I have bad judgement. Then again, maybe I was feeling softhearted. Those twenty-three, they were my favorites. The attention they needed. "Oh, honey, it's not your fault." "Yes, I'm sure this is the first time this has happened to you." "No, I don't mind just cuddling." Those large, cumbersome man hands taking that flaccid divining rod and trying to make it come to life. In the end, it makes up for every time one has twisted my nipple. *Flashback. The sting is still in my cheek and the belt is laughing at me from the floor. He's in his chair. I hear the pop and fizz as he opens a beer.*

Maybe I'm a bitch. The first boy I ever slept with was Gary Anderson. Yes, *his* name I remember. We made out in the back of his Dad's rusted Datsun. He pulled my cardigan up to expose my plain white bra and the teenage breasts it contained. "Aw, man," was his reaction and he let out the hot fetid breath of too many cheap beers in plastic cups. He couldn't get my bra off. I had to do it. Then he put his hands, with the auto shop grime under his fingernails, on my uncertain chest. Cold and clammy. I had imagined they would be warm and tender. He grabbed at them like they might dissolve before his very eyes. We kissed and our kiss was different. His tongue went deeper. I wanted to spit it out, but we were supposed to be in love, so instead I swirled mine around his, pretending to enjoy the dance. Something hard was growing inside his pants, against my leg. *Flashback. Uncle Danny spanking my bottom on my seventh birthday. The play soda pop dispenser was the most expensive gift anyone had ever bought for me.* I didn't know why was I thinking of Uncle Danny, ugly red-headed Uncle Danny with the lazy eye. Gary started speaking in a man voice. "Do you want it? Do you want me to give it to you?" I didn't, but I half-nodded in the jammed backseat that I did. This was supposed to happen sooner or later. He pulled up my skirt and bumped his head on the interior light while trying to maneuver out of his jeans. "Fuck," he said. Yeah, that's what we were doing. I had never seen a penis before. Never. *Flashback. Tight curly red hair, big white hairy thighs telling me what to do.*

"Touch it," Gary said, his boy voice back, unsure. I didn't want to. I imagined it to be slimy like I imagined a snake. But I put my fingers on it anyway, not certain how to hold it, even more uncertain what to do with it. I was surprised by how soft the skin felt, like the first time you touch deerskin gloves. Gary moaned and pushed himself into me. It took several tries and by the time he was inside me, I was walking on a beach

182

alone with a gentle wind whispering in my ear, the Datsun, the bouncing, the sweat, all miles away. Alone—until there's Uncle Danny at the beach laughing at me, running and trying to catch me.

I start sweating, but not a good sweat. Gary is Uncle Danny. Uncle Danny is Gary. His hand is over my mouth trying to stop my screams. I feel a heat inside my body and a tickling trickle of thick liquid on the folds of my skin. It's over and Gary is repeating, "Oh, man. Oh, man." He's using his red T-shirt to wipe off his penis. Only later does he get teased about the stain on his shirt. I sit up and just let the liquid run down my leg. This is the first time. Please God, let it be my first time.

The Boy Who Sits
Danielle Rado

There's a boy in my class who sits. I mean that's all he does. Every day he sits at his desk with his head down. When our teacher, Mrs. Goode, asks us to pull our desks into a circle, he stays put. Mrs. Goode says, "John, are you going to join us today?" and he lifts his head, like my cat does when he's sleeping and I call his name, then turns away, settling it back down on his folded arms. He won't do any assignments or even take the tests. Mrs. Goode tucks the stapled sheets or hardcover workbook under his arm when she passes them out.

My favorite workbook is our Reader, with hundreds of little stories, often with a boy named John. But I know this John doesn't do things like help his father on the farm, sitting on the lap of the dusty overalls and trying to turn the big wheel of the tractor; or visit his grandparents in Albuquerque and learn about Pueblo Indians; or fall off his bike and have friendly doctors show him X-rays of the broken arm, which he brings to school the next day in a cast that we all sign. Though what would we have to write to him? Besides, he'd keep it tucked up in the sleeve of his big sweatshirt, the one with the hood he often pulls up over his face.

After reading the story "When I Am Taller," we have to write one of our own. When I am taller I will…. People in my class giggle as they imagine themselves driving cars, or dunking basketballs, or smashing buildings. John could be taller right now if he would only stand up.

When I'm half way through with my story—when I finish writing about being able to reach the glasses above the counter or turn away from a grown-up's lecture, or walk right past their wagging finger and out the door, out to my car, and drive away—I pause, lift my head, lean back, look around. I notice that John's watching us—from the back of the room he's staring at our hunched heads. When he sees me looking at him he sticks his finger up his nose. Mrs. Goode tells me to turn around and then reiterates her policy on cheating. It is not tolerated.

I try not to look at him anymore. I return to my paper, but all the pictures I had in my head are now just flat letters on the page. Then the boy next to me looks over and hisses through the space between our desks, "When you're taller, you'll still be short." My face turns red and my paper clouds over, but what he said is true.

When we're done writing we pass the papers forward. The boy in front of John turns and grabs his. He writes John's name on top of the blank sheet like he's been doing all year. The students in the front row tap the papers on their desks and hand the evened piles to Mrs. Goode as she walks by. When the papers are collected we return the Readers to the long low shelf at the back of the room. Mrs. Goode snaps closed the one that John has propped open in front of his head, which is buried in his arms on the table. She hands it to me as I walk by. John doesn't look up. Some students linger to straighten up the books, others have already gotten their lunches or money and have lined up by the door. Only when the line is straight and silent will we be allowed to go. Mrs. Goode asks, "John, would you like to join the other kids for lunch today?" and he shifts his doughy body, this time rising momentarily, and settles back down again. Maybe he mumbles "No." Then we're dismissed.

He's has been like this since kindergarten. Maybe even before he came to school he'd sit on his parents' couch and refuse to raise his head when they called him for dinner, or when they yelled at him for not cleaning up his toys, or when they stood in front of him and said, "We're going now. Let's go," only occasionally peeking out from his lowered hood to look towards the monotone color and sound of the television set.

One day I have to stay in the classroom for lunch and recess because I forgot to do my homework. That's how Mrs. Goode tries to teach us lessons. Other lessons are like the one about diagramming sentences, about how in order to understand the meaning of words and sentences we have to understand how they work together, which words need each other and how words behave. By this point her fingers are intertwined in front of her face and her hands slowly lowering in front of her. Sentences should make sense, she says, convinced that miscommunication is only a by-product of slipshod word choice and lazy sentence construction. As everyone files down to the cafeteria I go to my locker and retrieve my bagged lunch. Mrs. Goode, John, and I sit at our desks, grading papers, ignoring papers, writing papers, and wait out the period. I diagram sentences from my reader.

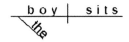

Once, when I was smaller, I asked my dad about John. I could still fit easily on his lap and if he wanted to he could have folded me up into a neatly packaged self.

"Dad," I said, "There's this boy at school."

"Your boyfriend?" He poked my ribs, but I wasn't in the mood.

I said, "No, just this boy. He never does anything. He just sits there all day."

"Aren't you supposed to sit during class?"

"Dad!"

"All right, all right. Don't get excited."

"But he doesn't do anything. Ever. He just sits there. No homework. No class work. He doesn't ever turn anything in!"

"What does it have to do with you?" He took care to emphasize every word, as if they each held valuable information regardless of the sentence they were in. "It only makes you look better."

"That's not the point."

"What else is?" He became serious and lowered his head so that his face was close to mine. He was like my desk, making me sit a certain way, making me look a certain way. But before he could speak, I twisted and pushed against his chest until he let go of me. My feet still dangled far above the ground but I wriggled back and forth until I began to slip from his lap, my pants riding up me as I slid. For a moment I stopped, the corduroy of my pants clinging to his own. I had to

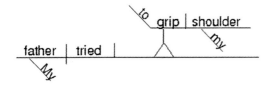

to steady me when my feet hit the floor. What's the problem? he asked, but I ducked his hand, stumbled forward, steadied myself and ran.

John has nothing to eat for lunch and I have tuna and carrot sticks, neither of which I feel like eating as I fill in the answers to last night's homework. I leave my desk to make an offering. He lifts his head and turns his sour face at me.

"I don't like tuna," he says to the soggy white bread and mayonnaise soaked fish I hold out in front of me. This may be the first time I've really heard his voice, though that can't possibly be true. I doubt he'll like carrots. Mrs. Goode relieves me from the immobility of sudden rejection by calling my name. She tells me,

187

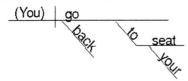

At the end of the day, at the end of the year, at the end of several years, we leave to go do some of those things one does when their taller—get married, find employment, buy expensive items—but John is still seated at that desk, exactly the same height, with a barricade of books around the hood pulled over his hunched head, a little more than a still life, crystallized in silence until one day the teacher, an older Mrs. Goode or someone else, comes over, taps his shoulder, and says, "John, would like to join us?" And instead of shifting his head and grumbling, instead of rising like dough then deflating, cracks will race from his shoulder around his entire body, making it look for a moment like he's covered in cobwebs, until he crumbles, not like breaking glass but like a lump of dried dirt, the sun-baked shell of him shattered, the inner shell of him laid open in a heap on the ground, revealing nothing but a slight smell of dust and a mess for the janitor to sweep up.

Years later I've managed to have a real job and this cozy house with a fenced-in yard. Each summer I try to hold the flakes of rotting wood in place by putting a fresh layer of whitewash on the fence while I imagine larger plans for my yard—perennials over there, small junipers along the back, maybe a fruit tree—but by the time I finish with the paint I find myself satiated with just the imagined yard.

This winter, before I have begun picturing the blooms, a new cat decides to come into my yard. He sprays the front and back doors with a quick mist, and rubs his face along the fence, slowly moving his cheek against a post so his lips pull back and reveal the hint of his brown teeth. He does this even if he sees me watching through the glass, especially if he sees me watching. His hair is matted, the white fur showcasing the dirt, the orange patches faded. He's worn and stocky. He stands outside the windows and baits my cat, also male, into coming outside and fighting, into protecting his turf, protecting his female. My cat hisses and spits at the sliding glass door with such ferocity that sometimes I think the tomcat is inside my house, that he's passed through the window like light and has tried to lay himself on my floor, as my cat would, to bask in the leftover beam.

My boyfriend wants to come over and take care of the problem. "I'll take care of it," he says. He suggests startling it off by firing a gun. I tell him I didn't know he had one. He says he doesn't but that he can get one. Then, when I say nothing, he says he can use the garden hose and spray him. I remind him it's winter, and the hose is frozen in its curled position.

"A trap then. We'll catch him and give him to the pound," he says, then adds, "Do you want me to get one and bring it over?"

"Not now," I say.

I latch my back door and look out the window. I can't see anything but my fence and thinned rhododendrons left by the previous owners outlining my tiny yard. He's too big and orange to be hiding behind them.

I call the pound.

I'm in my kitchen, the phone book lying open on my counter top. This number, the first of three for local pounds, is indicated with a penciled arrow. I practice what I'll say:

A cat, a lonely cat, has come to my house, my home, looking for something. At first we didn't mind. He seemed harmless, but now my cat comes home with cuts and bruises. He lets out a pitiful growl if I accidentally pet one under his belly or along his side. He's had to have his ear bandaged. He's afraid to go outside. He looks at me accusingly. Our relationship is strained. We've never fed or pet the other cat, but still

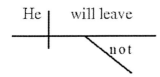

While I'm waiting for someone at the pound to answer the phone, my cat jumps on the counter and stretches his neck towards me. I lean my head down and he presses his forehead into mine. His purr turns to a low growl as his ear accidentally touches me. He jumps down and stands by the door. I slide it open but he runs in the opposite direction. When someone on the other end answers I explain my situation.

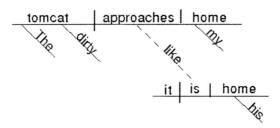

"Yup," the man says, and then is silent.
I explain further, "I need to get rid of him."
"Probably feral."
"What's that mean?"
"Can't adopt him."
"I'm not trying to adopt him. Can't you do anything?"
"We can come out there and catch him, but we'll have to put him down."
"I'm not trying kill him."
"Feral, you know." Now he's silent, waiting for me.
"I know, but what—" I ask.
"Probably wants to take over your house. You got a cat, right?" He says this like I should know exactly how animals

behave, like the key to their behavior lays in the strict observation of their habits, like all the workings of their brains are showcased in the way they prance, the way they lick themselves meticulously, their scratchy tongue pulling over their fur, the way they run or walk to or away from you, the way they make gurgling noises in their throats. My cat has watched me since the day I got him. All he knows of me is when I like to wake up, when I like to go to sleep, and when I leave for and return from work. He's happy when he's right, and so am I. We've watched each other for years. But there was no time to watch for this cat, because suddenly we're barricaded in my house, my cat and me, attacked by the scent of urine that circles our home, an olfactious sign of the tomcat. My cat has tried to drive it off by rubbing his cheeks against the outside corners of the house and my legs, by peeing all over the yard. His efforts fail.

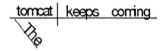

He goes on, "He was probably doin' the same thing to someone else, so they caught him and dumped him near your place." Again he speaks like I should know this, like the key to understanding people's behavior lays in the strict observation of their interaction with animals, the way they croon to them, or yell at them, the way they demand, the way my cat's tongue moves to my hand when I reach to pet him and for a moment I mistake that for affection.

"They can do that?" I ask.

"Har har," he goes. "Yup."

"Is there any place I can bring him?"

"If he's feral he's got to be put down," the man says.

I hang up the phone. I won't bother calling the other pounds. I open the back door and call for my cat. The tomcat cat comes running. Unlike my cat he's not careful to step only in the previously made prints in the snow, a technique that slows him down and winds him through tortuous paths in the yard. Instead the tomcat charges directly at me, his weight easily breaking the thin layer of ice that's formed on the latent snow. The cat must weigh under five pounds, due to malnourishment, due to banishment, due to long treks from house to house, but he charges at me with his confident tail straight up. Is this what scared the other people? Did they have to mount an assault with spoons banged on pots, an army of noise against an undomesticated domesticated animal, much like my boyfriend's strategy the last time the tomcat was this close, when he pushed me aside, squared his shoulders in the door frame and flailed his arms, yelling, "Get! Get out of here you fucking thing! Get the hell out," and slammed the door. Then

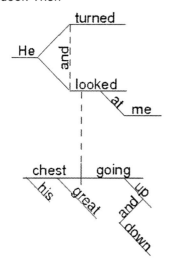

in his excitement. He didn't see the cat trying to run off so fast that he slipped on the ice of the back stoop, twisted over and fell to the ground, nor did he see my cat curl himself into a tight little ball under the couch.

"Damnit," I said, "You're scaring him."

Now I do nothing and as he gets nearer. He's making little noises, purring louder and louder as he gets closer and closer to the door. I haven't shut it yet. I'm almost tempted. I tell the tomcat, "If I didn't already have a cat," but reach my hand towards him anyway, reaching behind his ear to scratch. He hisses and spits and digs his canines deep into the flesh between my thumb and forefinger. He runs to the edge of the yard, turns around and looks at me. I cup my hand in my other one, then try to pinch out the blood and saliva through the little holes. I suck at the wound and spit out the door, the warm saliva, both of our saliva, melting through the ice and sinking into the snow, a hot little hole burrowing into the white blanket, a mark that'll be gone with the first hint of warm weather.

I shut the door and the tomcat trots back to its large window and looks into the house, then at me. He turns and sprays a fine mist at the base of the door and stalks off. I go to the opposite end of the house, to the front door and call for my cat again. He comes running up behind me and together we stare out onto the snow, the layer that managed to melt now freezing in the fresh cold of the evening. I close and lock the door.

My cat trots with me to the bathroom and watches me pour hydrogen peroxide over my hand and wince at the small white bubbles that rise up.

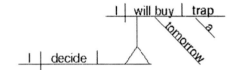

A nice one. One that's a cage and closes when the animal enters to get the food that I will set in there—something nice, maybe the canned food my cat has begun to shun, racing into the kitchen when he hears the can open so that he can sniff it, scratch around the edges of the bowl as if to bury it, and walk away—all without hurting him. Then I'll drive at least ten miles and drop him off in a wooded area, but close to houses. Maybe he'll find a house without a cat, owned by someone who won't mind taking him in. But I can't. I already have a cat. I work full time. Money's tight. He's not my responsibility. Tomorrow he won't be my problem.

Connecting Lines
Carol Smallwood

Blackboard partially erased: satyr, centaur, dolly, wr, h, wro, chimera, positive vs. neg, 000, right is pru, in clouds of smudges--lines left to right on green banked by cinder blocks.

--- 193

Supersleep helps you sleep. You should not do any activity after taking it requiring alertness, and use care when engaging in morning activities. All sleep medicines carry some risk of dependency. Side effects may include headache, dizziness, bowel irritability, and rash. For more check the product leaflet.

"Each person we meet, each place we visit, each event in our lives, and for that matter the universe itself in its far-flung glory, all confront us as bits of perception and memory, inklings and intuitions, and we seem compelled…to bind these scraps into a whole that makes sense." Scott Russell Sanders

----

To: Mary Ann Anderson <maa@penwoods.net>
From: Carol Smallwood <smallwood@tn.net>

Subject: Tuesday, December 6

Dear Mary Ann,

Many thanks for the neat info you sent for my horse friend. I'll be sure and give it to her. She is taking 18 hours right now so haven't gotten together but will after semester is done--she is going in for a hysterectomy so will need something to cheer her up!

Love, Carol

Indulge in light floral enriching mist. Quickly absorbs leaving skin delicately scented, sensual. Generously spray lines all over. Also good for repelling insects. Ingredients: Isopropyl Palmitate, SD Alcohol 0-B, Purified Water, Fragrance.

194

When Mary Ann came the last time, she wound yarn around a piece of wood and I asked, "What's it called?"

"A spindle. It's been used thousands of years."

It spun with just a nudge and wound skeins much to the delight of Kitty who watched with itching paws. It had a soothing, hypnotic effect and I thought of millions of women--a comforting procession of women doing the same thing in caves by fires and then, candle light.

As children, slim fingers were prized so we clipped metal hair curlers on ours for hours unaware that women in China used to bind their feet.

When my daughter first went to nursery school, I was uneasy when she drew lines into blocks instead of drawing flowers like other girls. It made me think I hadn't done my job although I knew she was used to playing blocks with her brother. Should I discourage it before a nursery mother commented? And while a part of me admired her doing it, another said she'd have an easier future if she conformed: common sense said not to make a big deal of it.

Date: Tue, 06 Dec 2005 08:42:42 -0500
From: Mary Ann Anderson <maa@penwoods.net>
X-Accept-Language: en-us, en
To: Carol Smallwood <smallwood@tn.net>
Subject: Tuesday, December 6

Hi Carol --

I got the superwash merino fiber to dye for out "dyeing and color day out". Will spin down stairs while the fiber is being dyed. I figure one day per color.

The tops of the mountains are getting pretty light - need to pull Tony in before the sun gets in his eyes. Probably should pull my winter jacket out of the closet too - it is 45 out there, and while it has been colder, I feel colder this morning.

Best I get out there before the sun is up.

Love,

Mary Ann

Leo, Orion, Pegasus, Big Dipper, Ursa Major, Ursa Minor are constellations that form pictures if lines are imagined connecting them. Dot-to-dot pictures may also be drawn connecting spots of frost on windowpanes.

It's a toss up which clerk
you get standing in
postal lines: the one always
smiling; the frowning one
you think more sincere.

Both have the tone of
priests in confessionals when
uttering, "What's inside?"

When finished, you pretend not
to see others still in lines,
departing with downcast eyes.

To: Mary Ann Anderson <maa@penwoods.net>
From: Carol Smallwood <smallwood@tn.net>
Subject: Tuesday, December 6

Dear Mary Ann,

It is VERY dark out this morning and sprinkling enough that
the back deck is wet away from the overhang and so is the
sidewalk out front, but there are no puddles in the driveway,
so either not much has come down or it has come down so
slowly it has sunk down as it arrives.

** Ah--hopefully you will get lots more your way yet. None
here in Michigan.

I had to turn on the light to be able to see the keyboard enough
to place my fingers correctly to type.

** Ah, shorter days indeed

I took a long nap yesterday afternoon -was so very tired! Feel
better today! One does need a Sunday every week to get
rested for the next one!

** Tried sleeping with no sleeping pills but had to get up and
take some. Have to fast for blood test which I dread because
last time they had to poke four times because they said chemo
made veins hard to hit.

It was strange - it was about 63 when I did chores last night
and it felt cold to me!!!

** How have the PA crops been?

I was going to go to Joanne's after mass, but found that my coupon had expired, so I decided to wait until I got another. I'm trying to get in supplies to make that small sample of the Watercolor Quilt. This kit makes one of the pieces that together would form the Flower Garden Quilt. The flowers are appliquéd on.

** Whew--sounds like a lot of work to me! Slow kind.

What I would like to make is the next one - the Birds in the Garden quilt with each section featuring a bird. You sign up and get 1 kit a month ($19.99/kit) except the last kit contains all the borders between squares so it $44.99. If you mail order it, there is about $3. postage on each. That makes a mighty expensive quilt.

** I guess! You should've saved those clothes you tossed!

I've got to start finding homes for stuff in my kitchen because the spinners are coming. Stuff gets to the kitchen and if I can't think where to put it, it stays there. And stays there. Is it Mouth or Month that has no rhyming word? Do you have a book with works that rhyme?

**Yes. After working with that sort of thing you sort of float off to another land.

The men on the submarine got out safely - lets hope the astronauts make it home safely also.

**YAAAA! Probably a Blockbuster movie shortly. Last night I watched a movie about the Colosseum. You can still see the four levels: the upper for standing women, the poor, and slaves--tickets were numbered pottery shards. Five thousand animals were killed from dawn to dusk performances in one day, whole species of animals were lost in the slaughter. Eighty thousand people at one time watched tens of thousands of people die and to make sure they weren't faking death, branding irons were applied. Considered large even by today's stadiums, it had elevators, a retractable awning. It became a symbol of Romanticism in the nineteenth century.

Love
Mary Ann

Love, Carol

Line upon line
spun off easily in dreams
that on waking,
turned into balls:
bouncing off reason
they tangled.

198

In the library study carrel, I felt tendrils extending from my mind seeking other minds inside books. My sense of smell, hearing, sight, taste, and touch sharpened in the hope of meeting minds, some occurrence of alchemy. One page weighs hardly anything, but page after page compresses. So much yearning to catch the gold, dizzy from circling, grasping for brass rings while the earth spins faster than could be imagined. I saw thousands of medieval alchemists bending over experiments saying, "Just one more try and I'll find gold—just one more time," only to find no gold--and yet aren't they to be envied for having dreams--and acting on them? And how much good does it do us now to know the earth spins? After a while, the tendrils became lines as straight as geometry problems of some gigantic book which turned to rays from stained glass cathedral windows.

When I left, I saw a rainbow prism on the floor and walked back and forth trying to see what made it, careful never to step on it as if it'd crack, yet never discovered (no matter what angle I looked) what made the brilliant purple, blue, pink, and yellow.

To: Mary Ann Anderson <maa@penwoods.net>
From: Carol Smallwood <smallwood@tn.net>
Subject: Thursday, December 8

Dear Mary Ann,

What happened to the 7th??? Did I spend two days on the 6th??? Or did the 7th just sneak past? Anyway, the little calendar says it is the 8th!!! It sounds as tho even in your comatose state, you just kept going like the Energizer Bunny they show on t.v. !!!

Let's see - Doug's boys (Doug fixes my computer) sweaters are finished, but only Ian's is deliverd.

Joshua's is ready for a placket, buttons and a few last minute ends to be worked in.

Joanne's sweater needs to be seamed, Mega-ends worked in, placket, buttons etc. But the sleeves are both knitted.

Morgan's sweater back is knitted and the front is knitted to the bottom of where the placket is to be. I need to put half the stitches out of work, knit one side and put them on waste yarn. Then I'll do the second side.

*Good grief, how can you keep all those straight? What patience! YIKES!

Time for me to get on to other things. Sure hope you got a good sleep last night!

**I took a Valium left over from chemo. It did seem to quiet me down. I'll ask my doctor what he thinks when I get the &+#% shots but most medications seem to wear off and only leave headaches.

If I get too tired, I can't sleep! When I do, sometimes a few swallows of coffee to sleep. Each person's chemistry is so different - it is a challenge to figure one's own system out.

**Well, got my first Christmas card yesterday from someone I didn't send one to so hope Michigan Humane Society's new recruitments arrive quickly! It will be very sad to see my neat classes end and will miss them. Watch out for the ice.

Love, Carol

Love,
Mary Ann

Thank you for calling Clare Bank and Trust. We are your hometown bank for all your banking needs; you do not need to go further for affordable mortgages. The time is 3:17 a.m. and 20 seconds; the weather calls for snow with the temperature in the 20's. We have dependable lines of credit at the Clare Bank and Trust.

200

Capturing the moon
through lines of
Venetian blinds
is a matter of
adjusting the pull,
your head—
and timing

Anonymous Children
of Martin Luther...
(A-G of an Abecediary)
Debra DiBlasi

1. (...who was anti-semitic)
I loved the <u>BENEDICTION</u> most May God bless you and keep
you and make His face shine upon you two hours after sitting
and standing and sitting and standing and stifling yawns and
sleep and laughter too when the sounds of snores or farts
interrupted the sermon May God lift up his countenance upon
you and give you peace and hand-shaking and then we were
out the door that was old and wooden and rotting because
it was not a big church so not rich, and neither were we, no,
we were poor but on Sundays we each got a candy bar at
the little market on the long drive home because In the name
of the Father, and Son, and Holy Ghost my mother's butt got
tired too and so did her ears and maybe her heart though she
wanted to believe in God, after all there had to be something
better than five kids and no running water and a husband that
sometimes called her the same cusswords he called his cows
Amen.

2. gold foil
Each Sunday after a funeral of somebody we didn't know (we
didn't know anybody in that church except the pastor and we
didn't know him very well because it was a thirty-mile drive

from his house to ours and he made it only when my mother asked him, which was maybe once or twice, when she thought she was going insane, or when he thought we were hell-bent because we'd missed a month of Sundays) the church would be decorated with CHRYSANTHEMUMS left over from the wake

["wake   n. 13. a watch or vigil by the body of a dead person before burial, sometimes accompanied by feasting or merrymaking;" a watch, it says, as if the body might rise up and speak, might confess finally its sins or condemn finally the sinners; merrymaking, it says, as if Lutherans ever the hell made merry]

and the flowers would always be yellow, it seemed, and just beginning to fade, the tips drying up and going brown and curling inward like somebody in a coma closing like a flower closing for the last time, and I would stare at the mums in plastic pots wrapped in gold foil so thin it tore if you touched it as I drank the blood of Christ wine and ate the body of Christ bread and I'd be glad whoever'd died had not stuck around to see the flowers dying too, because they were sad in their homely pots, sad and out of place in a church that was airless and dark, the only real sunlight coming through the face of Jesus in the altar's stained glass window so bright you couldn't look at it straight, only sideways, and even then it hurt your eyes.

3. descending into sin

Worse than the old DREARY church was the new drearier basement of the pastor's house where we had confirmation class and where the windows were rectangles one foot high by two feet long that you couldn't crawl out of if there was a fire and they were basically useless anyway, these windows, because the pastor's wife who was very pretty and soft-spoken like wind loved plants and grew bushes and flowers and ferns around the whole house, blocking out the light completely so that the basement was pitch black when we first walked down into it, and I wonder now if the pastor wanted us to be afraid of descending into darkness, which was the phrase he always used to describe sin, though he was not as precise about sin as I would have liked, for example saying that getting remarried after a divorce wasn't a sin if the divorce was because the spouse was crazy, like his first wife who was, he said, crazy as a loon and maybe she was because he put her in a nuthouse and divorced her and then remarried the pretty wind-voiced lady who loved plants and adopted a child from Korea and named her my name, Debra, because she thought it was a pretty and simple name and once she caught me in the bathroom singing where have all the flowers gone and she cried because it was the early Seventies, after all, and there was a war going on and things were different then.

4. brother paul could've used some therapy
In the beginning our pastor only preached about life, you know: drugs and sex and rock 'n' roll and how Jesus would have fit right in with the Haight-Ashbury crowd because they were all fucked up looking for something better and that's what Jesus was dealing in those days – something better, his brand of dope – so of course there were all these Jesus freaks too, not just regular hippies, hanging around like some big party going on in the temple, and there's Jesus turning water into wine, or as the case coulda/woulda/shoulda been, Coca-Cola into LSD, and everybody tripping and seeing God, which is not what the pastor preached, no, not exactly, well not at all, rather he preached about everything that was going on now ("now" being 30 years ago – Jesus, has it really been that long?) and there wasn't anything anyone could do to change that fact, though they tried by demanding the pastor quit talking about life and instead preach straight from the Bible, especially from Paul's EPISTLES because, they said, Paul was so [self]righteous and full of love, they said [come on! Paul was mad as hell at the Romans for putting him in prison, and he sure as hell didn't think much of women or, come to think

of it, most of humanity if you read closely, which most people don't because they just don't read, don't know how to read, at least read what the words are really saying, not just what they mean, for chrissake], or other stories from the New Testament so they all could sleep better during the sermon and not have to pay such close attention to things that made them think hard because it gave them a headache and subsequently ruined their Sunday dinner of whole chickens and mashed potatoes with gravy and green beans and corn on the cob and homemade buttery rolls and apple pie with ice cream which is why so many of them were grossly overweight, while every Sunday we ate bologna and cheese sandwiches and Doritos because store-bought food was a treat after living on nothing but fresh beef and vegetables, so we liked it just fine.

5. everything has a fragrance

What does God smell like? is what I wanted to know but was too afraid to ask my obvious question, obvious because I was a country girl, and in the country everything has a scent: cow patties, grass, pond water, rain… everything smelling fine and full, and to smell a world like that you have to take it inside your mouth – talk about communion! – inside your lungs, inside your blood even, especially spring mornings right after the fruit trees blossomed a <u>FRAGRANCE</u> so thick and vast it could choke a lesser soul who'd never think to ask, What does God smell like? I'd wonder sitting in the pews that were old and scent-darkened by lemon oil and hands that gripped the wooden backs to keep from swaying or falling, and the hymnals were old too, the pages yellow and turning to dust though you couldn't see the dust yet but its scent was already rising from the thin paper under the black-ink notes rising to impossible heights, beyond the voice's range, like God was up there sitting at high C in a heaven you'd never reach and, damn, it hurt to try, vocal chords straining, the way I'd strain my nose to smell God in the motes of dust floating in a rail of light streaming through the glowing face of Jesus, thinking

God'd be there first – in the smallest things I could see – or else not at all since everything starts from the bottom up, as every country girl knows, but the motes and light were always too high to stick my nose into, because I didn't know yet that even the darkness, the skin, the voice is full of dust.

6. jesus as teen idol

The boys who went to church weren't better than the boys who didn't, they were just more scared of being bad, but not all of them because a few were bad whenever and wherever they pleased including in church, like this boy whose name I can't remember except that it didn't suit him, was a homely name and he was already handsome at ten and would be, you could tell, handsomer as he got older (though he never got much older, moving to another state and drowning in a lake after he dived off a pontoon and struck his head on a tree trunk floating beneath the water's surface just out of view), handsome in his bones, in his hands when he GROPED me in the church basement where we'd gone on an errand together to get some construction paper for a silly art project that had nothing to do with salvation and everything to do with keeping a pack of ten-year-olds entertained until their parents came and took them home – a thank-god salvation for the Sunday school teacher – and he kissed me too, my first kiss, under a poster of Jesus sitting on a rock with a little girl on his lap who looked a lot like me which, combined with that dead boy's kiss, is probably why for a long time, in fact through all my teen years, I had a crush on Jesus.

Getting on a Horse
Raphael Dagold

My mother is drawing a horse on the kitchen wall.
The horse is a gesture of a horse, drawn idly,
with scant, quick strokes of a bold pen or marker,
her left hand surer than her right, which cradles
the telephone, connecting her to someone
else, the horse a mind a mile away
dreaming of soft straw, light hooves, sweet apples.
Where *is* her mind, stroking the rough wood
paneling, boards really, nailed side-by-side
and stained dark—where is her mind
stroking the wood with her pen?
She is a girl drawing a horse.
After she leaves, the horse stays.
I stand in the kitchen
or walk through the door to the back yard,
I imagine her standing there,
I show my friends, I'm proud,
a horse, riderless, its owner away.

Seeing My Wife
at the Whitney
Raphael Dagold

Again I'm loving what I can not see, beating
my heart against it, the black thirds

of Steichen's early landscapes,
silver all-the-way dark and the shapes above—

tree-limbs, voluptuous clouds, rocks like minor gods—
reflected in each pool of blackness.

I'm working my gaze into platinum, silver,
into gum bichromate, direct carbon

prints which ache and ache me. My wife
is the sky when her face opens up. The clouds

are intricate mountains making and un-making themselves.
My wife is a sharp tack vibrating on the floor of my brain.

A woman whose hair suddenly glistens
waits for me to move so she will not break

my gaze, seeking shapes in murmuring crystals
of platinum, layered dark ground and boundless.

The Searchers
Catherine Sustana

Everything made my father angry—the pigeons nesting in the eaves, the sound of our chewing at dinner, and the way my sister, Francie, looked at him when she marched over to the TV one Sunday afternoon, clicked off *Rio Bravo*, and said John Wayne was an actor, not a cowboy.

I was lying on my stomach reading "Laughter Is the Best Medicine" in the *Reader's Digest*, and I held my breath while I looked up to watch my father's face. My little brothers, out of my father's line of sight, made gruesome, bug-eyed motions to show that Francie was going to get her throat cut.

We knew she meant a real cowboy would never have gotten laid off from GE. A real cowboy wouldn't live in a house where the radiators creaked even louder than the floorboards and seven people shared a bathroom whose door wouldn't shut all the way.

But my father didn't cut anybody's throat. He just got up and turned the TV back on like Francie wasn't even there.

Later that afternoon, he decided to shoot the pigeons with my older brother's BB gun. His aim wasn't as good as he expected. Francie stood in the window and watched him, her arms folded and her mouth set in a thin line of disgust, until my mother made up some chore that needed doing right away. After that, my father sat outside on an old aluminum lawn chair every day, bundled up against the winter, staring into nothing with the BB gun across his lap.

Francie headed west with the first cowboy who offered to take her to California. Now she sends us postcards with palm trees on them and tells my mother she's acting in commercials, but I know better. When she came back for Dad's funeral looking all skinny and hollow-eyed, she told me she was cleaning movie stars' mansions and pocketing the loose cash and jewelry they'd never miss.

"The trick," she whispered, tearing one of my father's prayer cards into nervous pieces, "is not to take anything too special."

I think about that when I'm alone at night, staring across her empty bed, out the window and far away to where the giant GE sign glares through the trees.

Last Christmas, she sent two gold bracelets for me and Mom. When I thought I was alone, I spun in circles in the living room, admiring the way the light sparkled off my wrist. But when I stopped twirling, I saw Mom standing in the doorway, her arms crossed, her mouth set in a thin line, and the kitchen trashcan at her feet. She held her bracelet up like something dead, then let it fall into the trash. And I knew she was thinking of Dad in the lawn chair, the way the wind made his eyes water as he sat there, small in the puff of his old down jacket, waiting for the perfect shot.

pushme-pullme
                Fern Capella

long fingers decide whether tonight I live or die.
do you deny your bone curled power?
enough strength to crush muscle to dust
and terror to trust, resistance to lust.
210 "business is booming," you are strange, my
unforgiving fruit, pushme-pullme, some creature
you've created to disarm my will, your ebb
it flows painfully away, your flow is forth,
this coming ebb, we pull painfully away breaking
day and still no rest, no quiet no confessions
nothing left, no alibi, no cheerio mornings,
a boy listens to your commands, cowers, your hands
break the silence. we can't name this union yet.
half our love is duty, the other half release,
have me your way, backwards, blurry, out of focus,
it written in my skin, let whore and slut, the salt of my sweat
initiate our morning wrestle. skin desires skin still
here's our secret – oh the scent of you – pure oxygen
some eunuch in the sheer rush of your touch.

stasis
Fern Capella

now we are all hung here,
our intoxicants shutter us past darkness,
all of us, hung here, waiting,
for who might come to the door tonight.
will we hear sirens, will we hear footsteps,
will the mountains make some god-awful noise
and the ocean come to greet us, each, personally,
our hands suddenly wet, our clothes washed away,
everything covered in what's coming for us,
climbing our doorstep, sirens wailing, mothers
unsure how to leave for milk, to leave
and take in sunshine, a stranger's voice, to breathe
without praying for the next breath, to quiet children
until we choke them so unwillingly, we don't want this,
and still we always knew, could not have known,
you and i stuck in stasis, in status, milking booze
and making love to empty faces, my wardrobe slips,
a lipstick slut, nothing satisfies us, waiting, held in space.

should we begin like this
Fern Capella

212

should we begin like this, small
children crowding hallways, standing
water below the bathtub and the ceiling
too low for your proud head, flies
would prey for days on the dead shark
in our toilet before, bit by bit, our murderous
senses honed for destruction picked up
the scent of death. should we begin in this
business of friction, you wear your gold
ring around phantom ink eyes, gold flecks
a sunset haze through all the rest, and mine
i have swallowed and leave inside, a trinket
to treasure in terrible weather, when all of
our wrong deeds have gathered together,
and taking control they leave us terribly, terribly,
terribly alone, should we begin knowing this,
any home we build will be washed away, death
becomes us, minutely, secretively, and we, victims
vindicated, rolling out our silver lining, chancing all we love.

More Like Ravel
John Kay

        Yesterday,
my son and I changed spark plugs,
distributor and wires, air and oil filters,
front brake pads, and put in a new motor
for the window after dismantling
the door. Today, clouds without
enough determination to rain drift
over the city like a funeral dirge,
leaving the air damp and irritable.
So I am in the grip of my headphones,
listening to a Bartok violin concerto,
feeling every sliver of liquid starlight
as it drills through the little speakers.
It took me forty years to appreciate
the strident whine, the clamber,
the hum, and the twisted wrists,
of Bartok. I had a friend in Tucson
who studied opera at the University
and sorted letters in the post office;
he would shake his head whenever
I declined to borrow his Bartok albums.
So what. Today, it is the perfect
music for half-lived days,
half-slept nights, half-dreamed dreams,
and half-loved women, when you
are only half-sure you want to live

another half-minute in the half-life
of a half-lit, half-rained on Sunday.
My wife is preparing split pea soup,
wrapping spices in a piece
of old T-shirt for bouquet garni.
Once the rhapsodies are finished,
I'll spend part of the last half
of the day at the supermarket, picking up
carrots and thyme for the soup.
But I can tell you, with full certainty,
my son and I had a glorious time together
in the garage, loosening nuts and setting
spark plug gaps. And following
the thunk of the nut into the oil pan,
the steady stream of buttery oil,
silk between finger and thumb,
like a French horn pouring itself, languidly,
can be musical--but certainly, more like Ravel.

It's liquid chocolate and Dave Matthews to my son.

Delivery
Joseph A. Soldati

[I help to deliver a calf in Veciattica, Italy]

The calf, wet and the color of its mother's
milk, finally slid into our hands. We laid it
onto the sweet straw as if it were porcelain.
In the old barn, our delivery room this hot
July morning, the fresh odor of after-birth,
the permanent reek of urine and dung
stung our eyes and shortened our breaths.

The old cow had had a hard time of it,
as had we, having to thrust our arms
into her hot womb and turn the calf
toward the light. This was my first attempt
at reaching into the slick silken cradle
of life, and I had, despite my clumsiness
and the blood, come through. Arnaldo, of course,
never flinched; he knew the bovine way.

From a cranny hidden from the dusty light
slanting through the small windows, Arnaldo
held up a bottle of ten-year-old Barbera.
I thought, if ever I need a drink, now is the time,
expecting some classic comfort. But not for me.
Holding the wine under the cow's nose,
allowing the vintage bouquet to stimulate
bovid brain, and the cow to raise her head,
Arnaldo tilted the bottle toward the cow

who drank it so fast I saw his hand appear
through the green glass. In ecstasy the old cow
rolled her eyes; the new calf sucked greedily.

Sequels
Alan Ackmann

Ever since high school, when I staggered out of the wings in Ten Little Indians, I've been playing villains. It's not as bad as it sounds, really. Jack Nicholson got his start in horror movies. So did Kevin Bacon and Brad Pitt. So on my bad days I remind myself that a man with three Oscars once hammed it up on a blood-soaked soundstage, like I'm doing now. Then again, Nicholson got to play the hero, and he got to use his "hey, don't fuck with Jack" voice. All I've got is a rubber mask and a standing contract as Jacob Astor, resident slasher for the Spring Break films. No, that's not entirely true -- I've also got a problem. For the first time in three movies, after a total of twenty-seven killings, I'm being asked to show my face, no mask, and that scares the absolute shit out of me. First, it could erase any shot I've got at being a real actor. Second . . . well, I'm not exactly sure how someone goes about acting that homicidal anyway. Gus, my director, tells me not to stress about it much; I've got a "naturally creepy face," he tells me. Thanks Gus. Still, I better get it straightened out. After all, we're three weeks into shooting, the body count is rising, and I've yet to feel anything but ridiculous.

And wouldn't you know it, that's just problem number one.

It's a heavy load on set today, and we're about ten minutes away from the next take. I'm patting at my cheeks, and the light of a cracked make-up mirror is heating my fake blood, which Marnie spent two hours painting on this morning. She did a good job, too; I've got some scarring under the eyes, and a big gash across my cheek. For the moment, I don't even recognize myself. I wrinkle my forehead in what might very well be menace, then rest my eyes for a moment. When I open them, problem number two is standing behind me in the mirror. It's Vickie Greenway, herself the veteran of three Spring Break movies, and the closest thing we've got on set to a legitimate actress. She leans in, whispering over the carpenter's pounding. Our last take was awful. Vickie tells me: "That was great."

"Sure it was," I mutter, turning around.

Vickie leans beside me, chest pushed out. "No, it was, really. You're breaking hearts. I swear, the vulnerability was positively peeling off of him."

I pause, and then say, "Vickie, he's a fucking psychopath."

"Oh" Vickie says, eyes sparkling. "Well, in that case, I think he's a very well-rendered psychopath."

For a second, I imagine that we're having what most of the waiters out here passionately refer to as "a moment," before I remember that, with Vickie, it's often hard to tell. For four weeks of shooting I haven't been able to figure out if she's teasing me, or if she's about to drop down on her knees at any second. But I don't have the energy to decide right now, so I tell her that I'm concentrating. She shrugs, then walks away, thin hips rolling beneath her satin nightgown, and I want to slip my palm across her stomach, feel the fabric slide beneath my fingertips, up between her tits, between her legs, and then I shake my head. Vickie.

Fifteen minutes later we're shooting and she's splashing through the bog away from me, shrieking in fear. It's just as well, really. That night, my answering machine light is blinking, and it's Luanne, this girl I'm serious about getting serious about. She wants to meet for dinner someplace in the hills, a place I've never heard of, where she says they have divine stuffed crab. That's an improvement over her usual suggestions, which mostly involve burgers wrapped in lettuce. Shit like that. Before she hangs up, she tells me she loves me, and I smile. Luanne's nice. And at six months, she's also my longest relationship ever. That makes me proud, you know? I'm an adult. All the same, as I pick up the phone to return Luanne's call, I can't help thinking about Vickie . . . she'd be great in bed. Hell, I bet she'd be a screamer.

Like a lot of people out here, Luanne considers herself an artist. Our first date had been an exhibit of "Ohio Pastorals" that some transplant from the Midwest must have cooked up over an espresso. The date had been her idea. As we'd looked at the paintings, which were mostly things like silos and old bridges and plows, Luanne held my hand, and every word she spoke seemed personal, like she was sharing childhood memories instead of opinions. She talked about how the paintings reminded her of the "plights of workers", and the "desperate, soulless struggles huddled within the anonymous Midwest." And she had a sadness in her voice that moved me. That night, after sex (gallery silence made her horny, I found out later) she'd climbed out of bed abruptly, then walked naked across her creaking, hardwood floors and returned with a black portfolio, which contained "her work." These were her "embodiments," she told me, her expressions of her sentiments, her truths. In one of them, I saw a vast, receding plain of purple covered with sticks, which looked like those twig clusters from The Blair Witch Project. Luanne told me that the twigs actually came from a gulch behind her old apartment in Palo Alto, and that in her art she'd given the plants an ocean, water that they never had in life. I said I thought that was beautiful and smiled.

"I don't know what you're stressing out about so much," she tells me that evening, as we're standing in front of the movie theatre. "At least you're working. Did you know our night janitor at the gallery has a performance degree? He's been out here three years, and the only work he's gotten has been modeling for a one-nine-hundred male sex number - some kind of late night advertisement."

"Do you get to be in the union for that?" I ask.

She takes her eyes of the marquee. "Very funny. You laugh, but he's a good-looking guy. If it weren't for you I might just dial him up myself one night." She smiles and pokes my ribs. "Kidding. The point is that you're working and he's not. Besides, your job sounds like fun."

"It's fucking Spring Break Six. Not one or two, or even three or four or five. Spring Break Six. And I have to show my face --"

She sighs, then interrupts me and returns to her list of movies. "You keep saying that. You never minded being seen before."

She's got me there. Back when we were kids in Detroit, Gus and I had started making horror films using a Hi-8 cam we found in Gus' attic. I starred in most of them. After college, we scraped some money together and shot a low-budget flick in the hills of West Virginia. And it had been fun. In fact, it had been a blood dripping, tit popping, chick screaming blast. And when Gus got tapped as the director for Spring Break Four a few films ago, he managed to convince the studios to let him cast his old buddy Eddie as the new man behind the mask. They went for it on account of the fact that I had the same body type as the old guy (six foot four, broad-shouldered, built) and the fact that the old guy was in prison for beating the shit out of a prostitute. Fun town, yeah. So out to L.A. I came. Then, when Gus got the idea for Spring Break Six ("This time Jacob's on an island!") he managed to bring back Vickie Greenway, star of the original three films, and convince the studio and the public that it was time for the mask to come off.

"I guess I'm just ready for something more." I say.

Luanne turns to me, and takes on the same tone she uses when she's discussing art. "Listen to me, okay? You're fine. What you are doing fills a need. Most folks should be scared, occasionally. Most people either live in ignorance, ignoring everything that should legitimately terrify them, or else they stay inside, deluded, scared of things when they have no real reason to be. Your work satisfies both types of people. It's an escape, and a reflection of society. Besides, I'll bet you're terrific at it."

I think about Vickie, earlier that afternoon, telling me how wonderful our last take was. Unlike Luanne's argument, Vickie's crap is something I can buy. I say, "Thanks, honey."

Luanne smiles at me, and touches my cheek. "My little serial killer," she says. "Now come on - I think I know what I want to see."

Since I vetoed the seafood restaurant in favor of Luciano's, an Italian restaurant where Francis Ford Coppola sometimes eats (nobody eats seafood in this town, anyway, on account of the mercury) Luanne got to pick the movie. She picks this grand, historical drama that stars Meryl Streep and Joseph Fiennes, and has something to do with the French Revolution. It's not the kind of movie I'd usually go see, but it is the kind of movie I can usually respect. But as I watch, I start wondering if maybe, for the next movie, they should send Jacob Astor through a time machine, and have him slowly whittle down a village full of oppressed peasants using nothing more than hand-axes and pitchforks. It could be the start of a series - Jacob Astor in Ancient Egypt. Jacob Astor meets the Mummy. Jacob Astor and the Pirates of the Fucking Caribbean. I get so wrapped up thinking about it that I stop paying attention to the movie, and when I finally start focusing again somebody's on a scaffold, making a vague speech about how they will stay true unto their heart, their country, always. Then, bang, the guillotine comes down and we get a close up of the severed head.

Luanne is moved by the movie, so she decides she wants to stay over that night. I stay up running tomorrow's lines a little while, but the more I say them the more ridiculous they sound. Since when does Jacob Astor talk, anyway? It's like a different fucking movie. But I try to be as intense as Joseph Feinnes. It's worse then, so I give up and go to bed.

The lights are off in the bedroom. As I slip beneath the covers, Luanne nuzzles my shoulder and says, "You know, I could hear you talking out there. I think you're really good."

I settle in, surprised at how much I want the reassurance. "Yeah?"

"Yeah," she says. "I think you'll figure it out just fine. I think if you really work at it you can be any kind of actor you want to be, someday."

Fuck you, I think. Almost immediately, I feel bad about it. Luanne didn't mean it the way that I heard it. She nuzzles me again and since it seems like I should, I put my arm around her. After a minute, she starts rubbing her hand on my stomach. Then she nibbles on my collarbone, which she's gotten real good at in the last six months. I feel her tits against my side and, all of a sudden, any annoyance or frustration disappears. And as we start going at it, I think: This is real. This is genuine and beautiful. I'm going to have to remember this if I ever do a love scene with somebody.

Cut to the next day. All morning long, take after take, something is just not right. I blow my lines, I miss my blocking, and after one particular take, where I'm supposed to pop up out of a sewer with what the script describes as a "twisted scowl of rage," Gus tells me my face looked like I was trying to shit a tennis ball. Eventually, he throws his hands up in disgust and calls lunch. I sit down by a dented radiator, more mystified, more frustrated, than ever. Across the soundstage, Vickie is chatting with a crewman, probably grousing about getting some kind of rare fruit for her trailer. I'm angry for a second. It's not like I'm the only one who's fucking up. Most days, Vickie's acting seems as fake as mine. Then I decide: Fuck it. Acting is about making choices, so I make the choice to stand up, walk across the set, and put my hand on Vickie Greenway's shoulder. Her smile kicks up a few watts, and the crewman staggers off. I wait a bit, for good, old-fashioned flattery. On cue, she says, "Listen, I think you're positively brilliant out there. Positively brilliant. It's something about how you're walking . . . hmmm . . ." She smiles. "Or maybe it's just something in your face."

Her fingernail grazes my cheek lightly, and she grins. Then, for no reason, no reason at all, I just start going into it. I start wondering out loud whether I'm coming across as anything but a complete blank, and whether the audience is even going to buy seeing Jacob Astor's face after so long, and whether the whole picture is just a raging mistake, really. Vickie narrows her eyes, her smile fading, and she looks just serious enough that I start worrying whether there's some truth in what I'm saying. When I'm done, I shrug, like it's all just standard actor stuff, and I'm not really terrified. Then Vickie cocks an eyebrow at me. "But you need this," she says. "You need to be seen."

She takes me to this restaurant near Culver City, the Ninety-Fourth Aerosquadron, which is a converted soundstage made up to look like a nineteen-forties airplane hanger. It's been in style since Casablanca got re-released, and looks reasonably classy, even if its not that far away from where Hugh Grant bought his blowjob. On the walls, there are jackets and propellers next to the signed celebrity photos, which explain that Seth Green thinks the chicken cordon bleu "kicks ass!" Beside him, there's a picture of Vickie, ten years younger. We're waiting for our food, and I'm in the middle of telling her about my influences (Brando and Sean Penn, mostly, early Al Pacino) when Vickie interrupts me, saying, "Shhh." She places her fingers over the top of my hand. "Don't look, but there's a photographer over to our left."

I glance out at the parking lot, where a man is waiting with a camera. I've never been photographed this way before, and I start getting excited. Vickie whispers, "Hey. Let's have some fun."

"Sure," I say.

"Kiss me," she says. "It'll get your name in the papers." And then, before I can say anything, she's all over me -- all tongue and hands and tits.

After that, things go well for awhile. I'm not too worried about Luanne seeing the photo. Vickie's not a big enough celebrity, really, to make the papers, and Luanne doesn't read anything but art journals anyway. But when Vickie and I are on set I stop worrying so much about how I look, and how I come across. Even though I still feel like a fool, I have some fun. It's all just mugging, all just cinematic trash, but the joy comes back. So what if I feel silly, like one of Hitchcock's glorified props? It's just Jacob fucking Astor. Vickie and I start eating lunch together in her trailer, and she tries to get me started on this microbiotics stuff, explaining that if you eat food cooked over a certain temperature it destroys its goodness. Or something. But I don't like raw chicken. What we talk about 223 expands, grows deeper, and I'm so focused on not thinking about Luanne that I forget about Saturday night, which is the debut of the most recent exhibit at her art gallery.

These are standing dates, and I scramble to find a tie, then curse myself for living in LA and not owning a tuxedo. Forty-five minutes later, Luanne glides down her stairs in a sleek, form-fitting Dolce and Gabana that makes her little tits look larger, and has a slit up one side that makes me want to jump her then and there. At the bottom of the staircase she spins, and smiles at me.

"I feel like I'm underdressed." I say. "I mean . . . you look great."

She curtsies, flashing pale thigh when she lifts the hem of her dress, then swats me on the ass as she walks past. "Nice save, Romeo. You look great, too."

By the time we get to the gallery, though, I'm surrounded by tuxedos, evening gowns, platters of hors d'oeuvres, and the hushed enthusiasms of Melrose art groupies. There's a chamber orchestra in the corner, fiddling away and turning up their noses like they're the fucking philharmonic. In the corner, the latest teen actor to be a six month heartthrob on the CW is being chatted up by some of the patrons, who've sucked themselves onto him like leeches. This depresses me even more, both because it's wrong and because it's not me.

Luanne's off by the bar, chatting with her gallery friends, so I decide to figure this art thing out for myself. I wonder what it would be like to be here with Vickie, her famous tits pressed up against me. Then I start to notice other girls, and think about what it would be like to be with them. And then the beauty explodes. Across the room, standing like a statue by the shadow of an archway, a blonde in red is sipping her champagne, the glass of bubbles floating to her lips. On the opposite side, a brunette goddess (shorter, slightly plumper, with cropped hair feathering the delicacy of her features) is running painted fingernails along a velvet rope, which blocks off a painting that looks like a vortex. And by the bar, her limbs angled with mathematical precision, a reedy, thin-lipped, femme fatale is eating olives. She looks alone, like she's not supposed to be here, and I want to ask her to leave with me, to drive off in my girlfriend's car and go find all the mysteries this city promises. That'd be something different. Yeah.

224   Instead, I turn my head back to the wall and see a spiral of curves. I try to follow their patterns to a place where I don't think about the shorthaired girl, the blonde, or the leggy, perfect redhead - where I don't think about Vickie, and life is simpler. After about twenty minutes, Luanne comes up behind me and rests her chin on my shoulder. In that moment, though, she could have been anybody.

"Look at it," she mumbles. "Isn't it wonderful?"

I can always tell how much Luanne likes the art at these things by how much alcohol she drinks. Apparently this guy's such a genius, I'll be driving home tonight. Once we get in the car, Luanne leans her cheek against the window, dress wrinkling around her. I hope she doesn't puke. When we get to the street outside of her place, she slurs me an invitation up, and I help her to the sofa, and then leave to take a piss. When I come out of the bathroom, Luanne is sitting on the floor in her underwear, the apartment cluttered with her canvases. She gestures over to me, pinwheeling her arms drunkenly, and I wonder what I'm doing here.

"Look at these." She tells me. "Look at them."

Luanne is leaning over a painting almost two feet square, the pale expanse of her back standing in relief against a forty-five degree angled streak of turquoise, which she says represents desire. She reaches up a bony arm, pulls me down towards her, and rests her head in my lap. I stroke her hair absentmindedly. She asks if I think she's going to have an opening someday, in her own gallery.

I follow the script. I smile. "Of course you will," I say.

Before us, her catalogue of paintings lays spread like a series of psychological tests.

"I love you," Luanne mumbles.

Even though she's too drunk to understand me, probably, I simply nod.

A few weeks later, over a plate of almost bloody beef, I lean across the table towards Vickie, place my mouth over hers, and shut my eyes. Her body tenses up. For a moment, I think, she accepts it, before she places a palm on my chest, pushing me away.

"Not here," she says finally, quietly. "Tonight."

That night, she throws me to the bed, knocking off her collection of stuffed animals. She's on top at first, and naked before I even know what happened, crazy. She's kept her body strong. Even if her tits aren't as firm as they look in costume, she's got muscle. And it's hot, athletic sex. Then all at once, when I'm just about to come, Vickie climbs off of me and gets down on the floor, pulling me down with her.

"I want you on top," she says. "Fuck me like you fucking mean it."

She's quiet at first, lying there. Almost whimpering. Then she hooks her legs around me, and gives me a look like I've seen on a thousand posters. I start going faster then, and she's moving her hips. She starts moaning louder. We feed off each other, her clawing at my back, digging, her thighs squeezing. And by the end, she's screaming her goddamn head off.

Afterwards, Vickie and I lie there together on the floor. "That was great," she tells me. She pulls down an ergonomic pillow shaped like Pac-Man, and offers it to me. I decline. She puts it behind her head, so that the mouth is on either side of her neck. Vickie's room is decorated in her movie posters, at every angle, with a framed picture of the original Spring Break by an antique dresser, so her nineteen-year-old face stares down at us. We talk for a moment about nothing. Movies. The Oscars. It's okay. Then, without warning, a heavy sense of panic hits me, something new. It's terrifying. And I want to do anything that might make it go away. And so we fuck again.

Later that night, from Vickie's bathroom, without knowing exactly why, I give Luanne a call. It's been almost two weeks since the exhibit opening. She's gotten over her envy, and has begun to paint with fury. She hasn't really noticed I've been gone, I think, but all the same her voice sounds thrilled to hear from me. I realize that I don't want to talk to her for very long, but before I can say anything Luanne invites me over to her place. She's got a new batch of swirls and angles, and wants me to come take a look at them. I tell her I'm not feeling well. She offers to come over and help. I tell her I've got work to do. She offers to help me run lines. I tell her, frankly, that I'd rather just be alone. She tells me to take care of myself, that even stars need resting.

I tell her good-bye.

226   When I get on set the next morning, Vickie behaves as if nothing has happened. No. That's not quite right. There is a change. The gentle flirting that we've had since shooting started, since the first shirtless scene that I had in the film, is gone. Vickie's attitude has changed from seductively coy to distinctly indifferent. We do our scenes, no more, and remain remarkably professional. And pretty soon, it's driving me crazy.

I start thinking about her at night, looking at my ceiling. I start trying to call her at home. After a week, I start wondering if she's avoiding my calls, so I go up to her place in Laurel Canyon. It's this Moorish kind of home, with lots of columns, and its set back in the hills. There's a high security fence spread across the driveway. Through the bushes, I can see the lights are on. I pull out my phone and dial, but Vickie doesn't answer.

And the whole time this is going on, Luanne keeps trying to get ahold of me.

Then, one day, the schedule calls for Vickie and me to shoot the climax scene in the movie. When I get on set that morning, I see Vickie by the make-up mirror, touching herself up, and I enter the frame behind her. She looks at me in the mirror, her mouth closed, then turns around. "I tried to call you last night," I say.

"You try to call me every night."

I'm not sure what to say about that, so I shrug. "I was just wondering if you'd like to get together sometime. You know?"

She stares at me. Like always, its difficult to tell, but I think she looks disappointed. She puts the cap back on her lipstick and looks at the concrete floor, then back at me. "Come on, Eddie? What kind of good do you think its going to do to ruin anything?"

And then she brushes past me, walks away. Half an hour later, we're on set. Vickie has fled to the bathroom after I've killed the only man on the island with medical training, and the heliport outside is wired with explosives, ready to detonate us both. After thirty seconds of kicking down stall doors, it's down to the final one, and I bust the thing off its hinges. When Vickie sprints around me, trying to get past, I trip her, and she crashes into the sink. It's not in the script, but when she gets up I stab at her again, and she slips across the tile. I know the scene is gone now, but I keep coming. Vickie raises an arm and Gus calls cut. Some of Vickie's people, including her bodyguard, rush over. Vickie scrambles up off the floor, padding at her elbow, and shrieks: "What the fuck is wrong with you?"

Gus waddles over, cheeks puffing, and Vickie gives me this look like she's gonna tear my arms off if I don't apologize. So I say, "What the hell is wrong with you, huh? That's my mark. Step. Stab. Jesus Christ, maybe you'll actually get into character now!"

Gus turns his fat face towards me. "Jesus, Eddie."

I throw my hands up. "What? What? It's like eight takes on this one fucking gesture! I'm just trying to get the goddamn shot!" I step towards her, reaching for the towel, saying, "Oh come on, Vickie, it's fake blood on a plastic knife. You're fine."

"Just stay the hell away from me!"

Gus puts his arm across my chest and leads me over to the snack table, while Vickie hollers at crewmembers. He says, "Eddie, that was uncalled for."

"Fuck you, Gus!" I shout. Gus stares at me, pissed as hell, and I understand I've gone too far. I take a deep breath.

227

I say, "I'm sorry, huh? I just got a little carried away. It won't happen again."

Gus looks like he doesn't quite believe me.

On the next take, I improvise. I lunge at Vickie, like I'm teasing her, flipping the knife back and forth in my hands. Even though it's not in the script, I start laughing. Then I just howl. When I dart at her again, I deliberately miss my mark. I aim for her face. Gus calls cut. I make with the apologies real quick, then shoot Vickie a look, to let her know I knew what I was doing. And damned if it didn't work. The next take we shoot, it's fucking perfect. The next take, she actually acts like she's fucking afraid.

That night, I prowl the apartment alone. For the first time in months, I'm not wandering around like some prop, and it's intoxicating. Jacob Astor feels real to me now; I don't feel ridiculous. I feel strong. I can't bring myself to care. I go back over scenes we've already shot, and growl the lines again. I take a swig of beer and laugh, shirt off, Zeppelin on the stereo.

And then the doorbell rings.

I open it, and it's Luanne. She's got circles under her eyes, and her black portfolio is cradled underneath her arm. It takes me a second to recognize her. She walks into the apartment without being invited, lays the portfolio on the counter, and turns to me, her face wrinkled with concern.

"Are you okay?" she asks. "I've been trying to call you."

"I've just been busy," I say. "I take the phone off the hook when I'm working. And we've been having a lot of late nights recently, so . . . " I kiss her forehead. "I'm sorry."

She looks away.

I press mute on the CD player, and then turn towards her and shrug. "I said I was sorry."

"Eddie," she says, "what's gotten into you?"

"Nothing," I say. "I've just been busy. Like I told you."

Luanne's face is all hangdog and hurt, and she's running her fingertips along the black leather of the portfolio. In the florescent light of the kitchen she looks pale, awful. I almost ask her to leave, and then decide fuck it. I know what to do now. I know what she needs. I walk across the apartment, run my palm along her cheek, and tell her I'm sorry all over again. I tell her I missed her so much it scared me. Then I take her in my arms and kiss her, nuzzle her neck and her breasts. Then, just when it seems like she's getting into it, I stop. She looks at me, confused, and I say, "No. First I want to see the work you've done."

We're on the floor together, then, her portfolio spread before us. Apparently envy and heartbreak didn't do much for Luanne, professionally, because this is all the same crap it's ever been. Dark, descending spirals falling to the center of the frame. Nothing. I tell her I'm moved, dazzled. When she zips the portfolio closed again I tell her they're every bit as good as the ones we saw at her gallery, better, really, and her eyes mist over with happiness.

Then I take her, gently at first, the way she likes it. But pretty soon she's wild for me, really wild. We go into the bedroom and I turn the lights off. Luanne's not a bad fuck. Not really. In fact, she's just what I needed.

When I'm done, we lay there, the ceiling fan swirling the shadows around us. I don't say anything. Luanne sits up in bed, and behind her through the window I can see all the lights of the city, twinkling. Luanne doesn't seem like she knows what to do. I get out of bed, naked, and walk to the bathroom. When I come out Luanne has her knees pulled up to her chest, her head down, the covers wrapped around her. I glimpse my own silhouette in the mirror and it startles me, like for a second I was looking at someone else.

When Luanne looks up, I tell her I've still got work to do. I tell her I'll call her soon. She dresses, gathers her portfolio, and leaves. She doesn't say anything. She doesn't even look back.

I guess she knows.

Water Balloons
Anne Germanacos

Last night

I fucked him so hard that afterwards he got up for water, and when he came back from the kitchen he was still coming. He had to wait until his throat stopped making noise before he could swallow.

Today he spent four hours outside digging in rocky soil, preparing to plant things. Here, in Greece, they say the weather changes with the new moon.

We finally got rid of that student, the mad girl. In the calm following that particular storm, we come back to each other and our lives. I wouldn't want to dig beside him, but I understand why that's what he needs to do: the plants won't hold him responsible for damage.

Today

the sea tosses so wildly, there's a sea-churned demarcation that looks as if it's been made with a knife: the water closest to shore is celadon, farther out it's midnight. The line curves around, currents rendered visible, just like the girl, our (former) student, whose body was marked with strange symbols and signs.

The students

had been told to bring sweaters and a warm jacket, but the thought, *Greece*, wouldn't square with that. So they sat in the classroom shivering, bundled in acrylic blankets, holding their hands against the one heater.

That first cold morning of classes,

I noticed the girl with the unusual bracelet. Up close, I saw it wasn't a bracelet at all but flesh a little darker than the rest of her skin. Burnt. That central circle had most likely been made with a hot nickel or quarter. It looked like a bracelet a spy might wear: hardly there.

(I tell myself :

You have no such bracelet yourself, you have nothing akin to it.)

The boy student

watches himself drop. Like an object that can float only after it's almost drowned, he goes deep, wanting without wanting to lick her bracelet. He catches himself with her wrist in his hand, still dreaming, and forces himself awake. Does it make him homosexual, he wonders, to wake up with his tongue curling toward a mad person's wrist, even if it's a girl? The maddest person in his life until now has been his father. Where does symbolism start and end? (And who decided that he's bipolar, anyway?) The others paint her evil. He thinks it's kinder to call her mad.

After she was sent home,

the boy handed me his poems, saying: "She didn't really leave because of her appendix, right?" I smiled a little, trying to show him that I would've liked to say more, but couldn't: The parents of such cases as the girl were always vicious in their threats, and often litigious.

Her Wrist (his poem)

She burnt the bracelet onto her wrist.

Not her wrist, her thigh. And he did it to her.

She put pennies on his chest, seared the fine dark hair.

He let her cut the curls from his head.

Her wrist was once a bouquet of sores, now it's a flesh-colored bracelet. And where the watchface would be, a quarter-sized circle.

He finds her easy to like.

My husband asks me

to open the door to his musty, pearl-colored chapel on the hill, so I take the key on its red buoy and climb the steps past cacti, yellow crocuses, and daffodils. I push against the door and a puff of stale incense comes out. All the saints plus Jesus and the Virgin Mary stare off into space: they never have anything to say to me. At this moment more than any other, the anachronism galls.

I leave the door wide open so the room can be exposed to the sun and light, then jump down the stone steps quickly.

She was the only person

who brought Manolo Blahniks. The one time she wore them was in her bare-walled room. Huddled beneath a dirty acrylic blanket, she wore the shoes with a Cosabella thong, braless. Her roommate told me later that she turned her own face to the wall.

"What was she looking for, anyway?" She hadn't slept through the night for weeks. In the dark quiet past midnight, when the whole village was dreaming, the girl had thrown things at her-- a toothbrush, a comb, a tube of depilatory cream-- screaming at her to stop screaming.

"A little action?"

Flirting (his poem)

The girl with the thick dark-brown hair was just going out for a cigarette--

she smokes like a chimney.

She was going to the bathroom--

she has the tiniest bladder on earth.

She walked past the long tables and the musicians.

Men handed her small glasses of foot-stomped red wine.

One black-shirted man with a trim dark beard poured the

whole glass down her throat.

She never drinks.

I'd drink anything she offered me.

Some evenings

all the students come to get their meds on time, a little marching troop just in from watching the Iraq war on TV. Other times my husband puts the meds on a chair, arranged so each student can take the pill swiftly, without exchanging a word with him.

The girl's last night here, he took all the medicine bottles upstairs with him, even Tylenol and Mylanta, put everything in a pillow case, and pushed it to the bottom of the bed. During the night, I felt him reaching for it with his toes.

Niko

the male nurse came in with two Ace bandages. I thought maybe he was going to wrap them around her belly--

something to do with keeping the appendix in view, or tight, or something else I couldn't figure out. But he wrapped one around each foot up to the calf, to enhance circulation. In American hospitals, I've heard circulation stockings with their monotonous ugly music. But her ace bandages were silent: so were we.

Niko returned to the room after the surgery with an exuberant smile on his face. The appendix was huge and ready to burst, he told us. "Would you like to see it? The appendix? It hasn't been disposed of yet, and I'd be happy to show it to you." My husband said that won't be necessary. Later, he said he believed Niko's claim that the appendix was monstrously distended, but I was vexed with myself for not taking Niko up on his offer: I'd wanted to know what her insides looked like. As it happened, we ended up seeing much more of her than was savory or desired.

The boy

sits in an overheated room in an underheated house trying not to plagiarize his sources for his history paper. "The Battle of Crete took place in 1941." How can you say that any other way?

One day

she went to town and came back with a glass fishbowl. In her knapsack were the goldfish.

Before feeding them, she took each one out and held it in her palm. She hummed to the goldfish, one by one. All day, the fish swam in circles.

The night before she left, she poured a whole jar of smelly processed food on top of the water, and by morning, all three of the goldfish were belly up.

She tells them

she could have gotten drunk with that one boy and cried rape as she had done before, at St. Edward's Academy. She could have used the kitchen knife on hair, thigh, or arm.

But instead she told them she was pregnant. When the doctor examined her, he found a sensitive appendix. Rather than performing an abortion, he removed the swollen thing. After recovering, she got her period together with her roommate and all the other girls around.

That school, she'd say once she was back home in B., was too much like a zoo. On the wooden-slatted stairs, their feet went knock knock even in soft shoes. Bars everywhere. Caged-in.

"Horses

are the love of my life" she said, "but I can't get near them because they take away my breath. Still, I'd sacrifice my life for one last ride, bareback and fast."

To compensate, her father had given her a tiny gold horse on the thinnest gold chain.

In the clinic, she woke up wiggling her fingers, expecting to find the chain wrapped in them like a rosary. She rang for the doctor and called out loudly: "Where's my horse?" Too angry to cry. "My horse. My hypoallergenic horse!" She shouted down the pale yellow corridor.

Because

he was smitten with her, the doctor had sewed it into the hole in her side. That, anyway, was what she wanted us to believe.

I suppose if we're brought to court, a simple x-ray would prove her instability. Niko, the male nurse, probably took the chain from her anesthetized fingers.

Only the maddest hope could have let her parents think she would survive here. And, of course, they lied.

The new moon

broke the boy too-- he set to work on his paper.

The reasons for the battle were:

He got to the bottom of the first page and knew he couldn't stretch it out to more than three. If I'm going to have to write papers at college, he thought, maybe I shouldn't go.

In the middle of the night,

when her roommate was snoring across the narrow space between their beds, she lifted her Cosabella thong to the side and, squatting above the sheets, squeezed out an elegant turd.

It's one thing

to say "mad," but another to see it walking around.

The question I ask: How did we get here? Everyone knows there are other ways to earn a living.

She said:

"All I have to do is ask my Dad, and he'll have a jet here in a few hours. Do you want to see it happen?" As she spoke, she twisted her shirt, unaware. Since the operation, she'd gained weight. Flab hung over her "Sevens," and if the shirt, caught in her fingers, went high enough, you could see the scar. It was the only one on her body that wasn't self-inflicted.

She and her roommate

filled balloons with shaving cream and threw them across to the boys' balcony. The boys threw back the balloons that didn't break. By the time we got there, the rooms were a mess, white foam dissolving into a soapy crud. We never got to the bottom of it.

Later she said: "Two weeks ago, they dropped a filled condom that burst a foot from where I was standing." She also said: "You're not saying I was *asking* for it, *are you*?" All her questions were double-edged, triumphant.

Water Balloons (his poem)

They were filled with water.

They were filled with shaving cream.

She hadn't taken her medication.

She'd taken four pills instead of two.

Her wrist, three years later, hurt where she'd cut it.

She hadn't placed a single penny on his chest.

She loved him. She didn't.

The water balloons wet the blankets.

The blankets were drenched by the rain.

They weren't her blankets.   237

She left her underwear, three pairs of jeans, four shirts, two

sweaters in a tub of water.

He waited for the sun to evaporate the water and dry her clothes.

Like a mother, he sniffed each piece as he folded it.

When

the boy laughed so hard he cried, I saw there was something like salt on his lashes. It was as if they were interwoven, almost knotted.

He'd seen my husband changing out of his dirty work clothes. As he laughed, he choked on his words: "That's just like my father!"

He wakes up

the next day, and she's gone. He's grateful she hasn't jumped from the balcony and left them with a mess, though he never really thought she'd do it.

Once she's gone, he forgets her, even in his sleep. He's never been so happy. He's not homosexual or mad, just a boy with a unique family.

Walking in cramped village lanes, he breathes in the blue of the sea. For seconds at a time, he knows nothing can touch him.

She kept saying

"I want to take a picture of everyone," until someone finally answered: "Well, go ahead. We're all here." But she stood there without saying anything, the camera sort of dangling from her wrist. This was the other wrist, the one empty of hieroglyphics.

She's got the new scar on her belly to remind her of us-- just a thin ridge of skin, something to fondle mindlessly.

Now

that she's gone, we return to our original questions: Why weren't we informed that her reproductive system was almost ruined by starvation? Why did they neglect to mention the incidents with the pills, the coma, the hospitalizations? And that she never stopped telling lies?

He

bites my lip and with my tongue I feel the rough edge of a partially chipped tooth. This time, I'm out of control.

I know we've done nothing wrong beyond trying to fix the problems of the world lodged in one maddened soul. It's pity, along with fury and terror that brings our own madness on. I can't let go of him; he won't stop.

The next consultant

asked: In your opinion are her problems characterological or neurological?

We say: Who knows where madness begins?

Two days

after she leaves, my husband finds the ewe with her new lamb. He brings them down from the mountain, pens them, wipes the skinny lamb dry, and leaves him on a blue towel in the sun. I put on rubber boots, and together we hold the angry, stomping ewe against the cinderblock wall.

This ewe is a first-time mother. Her udder, swollen and too round, is hard to grasp, but I manage to squeeze out some milk into a jug. Then my husband pours it into a soda bottle and adds a rubber nipple, and while I hold the lamb against my chest, he tips the bottle skyward and the milk goes down in a stream. We see the throat move. When he takes the bottle away, the milk stays inside the lamb.

We leave them there in the pen, bright sunlight all around, but the next time we go back, despite the nub of dark green liquid by its tail that tells us the lamb's digested the milk, we can see he's dead. My husband buries him behind the house, under an olive tree.

The hoofs are what stay with me-so sturdy already, prepared for business.

The ewe stomped for us to leave even when her lamb was dead. She nuzzled him-- head, rear, head.

Baby Lamb (his poem)

The lamb was born four hours before they found it.

The lamb had been wandering around for at least two days when his teachers found it curled up in a ball, unable to stand.

The lamb would never stand again.

With proper sustenance, the lamb would be fine in a couple of days.

They saw its throat open and close over the milk.

The ewe stomped on her baby's neck.

The bottled milk would make him strong.

It was a male, but they kept saying "she."

240 They called the mother "he" because she was so forceful and wild.

The lamb had tight curls at the back of his neck.

He died later that day, early afternoon sun shining on him.

The hooves were perfect.

At the Altar of the Kitchen
Judith H. Montgomery

There's a steady blessing, a pleasure
in scrubbing. Nicking each stuck crumb
out with a knife, deft surgeon after dirt.
Lined up on the countertop, little jeweled
gods carried in a basket from my home:
emerald cylinder of Comet, sapphire-
sparking Windex, flask of Simple Green—
liquid miracle alleged to spare
the earth that blooms relentlessly
beyond my friend's kitchen windowpane.
A soft click at her husband's cancer-
shadowed door, then she blows me a kiss
and shrugs on the somber winter coat. It's
today she inquires about arrangements. . . .
*
I have an hour, two, to scrub her kitchen
to a glow. To make each inch *immaculate*
(from the Latin, *without spot*). I slip
dried plates and glasses into cupboards
whose alder doors open, close, like wings
or valves of a spent heart. Slide aside
the cordless phone, the jar of wilting asters
cut days ago from her unweeded garden
beds. Now, scour each corner with a damp
cloth—unprint the thumbs from the swinging
door, at the youngest grandchild's height.

Each slight grease spatter on the stovetop, gone,
as I bend mind and muscle to the holy
office of perfecting her kitchen.
                    *

The only offering I can make—a gift
of labor, of rapt attention to setting
this one room to right. Hot ammonia water
slops my wrist. The chrome-rimmed kitchen clock
ticks above the sink. Kneeling to scrub square
by square the marks of hasty meals from blue-
white tile, I aim to make spotless what
was once the center of her home—as though
I could rid the room of every smirch and speck.
(O Lares and Penates, O Angels
of the Hearth.) As though this litany of work
could work to bring her ease. Could erase
the blotch that from his riddled bones
smudges daily deeper through her heart.

                              For C.P.

Rehearsal
Judith H. Montgomery

My hands love its heft,
secret in pockets. I slide
my thumb up, down

its hooded flicker-tongue.
Practice inserting   243
my schoolgirl bitten nail,

so, in the slit, and lever
the quick blade gasping
into light. Flip it, sharp

side down, palms closed,
to shut the metal tongue
safe home. . . .Today I'm

waiting in the long white-
columned school arcade,
nudged by rowdy teenage

boys flurrying to class.
They leap and jockey,
tossing paper planes

and what I guess are jokes
above my head. Self-
conscious in sweat, I rub

the sleek shaft nestled
in my pocket. It nuzzles
my clumsy palm. I need

some thing to do. Slip it
out, slick a thumb along
its length. Open it. It

shines in my damp hand . . .
then my father arrives,
jingling his keys,

looking for me. I
snap the naked blade
home—it bites the fat

pad of my thumb. Blade
and bitten hand hide
244   behind my dress. *What's*

wrong? Daddy's going to say.
I'll have to show him.
But he's too late. Already,

blood's begun to run.

Swimming to Staten Island
Michael Hardin

Black water seduces,
obsidian flecked with New York
upside down,
incandescent, fluorescent.

The ceaseless growl of diesel
dissipates with the howls
once his body
slides off the ferry.

I saw him a week earlier,
at Barnes and Noble in Midtown,
I needed Between Angels--
couldn't see what he picked up.

I recognized him as someone
from a dustjacket,
gave him that glance
accompanied by a nod

so subtle only the famous
can detect it. I wanted him
to know I knew the routine.
I had seen celebrities, Cristo

and Tom Cruise, in cognito,
had not blown their cover,
was not one to gush praise
or beg autographs. His picture

graced The Times, "Spalding
Gray Missing." I wanted to say
I'd seen him, tried to remember
which way he turned,

what book he bought.
A month later they found him
floating in the East River.
The instantaneous cooling of lava

becomes obsidian, stone so smooth
and deep and cold, you cannot help
but let your body slide in, enveloped
in the permanence of rock.

Who's Looking Out for Us?
Michael McCauley

The other news networks obscure the real story with jargon and buzzwords. XNN, the *X-treme* News Network, commonly referred to as "The Hawk," modestly reduces complex issues to a set of elementary, universally understood concepts. The other networks deceive the common man, alienate Joe Six-Pack, and run like schoolgirls in leotards from the tough, no nonsense angle. The Hawk remains uncorrupted by the powers that be, the suits, the biased puppeteers behind the scenes, and has a mind to walk up to the other networks, knock on their heads and say, "Hello, anybody home?" The other networks went to East Coast private schools where they wore sandals made out of marijuana. The Hawk went to a state school that kicked the other networks' asses in football. The Hawk's dad can beat up your dad. The Hawk has a black belt in karate but can't show off any moves because sensei told the Hawk it should fight only in self-defense.

At the top of each hour, that trusty insignia flashes across the screen, "XNN" in flames against a black background, spelled out letter by letter to the sound of a hammer striking iron, followed by the voice of a popular country star announcing the network slogan: "Tough, Accurate, Hetero." Distorted electric guitar plays at the start of each program; in fact there is always a session guitarist on set, plugged in, ready to punctuate a particularly emphatic editorial with a series of power chords. The network's highest rated program, *The News at Night With Buck Mayhew*, begins with infrared footage of a Stealth Bomber leveling a building inhabited by various bad guys and assorted evildoers. Then it's Buck, smiling at his desk, laser beams illuminating the artificial smoke behind him. Whichever program is on, the Hawk has us covered. The Terror Alert Level Indicator will never leave the top left corner of the screen, nor will the Bird Flu Death Ticker vanish from the bottom right.

When a significant portion of this country is flattened by a terrorist attack or hurricane, or even a terrorist hurricane, and order as we know it is buried beneath the rubble, and bands of machete-wielding savages set out in the night to commit unspeakable acts against our women and children, many a pathetic man will cower with his genitalia tucked. A few men will emerge from the wreckage with babies in their arms, jaws sturdy, soot streaking their cheeks like war paint. They will rummage through the debris for two-by-fours with which they will set things right again. These are the men of XNN, the kind of men we turn to in a time of crisis, or when we are having difficulty opening a jar of salsa.

248   Buck Mayhew wears an unusually severe expression tonight. The top story, "Countdown to Calamity," concerns Hurricane Dimitri, a Category 5 storm due to make landfall near Mobile, Alabama within the next twenty-four hours. Buck describes a worst-case scenario, wherein Dimitri strikes the coast and, instead of moving inland and weakening, becomes attached to Mobile's Southern charm and hospitality, camps there for days, and grows into a Category 7 storm. He segues into a live report from the forecasted disaster area. A promising young assignment reporter stands cupping his earpiece on the beach of Heron Bay, a resort town thirty miles south of Mobile.

In a single dramatic breath, Hunter Davis inhales the collective anguish of the Heron Bay residents, most of whom are securing windows and loading suitcases into cars. Their dread draws itself upon his forehead. His coarse, pack-a-day voice echoes local sentiments: people are praying for the best; a house can be replaced, not a life, etc. He relays a heartwarming anecdote about a middle-aged woman and her missing cat, Patches McWhiskers, whom she feared would have to endure the storm alone but was later found in a tree and rescued by a neighbor.

"Amazing," Buck adds at the conclusion of the report. "Sometimes tragedy brings out the hero in us."

* * *

The cameraman and an intern lean against the news van, yawning, activating the blue lights on their digital watches. Hunter Davis stands at the shoreline. "I'm counting on you," he says, looking out over the bay. The sea is calm yet. He walks across the sand toward the parking lot. The townscape shows no signs of life, but he remains undaunted.

"That's a rap," he says to his pudgy, disheveled subordinates. "Let's get some pussy." Of course he is joking. Neither half of the crew would know what to do with a naked woman if she fell on his cock.

Later, in the bathroom of his Ramada Inn suite, Davis marvels at the contrast between his face, caked with layers of makeup, and the rest of his pale body. He adores how the makeup emphasizes the indentations in his cheeks, a feature that suits his pull-no-punches, news with an attitude reporting style. He pokes breathing holes in the complimentary shower cap on the toilet and pulls it over his face. He enjoys a hot shower. Afterward he sits in the hotel parking lot, on the hood of his rented Lexus, hair wet and makeup intact, wondering what that Southern sky, unrelenting in all its moods, will throw at him tomorrow evening. But death he cannot fathom. It contradicts visions of his own primetime news show, the proposal for which is presently on the table with network executives. He is counting on the greatest natural disaster in U.S. history to give him the exposure he needs to close the deal.

249

He cruises empty streets to fusion jazz radio, looking for pretty legs on porch swings, but all the women have fled north. Subdivision gate attendants shoot Gestapo stares from their booths. He returns to the hotel, martinis on his mind.

The hotel restaurant bar is empty except for a man and woman leaning close at a table, whispering, gesturing, making faces, doing what people do upon recognizing him. So he does what *he* does; he dispenses with false modesty and sits with them. Close up he discovers the man is rather effeminate—a sissy, one might say—and after nodding hello Davis lets his eyes linger on the petite redhead.

"Do you watch much TV?" he says.

"We know," says the sissy. "XNN, right? The Hawk?"

"We couldn't remember your name," says the redhead. She has the kind of eyelashes cartoon seductresses bat rapidly.

"Call me Hermes." Before approaching, Davis hadn't made up his mind about that line, about comparing himself to the messenger of the gods, bringer of dreams to mortals, underworld escort. Is the comparison so far fetched? Apparently, for the sissy blows wine cooler through his nostrils.

"I think I've had enough," he says, coughing, rising from his chair.

But the redhead remains. "I'll be right up," she says. The sissy wags an index finger and leaves. His departure alters the dynamics of the room, gives Davis confidence he can will his perspective without objection. He can convince the redhead that he is a Greek god and that their table is a Venetian gondola.

He lifts his chin and proposes a toast to the last night of the Gulf coast of Alabama. They touch drinks. They exchange analogies to describe their understanding of the world. Hands over his heart he says the world is a rose that has collapsed upon its own thorns. She says it is a happy wino jerking off in a dumpster. He says, "What have we done to the Earth? What have we done to our fair sister?" She asks him to name the worst possible song for a pole dancer to strip to. He says *Blowin' in the Wind*, the Peter, Paul, and Mary version. She gives him the duck when he tries to smooch her in the elevator but in his room she attacks, kissing him a full minute before telling him to wash his face. When he returns from the bathroom she's undressed, her body striped orange from the parking lot light through the blinds.

He kisses the length of her and tells her to turn over. He asks if, instead of moaning and saying his name, she can repeat the XNN slogan, "Tough, Accurate, Hetero." Indeed she can. She can do many things.

Morning raids his room like a SWAT team. He answers the shrieking phone, mumbles into the receiver, hangs up, and puts himself together in the dark. At the sound of frantic knocking he hobbles to the door. The bald and bearded Remote Director of XNN's Special Projects Unit shouts himself red. The tirade continues down the hall at lesser volume and stops in the elevator when an acne-scarred, curly-haired young man boards, his backpack covered in antiwar buttons. The kid snorts and says, under his breath, "The Hawk lies," but Davis is too intent on studying his own reflection in the elevator doors to care about naive undergrads and their broad accusations, not to mention their trust funds and ironic flirtations with communism.

Outside the sky droops and steady wind blows swirling debris. As the intern brings the van around to the front of the hotel, the Director hands Davis a stack of faxes and debriefs him: overnight Dimitri veered north of his projected path, the eyewall is scheduled to strike Panama City this afternoon, and another team, already stationed there, has been assigned to break the story.

Davis, sobered by this last bit of information, straightens his posture and clears his throat. He asks which reporter is in Panama City. The Director says Mitch Larson, a new guy, newer than Davis, who has made an impression on the Executive Producer, who doesn't let cheap sluts interfere with his work.

At the beach, where he is scheduled to report Heron Bay's relieved response to Dimitri's change of tack, Davis opens the news van's rear doors, tunes in to *Early Bird with Graham Cartwright*, and sees grainy footage of Mitch Larson inside the brand new, state-of-the-art Hawk News Stormcopter. He is wearing a green jumpsuit and giving the thumbs up.

"We're headed straight for Dimitri's storm bands, Graham."

"Are you sure that's a good idea?" asks Graham, starched, coiffed, concerned.

"We're perfectly safe up here," Larson says. "As for Dimitri, he had better think twice about messing with the Hawk Stormcopter."

The studio guitarist plays a sassy solo.

Davis switches off the television and charges the beach, screaming like a delirious castaway. He throws fistfuls of white sand. He chases down a deflated beach ball and punts it, not very far.

By grounding him here to report good news, the network has closed one of the nation's most astute and critical eyes. When the likes of Davis are preoccupied with feel-good stories about heroic pets, who is left to defend the castle?

Mitch Larson? Does Mitch Larson carry a gas mask in his briefcase? Davis would like to know. He would like to know whether the American public trusts a pussy in a helicopter more than they do a hard-nosed watchdog who never travels without an energy bar, a small towel he can place over his face to screen out dust and smoke, a bottle of water, a flashlight, and a whistle to signal to police should he find himself trapped under a collapsed wall. He makes a fist, admires his forearm, and looks out across the bay. Good news is terrible news.

Later that morning he presses his face against the window of a conference room on the nineteenth floor of the Ramada. Behind him, his crew and others from the network help themselves to a complimentary lunch buffet. According to the latest information from the Special Projects Unit, they should have clearance to leave for Florida by midnight. In the meantime Davis is slated for another live spot on *Buck Mayhew*. The Heron Bay weather report calls for isolated storm cells, but nothing that should keep him from conducting interviews nor the crew from gathering b-roll footage. After lunch they roam aimlessly, the intern at the wheel, the cameraman asleep in back, Davis smoking cigarettes in the passenger seat.

"I want you to get on I-10 East," he says. The intern obliges, for the moment unable to defer to the snoring cameraman.

The pastoral American countryside rolls by: dilapidated fruit stands, adult bookstores, fireworks warehouses. Thirty miles later the cameraman rights himself and demands to know why they have just entered the Mobile city limits. Davis ignores him and tells the intern to take the next exit, which connects to a highway lined with strip malls and chain restaurants. A teenager in a foam pizza costume waves wildly at traffic. Red, yellow, blue triangles strung across car dealerships bob in the wind. The intern makes another right, as instructed, and coasts down a happy, tree-lined boulevard. Davis observes the soccer balls and tricycles left out in driveways, stick flags planted in gardens, swing sets, gazebos. He frowns. There is no danger here, no real news. He tells the intern to cruise the main drag again.

Eventually the commercial district becomes what used to be the commercial district. Streets become numbered and check cashing stores appear in clusters. Each block features an abandoned building sprayed with graffiti. In neighborhoods like this, Davis knows, real news happens constantly.

Nothing happens for an hour. The crew fidgets and grumbles, boredom having surpassed their fear of carjacking. Davis counts Beware of Dog signs, eleven of them, when at last he sees breaking news writhing on the sidewalk—a half-naked man holding a bloodstained t-shirt to his face.

"Though Mobile has been spared the wrath of Mother Nature," Davis says into his microphone, "manmade violence continues." He squats and asks the wounded man to describe the gunman. The man points to an overturned lawnmower in his front yard, says he had just repaired the blade, that he was giving the machine a test run and it fired something into his eye.

"Are you sure there was no gun?"

The man says to please get help.

"You'll be fine." Davis motions for the cameraman to cut.

The crew grows increasingly impatient over the course of an uneventful afternoon, whining about the futility of Davis' search for a headline. To placate them temporarily, he offers to buy ice cream. They pull into the parking lot of a falling-apart custard shack and enjoy vanilla scoops in the safe confines of the locked van. Davis remains vigilant, wary of letting each delicious lick distract him from the task at hand: to secure his future as host of the most balls out news show in the history of hardcore cable news.

Two police cars scream down the street. He tosses his cone into the glove compartment and barks at the intern, who peels out and follows the revolving lights. A sudden spell of erratic traffic sabotages the pursuit. Cars swerve, turn left on red, deposit sideview mirrors in the middle of the road. The cameraman shouts and points out his window at a massive funnel cloud dancing beside a TV tower in the distance. The nervous intern's arms shake and the van skids through an intersection in what appears to be the heart of Mobile's inner city. Davis spots a public building they can retreat to, a watering hole called The Old Brown Shoe.

A television provides what little light there is in the musty bar. A fat man resembling every construction worker ever featured in a commercial for headache relief oppresses a stool at the far end. The tall, lean bartender takes his time fetching a round for the drenched newcomers. Davis looks up from their wobbly table and on the television behind the bar sees XNN's Chief Meteorologist, Guy Jackson, standing

253

before the Hawk News Storm Radar. Looking sharp in his wraparound shades, Guy reports that the hurricane, after weakening dramatically this morning and afternoon, recently made landfall as a Category 1 storm.

In any other bar, in any other neighborhood, Davis would stand on the table and do a celebratory jig. Dimitri's winds are far too weak to cause the kind of destruction Mitch Larson can capitalize on. There will be a few casualties, statewide power outages, but nothing that calls for legendary statements with which a reporter can make television history. Davis takes a sip and has a silent smiling moment to himself. He recognizes that today is a story he will describe in his memoirs years from now, after all the honors and awards. These are the romantic days of grunt work and small paychecks, an innocent and simple time he will one day marvel over in the dark as his silky wife removes his Hanes Full-Cut Briefs. Suddenly his assigned story strikes him as a worthy, albeit small part of an illustrious career to come.

The tornado warning expires, leaving just enough time for the team to return to Heron Bay. They lumber out onto a street they would never walk alone, but with a getaway vehicle around the corner they casually take inventory of the squalor around them—a crumbling building, a playground overgrown with weeds.

A wild shriek disrupts the post-storm calm. More shrieks follow the first one, in short bursts interrupted by loud and desperate breaths. Davis cups an ear to locate the origin of the sound, crosses the street, and jogs down an alley. He pokes his head around the side of a brick apartment building and sees a scrawny man in a winter parka repeatedly punching a large woman in the stomach. She is on her back, beside a dumpster. She cries out again and the assailant stomps on her face. Davis turns to the crew and, in violent pantomime, orders them to get the equipment and start shooting.

The cameraman gets in his face: they are supposed to be reporting on the fucking hurricane. If they stay here, they should at least help the woman.

The man could be armed, warns the intern.

"If you really want to help this woman," Davis says, pushing the cameraman away, "then grab the camera and start rolling. You'll be helping millions of other women who suffer from abuse."

The intern asks him to explain how recording the incident will help other women.

"Because it will be on the news." Davis puts forth an ultimatum. Either they shoot the beating, or they shoot nothing at all and take heat from the network.

He squats behind a chain link fence opposite the apartment building, peering through the ivy, safely obscured. The crew sets up ten feet away. Inexplicably the intern drops the shotgun mike. The assailant turns around, pauses for a moment, smiles, waves at the camera, and resumes kicking the woman, who has stopped moving. Each dull thud of the man's worn high tops lays a brick in Davis' stomach. He feels the heat of a hundred eyes boring into his back, a hundred eyes peeking out from behind pulled shades. What devastating work it can be, pulling the wool from the eyes of the millions who will tune in tonight for another reminder of the danger threatening our livelihood at all times, of despair so intense it can be viewed only in brief doses. He closes his eyes, sticks his fingers in his ears, and hums a melody.

*   *   *

255

A stealth bomber obliterates a building occupied by villains, malefactors, and perhaps a few scalawags. Bitchin guitar heralds the king of evening news. Below his immaculate silver pompadour, Buck Mayhew's black eyebrows bend in alarm. Tonight, six people are dead and millions without power after Dimitri ravaged the Florida panhandle, which the President has already declared a Federal disaster area. Though Dimitri made landfall as a Category 1 hurricane, risk analysts estimate the damage will cost billions. XNN's Mitch Larson is in Panama City with the story.

Over footage of horizontal rain and thrashing palm trees, Larson recounts Dimitri's trek across Northwest Florida. Then he's standing on a local street, wearing the XNN windbreaker, an ill-tempered hawk stitched across his left breast. He reports that Federal relief agencies will distribute ice, water, and other essentials tomorrow. The Governor has urged residents of affected areas to remain indoors, as the majority of hurricane-related deaths occur after the storm.

"We appreciate your bravery, Mitch," says Buck.

"Don't mention it. Dimitri was a total sissy, if you ask me."

"I hear you loud and clear, amigo." Buck holds up a wrist and lets it flop in sissy fashion. He shuffles papers and turns toward camera two, his now hopeful expression promising a lighthearted story. He says residents of Alabama's Gulf Shores are returning home in droves, thankful their homes are still standing. As XNN's Hunter Davis reports, some are calling Dimitri's sudden detour an act of God.

Footage plays of a fat man in a dark and empty bar putting out a cigarette. Davis' voice narrates: the consensus among the people of Mobile is that divine intervention saved them from Dimitri's wrath. The fat barfly looks into the camera and says, robotically, "I think it was divine intervention."

Davis stands in an alley, surrounded by dreary apartment buildings. His eyes narrow into skeptical, critical slits. Accusingly he asks, "But where was divine intervention when a local Negress was getting her teeth kicked in? An hour ago I happened upon a domestic dispute turned violent, a stark reminder that, often, the greatest threat to our livelihood is not Mother Nature, but our fellow man. A warning to our viewers: the footage we are about to show contains some upsetting and, frankly, gruesome images."

Video of the beating plays. After a few seconds it is aborted, but they are long seconds, during which Buck utters an unscripted, "Jesus Christ," and, "My God, what is going on?" He nods at someone behind the camera, realizes he is on the air, and assembles his face into a practiced look of moderate disconcertion. "Where is the woman now?" he asks Davis. "Is she okay?"

"She's unconscious." Davis squats beside her slack body. A crowd has gathered behind him. "While the beating was certainly disturbing, it was even more difficult to watch bystanders turn a blind eye. Not a single person came to her rescue."

Smiling faces and waving hands pop forth from the periphery. A child swings from a fire escape. Davis rises slowly, looking out from our television sets like a prophet unable to comprehend what the desert has shown him. He looks at us, his back to the witnesses.

We watch natural disasters and unnatural disasters with equal fascination. We watch the Hawk with a sense of relief, knowing in less than a week that beloved group of hard-hitting, square-jawed messengers will have put the latest disaster on the shelf, so that we may concentrate on more immediate concerns: the broken seal on a jar of mayonnaise, the discoloration on a patch of skin, the other person on a clattering late night subway car.

The other networks give only one hundred percent. The Hawk gives one hundred and ten. The Hawk goes all the way on the first date, every time, while the other networks are lucky to receive half-hearted palm jobs. The Hawk leg presses seven hundred pounds. The Hawk touches its female coworkers' asses at the office without penalty. The Hawk parachutes out of an airplane, lands on top of a mountain, and snowboards safely to the bottom, fists pumping.

Measuring the Divine
Bill O'Connell

This morning the sun over the sea heats up
each cottage, the white trim
around the windows and roofs
softening, shingles graying
in the salt air.

Swallows on the telephone line
perch at attention
because that's the figure
we've given them: the local landscape
straightened out, plumbed
until it squeaks.

It doesn't matter that the sea
shapes the shore, fills in
glacial cavities. The swallows
shoulder the sun: the hum of the wire
calms them. If they filled
a tree instead
they might be the flames
of a chandelier.

Everlasting God
Just Out of Reach
Bill O'Connell

The sun is out. Winter birds
sing. The icecap melts
into water, sunlight, air.

We rose from old bones,   259
from the sediment of dying things:
fins unfolding legs,

wings. Each thought
a litmus: Beethoven's bass line
under Duke's fingers, the black

keys triangulating passion.
Longing, that bitter purse,
our most fervent chore.

Night Poem
Bill O'Connell

1.

What could be better than this? The night
spread around me. Bicycles
where they fell, raccoons
maneuvering between them. Two deer at dusk
by the lagoon, the yearling
split off from the mother by my intrusion,
her feet jigging on a spit of sand.
The grey fox who appears
again and again in the real
is symbolic by distance. Even as I speak,
a boy kisses a girl by the trampoline.
My own children in bed, my wife.
I'm rooting for stars like a pig in muck.
Sleep won't help, the dawn always
our last hope made new.

2.

The fleeting sadness of ordinary life
is a gift. The translucence of loss
attracts us. Breasts through blouses
carry the eye. Sun through fog, tall
sea grasses bent by the breeze.
When I return to the cottage, the children

will be waking. The heat of day
beginning to build. We will feed and clothe
and shelter our love like a house
in constant need of repair. Death
waits for us to falter. Calls in
loneliness and despair. We fight
each demon as it comes
like a village armed
with pikes and grog, howling
insults and prayers
at the edge of suburbia.
A hand squeezed in the night
reminds us of who we are.
A whisper met by lips.
Worries spoken out loud.

3.

Who will be at the tallying?
The cormorant and the osprey.
The bartender with a fresh drink.
Mrs. Barry singing "Hello Dolly"
at the piano. My father so desperately
waiting for us all, with his father,
and the legion before him.
I remember the day I was married,
my father alive, the air
humid, people dancing out doors
past midnight. It was like
the old neighborhood revived, brought
west. Some folks camped overnight.
I lay in bed with Robin opening
envelopes of money. This
is how we begin, a downpayment
on the world. The next morning
the canoe half-full of booze.
Some hardy souls
returning to drink it.

4.

I don't need to tell you
how death visits the late nighters

who can see beyond T.V. Some sense
of the Milky Way. The shore
with real waves crashing: have
you been there? I'm talking
about the heart's aorta, the muscle's
fervent pull, the young couple,
black with water,
standing up in the surf.
How many sunsets are like this?
Children's bodies clashing on the court,
you among them, passing under the basket
like a ghost. Lofting the ball
to the six-foot-four fifteen year old
who completes the play.
High fives after, and you know
he's giving you a break—

5.

There's no solution like three olives
at the bottom of the glass. Better
than all night to think about it.
In the distance, waves
pound the shore. No one is there,
all the young lovers gone home.
Just you and the sea breeze.
Mosquitoes reminding you of your place.
You hold your position like a guy
under the basket doubling down
on the big kid from the next town.
Sweaty shoulder against shoulder.
He's smiling as he goes up, his youth
overmatching. His sweaty breast
against your eye like wood.
You are happy to be there, legs
churning to a stop, eyes
eyeing the hoop, the bodies
crossing high over the rim,
falling gently like laughter at your feet.

6.

O.K. midnight, settle your mind.
Tell the willows to stop talking.
Everyone I love is asleep.
I am freed from their imaginations:
how their bodies lean towards me,
families spreading across the landscape, ocean
to ocean. My great-great grandfather, Michael,
slit his throat in Connecticut.
He survived famine and the crossing from Cork
but couldn't get past the rubber factory
shutting down. His son married Mary
from Skibbereen, producing thirteen.
My own mother had ten. How many women
had more? Medicine women
holding the future in their wombs
with little clue. What they wanted
excised by history. Dear mother,
I have been unworthy!
Every Mass you attended, your conversations
with God. Your son the sculptor
should make a statue to you.
We'll turn the old house into a park.
Build your legacy like a stone wall.

7.

You have been to the end of everything.
It's like this night, the mind's wind
eternal. Nothing coaxed from the ground.
All your life you think youth
will save you: not yours (after awhile)
but some new thing. You are not that lucky,
the imperfect all around us. Sound and words
mixing on the tongue. You are willing
to exist—to fight for it.
All your senses work: no excuse
or a pension. You take up a hammer
and nail, learn that musical
score. You kneel at the altar
of a stranger's church and sing hymns
not at all familiar.

8.

I have no excuse for error: each day
is a boat I pull closer to the sea.
How easily I could slip into this
watery grave. Even now, past midnight,
the grey fox has no victims. He trots by.
I am inordinately alive!
Who is my master? Not the town.
Not the planets aligned against me.
Not my son who loves to ride with me
in the old pickup. Everything is measured
against that. My son's face
morphing between
boy and man. My face in the mirror
looking out, immortal.

Stuffat tal-Fenek
Mia DeBono

Mara Ghanda Sebat Erwieh
A Woman Has Seven Souls

1951. The MS Florentia set sail from Malta. Across the Indian Ocean sailed Juza, a slender black haired woman with inscrutable eyes that struck poisoned arrows into the blood of men. The last image she saw of the immigrant ship as it delivered her and her two children to the harbours of Sydney, was that of a husband running to greet his Tunisian wife whose baby had died at sea. The woman, dressed stiffly in a black dress, said nothing to her husband as he approached her. The woman just limply stared into her own memories, untouched by the presence of any life that remained around her. Juza watched as the woman stood like the Madonna of death; her eyes gazed downward, arms outstretched, palms face up, hands empty.

Juza's husband Carmello greeted her and their children with a bag of oranges and drove them to their new home, an immigrant ghetto bordering the outback. Juza felt the inside of her womb twist with an ache as her husband showed her the rabbit hutch he built. "Rabbits in the bush have a gamier taste than the rabbits in Malta," he proclaimed.

Juza looked at the lines on her outer hands, her skin was still soft, gentle. She looked at the encroaching town carved out along the edge of the Australian bush. It was not a town she thought, but a dirt hole lined with outhouses. Feral rabbits hopped freely around the roads, aboriginal children shit barefoot outside their homes, and the buzz of all the dark haired immigrants inside their tin huts could be heard like a contagious disease bouncing off the metal roofs. "The black menace," an immigration officer had called them.

Juza walked down the road to skim the outskirts of a neighborhood that was now hers. What she saw was that her life would become a series of unworn skirts, that the only dresses she would ever wear would be sewn from the blackened threads of the outback. What she saw was the women of the periphery had black hair. They had black bruises around their ankles and black dirt under their nails. Some had black in their eyes and black in their hearts and some even had black on their skin.

1962. Juza's long fingers sew a new dress for her daughter Lourdes. The veins pop out on her hands leathered and waxy from the Australian sun. Juza pricks herself as anxiety sets in. Her boy child has not come home from school.

"Lourdes! Lourdes!" Juza screams.

Lourdes, eleven has long black hair. When it is sunny, glints of auburn that match the freckles on her shoulders can be seen. Her hair is parted into two even braids. There are very strict rules at the girls' school. The nun's have very little patience for wop children.

"Lourdes! Eh-ya-ow! Where is Junyano?" Juza screams.

Juza leaves Lourdes, the eldest girl to tend her elder and younger brothers. Juza searches the neighborhood for several blocks. She checks his friends' houses, the swings, and the food stands. She looks out to the edge of the bush and checks the rabbit cages at least four times. Meanwhile, Lourdes washes her brothers' faces and puts them to bed.

Carmello has had a hard day.

"Come take off your father's shoes," he says.

Carmello sighs a tired earthy shade.

Lourdes kneels down in front of her father's rest chair. She takes great pride in removing his shoes for him every evening after work. She slips them off and sets them aside. Carmello sits back in his evening chair and scans the paper for the horse track scores.

"Win, place, show!" He teases Lourdes and lightly pulls one of her braids.

Lourdes smiles at him.

"You always pick them for their names Lourdes. You bring me luck at the silly names you like! Now go get ready for bed," he says.

Lourdes smiles again.

She puts on her nightclothes, tucks a scapular beneath her undershirt, and sits looking out the front window as she unbraids her hair for the night.

"Lourdes, come take off your father's socks. I'm getting too fat to bend down," he says.

Carmello laughs on the warm side.

Lourdes does not move. She is fixated on a dirty blonde haired man wearing a white T-shirt and a cap. He slowly drives near their house in a cab. He stops. Her missing brother Junyano is sitting in the back of the cab. Junyano does not look towards his house, but sits looking forward. The man driving the cab turns to look back at the boy his car possesses. Lourdes notices their mouths do not move. The man driving the cab raises up his hand and slams it down on the seat in front of the boy.

It starts to softly rain. Droplets of water splatter the windowpane Lourdes looks out of. The water also splatters the car window that frames Junyano's boyhood head. The beads of water slowly start to trickle down the glass. Junyano turns his head to look in Lourdes' direction. They both look at each other through weeping glass.

Juza screams.

"Junyano! Junyano!"

Juza runs down the street in the rain at dusk. The man driving the cab turns on the headlights. Junyano opens the door to the car and carefully steps out, gently closing the door behind him. The man in the cab meets the daggered gaze of Juza. Juza runs towards the cab reaching out to grab onto her boy child. "Junyano," she calls out. She puts a knuckle into her mouth and bites down hard. Junyano is large for his age. He is always making jokes. His family name is imbufo, "The Clown." He is almost the biggest in the family. He is nine and beginning to grow a mustache.

Juza screams.

"Imbufo! Kifintee, imbufo? Eh-ya-ow!"

She pulls the fist out of her mouth and uses it grab onto Junyano's thick face. His upper lip hair beads with the salty sweat of the Dead Sea. Junyano looks down. He starts to cry and roughly lunges his arms around his mother's waist. His cries are audible to Lourdes still watching out the teary window. Juza looks at the man in the cab. She starts to run towards him shaking her fist raised to the heavens.

Juza screams.

"Inyorunt! Inyorunt! Intee uhrufsodmuk!" She calls to her husband.

Carmello stands up. Lourdes instructs him.

"Mum is calling you, something's wrong with Junyano!"

Carmello runs to the window and sees Juza pounding her fist on the cab. Carmello stumbles out the front door. He is only wearing socks. He slips on the wet grass and falls on his bum.

Juza screams.

"Moratalla! Intee demonyo, moratalla! Carmello!"

The man in the cab drives away. His car turns off the street. Juza tries to run after it with cursing fist still high in the air. Blue-eyed Australians pass by whispering.

Carmello lays bruised on the slipped grass. Junyano cups the back of his bum with both of his hands. A light watery stream of blood tinged fluid trickles down the back of his right leg. He is wearing shorts and socks pulled up to his knees. The blood tinged fluid stops as it soaks into the back of his right-legged sock.

Lourdes walks outside in her sleep clothes. She softly pulls Junyano into the house with her. She gives him a bath and washes his bum in warm water. He vomits in the tub.

Carmello takes off his socks and retires to bed.

Juza walks into the backyard dampened by the rain. She unlocks the rabbit cage and sits for a time with the rabbits. She pushes rain-frizzed hair out of her face. The blue-eyed mob has cornered them in a pocket of the world where the cracks are wide. Juza feels as if they have cut out her eyes and left her screaming and blind. She feels like the sinewy orbs have been wrapped in a dirty rag and put in her left hand; the idle hand. The hand that does not read or write. The hand that cannot steer or downshift. The hand left holding the flag.

Juza sets one of the rabbits free and gets up to leave the cage.

As she goes back towards the house, Juza spies a lizard on a log near her children's outdoor toys. She gets the small hatchet hanging on a nail outside of the rabbit cage. She walks over to the log with the small ax raised high up to God. She quickly grabs the lizard up by its tail and slaps it over on to its back. She slams the blade down onto its throat. The lizard's chopped head lies on the log looking up at the rain. Juza tosses the tail end of the lizard into the bush and takes a rabbit from the cage. She cuts the head off the rabbit, skins it, hews it, and hangs the hatchet back on its nail. Juza walks into the kitchen to wash the blood off her hands. She then begins to prepare tomorrow's dinner.

Lourdes washes Junyano's face and puts him to bed.

Stuffat tal-fenek. Rabbits cut into pieces will make a very hearty stew.

Jarvik
Stacy Tintocalis

1.

"Like smoke," he says. "Yes, like smoke." He is speaking about her eyes.

Conveniently, he'd placed his wedding ring in his suit pocket while walking over to her. She knows the move, has seen it dozens of times, the way a man will slip his hand into his pocket and fumble beneath the fabric until his thumb has worked the ring over his knuckle.

She puts on her best blush. Yes, even that too is fake. Reddening her face, feeling it heat up, she rests her hand under her chin, one finger bent over her lips. "Is that good?" she asks. "Smoke in the eyes?"

"No. The color. Eyes the color of smoke. That's very good. Very...warm." He turns to the bar, flags the bartender. "Two more," he says, pointing to his drink and hers.

When he first saw her, he came from across the room, no hesitation at all. So what if he's slightly overweight. She doesn't care. They all have little imperfections. Tiny defects. She likes the way they're insecure about them, especially in private.

"You're not married?" he asks.

"Divorced." Nodding. "It was an air force marriage. We were traveling all the time. Anyway, you don't need to tell me. I can tell you're not married."

Smiles. Silence. This one is good, she thinks. Not even a flicker of hesitation. Not even a blink.

"We don't need to talk about that," he says.

The drinks arrive, and they toast. To what? To new friends. Classic.

There is talk of work and the convention in the hotel and the long hours spent on the road. This is the dull part, where she pretends to make the conversation friendly and innocent. Bartenders must overhear the same conversations repeatedly. Never, not once, has she seduced a bartender. They've seen too much. Nothing about her would be fresh, new, exciting.

2.

In his room, the air conditioner is on high. His suitcase is open and overflowing with socks and underwear. A suit hangs on a door hanger. Shoes are scattered over the floor. A miniature bottle of wine, empty, sits on the nightstand. There is a deck of cards on the table, a half-played game of Solitaire.

"Sorry about the mess. I've been here since Saturday," he says. "Here, let me get you a drink. I think there's still some wine. Or would you rather get something from room service?"

"Room service? Good God," she says. "Let's leave them out of this."

"My heart! Isn't that why I brought you up here? You aren't an industrial spy, are you?" He laughs. "Ha! No. Of course not. No. Let me see…" He unlatches a chrome case and pulls out the latest model of an artificial heart.

"This is our own design. The best heart on the market, much better than a Jarvik-7 heart, perhaps better than the AbioCor heart."

"I never knew they were so large," she says. "May I hold it?"

The heart is comprised of two clear plastic chambers, each with metal tubes and valves. She feigns interest in the heart. How heavy it is. How delicate. "And they put this inside someone? Fascinating. How 'bout some of that wine?"

"I bet you didn't know that the average heart only has a limited number of pumps in it. The artificial heart is flawless. It has an infinite number of pumps. It can go on forever. Your arms and legs can fall off, but the heart will keep going."

She takes the wine. "Strong heart, sick body? I think I'd rather keep my heart just the way it is."

"What company did you say you worked for?" he asks.

She sips her wine, looking away from him. "It's a PR firm in Los Angeles."

He is sweating now. A mistake, she realizes. Suddenly this man is in full panic, backing out, ready to get rid of her, a sudden rise in his conscience. He's never done this before, she realizes. And here she'd been thinking he was an old pro.

"Hey, let me give you some of this wine," she says. "I can't stand to drink alone."

"It's funny," he replies. "I don't usually drink. Just tonight… I don't know why…I felt like having a glass of wine."

She sits on the edge of the bed, beside him but not touching. The artificial heart rests between them.

"Sometimes you need to let go and have a drink," she says, then picks up the heart. "Sometimes you need to forget about this goddamn heart."

3.

They aren't very interesting after sex. Explored territory. That's all. She finds her shoes in the half-light that seeps through a crack in the curtains, then her clothes, her bra, her panties. Quietly she puts them on.

The heart is on the floor, just sitting there. Tempting…but no, she doesn't take it.

Contributors

Alan Ackmann is a recent graduate of the MFA program in fiction at the University of Arkansas. His work has already appeared in *McSweeney's Quarterly Concern*, and is forthcoming in *Ontario Review*. He is a former editor of *Evansville Review*, and currently serves on the editorial staff of *Relief: A Quarterly Christian Expression*. He is currently teaching in the First Year Writing program at DePaul University.

Becky Aldridge is a writer and editor living in Minneapolis, Minnesota.

Diane Averill's first book, *Branches Doubled Over With Fruit*, (University of Florida Press) was a finalist for the 1991 Oregon Book Award. Her most recent collection, *Beautiful Obstacles*, was also a finalist for the Oregon Book Award, (Blue Light Press). In addition to local and national magazines, such as *The Bloomsbury Review, Calyx, Calapooya Eclipse, Hubbub, Kalliope, LUNA, Manzanita Quarterly, Midwest Quarterly, The Bitter Oleander, Pemmican, Poetry Northwest, Tar River Poetry*, and *The Temple*, her work appears in several anthologies, such as *The Carnegie Mellon Anthology, From Here We Speak: An Anthology of Oregon Writers*, and *Ravishing Disunities: An Anthology of Ghazals*, written by English speaking people, and published by Wesleyan/New England Press. Her newest collection, *For All That Remains*, is forthcoming from Fir Tree Press in April 2007. Diane is a graduate of the M.F.A. program at the University of Oregon, where she won the annual award for the best poem by a graduate student. She has taught at Clackamas Community College for thirteen years.

Matt Briggs is the author of three collections of short stories including *The Remains of River Names, Misplaced Alice*, and *The Moss Gatherers*. His first novel, *Shoot the Buffalo*, was awarded a 2006 American Book Award by the Before Columbus Foundation. Recent fiction has appeared in *The Steel City Review, Spork*, and *5_Trope*.

John Bullock is English and a graduate of the University of Virginia's MFA fiction program, where he was a Henry Hoyns fellow. He teaches at Ohio University and is managing editor of the *New Ohio Review*. "*Safe*" is his first publication.

Fern Capella is a singer/songwriter/poet currently residing in portland, or. she has been published in and toured with *hipmama magazine, the essential hipmama, fictions of mass destruction,* and countless others. she graduated with a bachelor's in experimental performance from new college of california's experimental peformance institute in 2005.

Raphael Dagold is a writer, teacher, photographer, and cabinetmaker in Portland. His poems and other writings have appeared in such journals as *Quarterly West, Frank, Indiana Review, two girls review, Shirim, Washington Square,* and others. Two short prose fictions appear in *Northwest Edge iii: the End of Reality,* and his photographs have won awards from the Berkeley Jewish Museum and have appeared in several publications. Dagold has won fellowships and residencies from the Ucross Foundation, Literary Arts, Inc., The Vermont Studio Center, and other institutions. He has taught writing and literature at Lewis and Clark College, Mt. Hood Community College, and in the Writers-in-the-Schools program of Literary Arts, Inc.

Mia DeBono is the author of the short stories *Metasphere* and *Nowhere.* She has also written several short plays including *The Millwheel.* She currently lives and writes in Oregon.

Debra DiBlasi (www.debradiblasi.com) is the author of *The Jirí Chronicles & Other Fictions* (FC2/University of Alabama Press), *Prayers of an Accidental Nature* (Coffee House Press), and *Drought & Say What You Like* (New Directions). Awards include the Thorpe Menn Book Award, James C. McCormick Fellowship in Fiction from the Christopher Isherwood Foundation, Eyster Prize for Fiction, Web del Sol's Best Web Fiction, and a Cinovation Screenwriting Award. She is president of Jaded Ibis Productions, a transmedia corporation, producing the new arts-as-entertainment, podcast *BLEED,* and *The Jiri Chronicles,* a multimedia project consisting of over 450 works of prose, poetry, visual art, video, audio, music, interviews, web sites, and consumer products (http://jadedibisproductions.com).

Gina Frangello is the author of the novel *My Sister's Continent* (Chiasmus 2006), as well as the Executive Editor of *Other Voices* magazine and its book imprint OV Books. Her short fiction has appeared in a variety of literary venues including the *Chicago Reader,* the anthology *Homewrecker:*

An Adultery Reader (Soft Skull) and many literary magazines such as *Prairie Schooner, StoryQuarterly, Swink, Blithe House Quarterly* and *two girls review.* She guest-edited the anthology *Falling Backwards: Stories of Fathers and Daughters* (Hourglass), has been a book reviewer and freelance writer for the *Chicago Tribune* and the *Chicago Reader*, and currently teaches fiction writing at Columbia College Chicago.

Anne Germanacos' poetry, stories, and essays have appeared recently or are forthcoming in *Madison Review, Descant, Quarterly West, Salamander, Georgetown Review, Pindeldyboz* and others. She lives in San Francisco and on Crete.

Lindsey Gosma teaches creative writing and composition at Arizona State University where she is finishing her MFA in poetry. Her work has recently been published in *Crab Orchard Review, Painted Bride Quarterly*, and as a part of the "*Moving Poems*" public arts project at ASU. Lindsey is currently co-directing *The Visual Text Project 3: Triptych*, connecting artists and writers through the process of collaboration.

Siân Griffiths earned her PhD in English with a creative writing emphasis at the University of Georgia, Athens last May. Her work is forthcoming in *Ninth Letter* and has appeared in *Quarterly West, River Teeth: A Journal of Nonfiction Narrative, The River Oak Review, Court Green* and *The Georgia Review* (twice). She recently completed her first novel, *Borrowed Horses*, and is currently seeking an agent and publisher.

Michael Hardin is Visiting Assistant Professor of English at Susquehanna University. He has had poetry published in or forthcoming from *Seneca Review, Connecticut Review, North American Review, Birmingham Poetry Review, Gargoyle, Texas Review*, and *Tampa Review.* He has published two books of criticism, *Playing the Reader: The Homoerotics of Self-Reflexive Fiction* (2000) and *Devouring Institutions: The Life Work of Kathy Acker* (2004), and he also has published articles on contemporary literature and popular culture.

Kristen Henderson's poems have appeared in *Birmingham Review, Bloom, Passages North*, and other journals. She has received an MFA from the University of Arizona, has recently finished her first full-length manuscript of poetry, and is pursuing a master's degree in social work at SUNY Albany.

Justin Jainchill is a third-year MFA candidate at the University of Idaho, where he serves as Co-Editor of *Fugue Literary Journal*. He is from Connecticut and attended Bates College in Lewiston, Maine, where he played on the varsity lacrosse and read a little too much critical theory.

Megan Jones lives in the cultural mecca that is Gresham, Oregon. Her poetry and short fiction have appeared in *Epicenter, Diner, Northwest Edge iii*, and *Bryant Literary Review*, among others.

Stephen Graham Jones is the author and illustrator of the picture-less books *The Fast Red Road, All the Beautiful Sinners, The Bird is Gone, Bleed Into Me*, and his most recent, the horror novel *Demon Theory*. More at demontheory.net.

John Kay lives and works in Heidelberg, Germany as an education counselor. He has an MFA from the University of Arizona, taught writing for the University of Maryland in its European Division for many years, and worked as a mental health therapist at Providence Medical Center in Portland, Oregon. His poems have appeared in many magazines, including *Kayak, the New York Quarterly, the Wormwood Review, Bellevue Literary Review, Texas Poetry Journal, Chiron Review, Pearl*, and *Jewish Currents*. He has three chapbooks, the most recent, *Further Evidence of Someone*, from Eyelite Press.

Aaron Landsman, a Brooklynite by way of Minnesota, writes stories and performances. His writing has appeared or is forthcoming in *Hobart, Mudfish, The Village Voice*, and *Contemporary Theater Review*. His theatrical work has been presented in New York, Minneapolis, Houston, Cleveland and Austin.

Cris Mazza is the author of over a dozen books of fiction, most recently *Waterbaby* (fall 2007). Her other fiction titles include the critically notable *Is It Sexual Harassment Yet?*, and the PEN Nelson Algren Award winning *How to Leave a Country*. She also has a collection of personal essays, *Indigenous: Growing Up Californian*. Currently Mazza lives 50 miles west of Chicago and is a professor in the Program for Writers at the University of Illinois at Chicago.

Michael McCauley's stories have appeared in *DIAGRAM*, *Painted Bride Quarterly*, and *Six Little Things*. He recently obtained an M.F.A. in creative writing from the University of Alabama. He lives in Chicago.

Judith H. Montgomery's poems appear in *Gulf Coast, Northwest Review*, and elsewhere. Her chapbook, *Passion*, received the 2000 Oregon Book Award. *Red Jess* appeared in winter 2006; her second chapbook, *Pulse & Constellation*, will appear from Finishing Line Press in summer 2007. She's working on new manuscripts with the aid of fellowships from Literary Arts and the Oregon Arts Commission.

Cindy May Murphy is an MFA candidate in creative writing at the University of Oregon. Her work has appeared or is forthcoming in *New Delta Review, Sycamore Review*, and *The Briar Cliff Review*, among others. Cindy lives in Eugene with her husband and several dead or dying houseplants.

Deborah Narin-Wells, formerly an English Instructor at Lane Community College, currently teaches Creative Writing workshops through the Young Writers Association. Her poems have appeared in *Poetry East, Poet Lore, Comstock Review, Red Rock Review, Many Mountains Moving* and others. She won the 2004 Lois Cranston Poetry Prize from Calyx. A chapbook, *Birds Flying Through*, was published by Traprock Books in February, 2006.

Greg Nicholl is a freelance proofreader and web manager for *The Cortland Review*. His poetry has appeared or is forthcoming in *Barrow Street, Natural Bridge, Smartish Pace, Feminist Studies, Runes, The Los Angeles Review*, and more. He is currently the co-director of the Rocky Mountain Writers' Festival.

Bill O'Connell is a teacher and social worker in western Massachusetts. His poems have appeared in *Poetry East, Colorado Review, Green Mountains Review, The Sun*, and many others. His chapbook, *On The Map To Your Life*, appeared in 1992. Available at oconnelle@cs.com.

Lance Olsen's most recent book is *ANXIOUS PLEASURES: A NOVEL AFTER KAFKA* (Shoemaker & Hoard, 2007); his publication here is an excerpt. He is co-founder of *Now What*, a collective blog by alternative publishers and prose writers (nowwhatblog.blogspot.com), and Chair of the Board at Fiction Collective Two, one of America's best-known ongoing literary experiments and progressive arts communities.

Robert Parham's work has been published by *Southern Review, Texas Review, Georgia Review, Shenandoah, Connecticut Review, Northwest Review,* and *South Carolina*

Review. His chapbook *What Part Motion Plays in the Equation of Love* won the Palanquin Competition. A collection of his poetry was a finalist for the Richard Snyder and the Marianne Moore poetry competitions. He edits the *Southern Poetry Review* and serves as Dean of the College of Arts and Sciences at Augusta State University.

Ritah Parrish is the author of two collections of fiction, *Pink Menace* and *Girl Juice.* Her work has appeared in various anthologies including *Northwest Edge III: The End Of Reality*, *Northwest Edge: Fictions Of Mass Destruction, Poetry Slam, Poetry Nation,* and *Shortfuse.* She has written and performed three one-woman shows: *I Think He's A Sociopath But The Dance Is Saturday Night, Bite Down Hard,* and *Thinking Outside My Box.* She lives in Portland - land of coffee & beer.

Paulann Petersen's books of poetry are *The Wild Awake* (Confluence Press), *Blood-Silk* (Quiet Lion Press), and *A Bride of Narrow Escape* (Cloudbank Books), which was a finalist for the Oregon Book Award. A former Stegner Fellow at Stanford University and the recipient of the 2006 Holbrook Award from Literary Arts, she serves on the board of Friends of William Stafford, organizing the annual January Stafford Birthday Events.

Jay Ponteri lives in Portland, Oregon. He has recently published short stories in *Del Sol Review, Eye Rhyme: A Journal of New Literature, Cimarron Review,* and *Northwest Edge III: The End of Reality.* His story "*The Quiet*" has been nominated for Pushcart Prize. He teaches literature and writing seminars at Marylhurst University.

Danielle Rado recently received her MFA in fiction writing from the University of Notre Dame. She currently lives and works in Richmond, Virginia.

Paul B. Roth lives in upstate New York with the sculptor Georgina Heksch Roth and their three sons. A graduate of Goddard College in Plainfield, Vermont from which he also earned his Masters Degree in Contemporary French Poetry, he has been the editor and publisher of *The Bitter Oleander* since 1976, publishing contemporary poetry and fiction in translation, along with essays and interviews of substance about poetry and the creative act in both full length books and as a Spring and Fall issued magazine. In 2005, *The Bitter Oleander* was recognized as Best Literary Journal by Public Radio and given its "Excellence in Writing" award.

He is the author of six books of poetry the two most recent being a 2002 collection of prose poems entitled *Adrift in the Infinite* by Cyrpress Books, who in 2008 will publish another collection of his verse entitled *Cadenzas by Needlelight.* Roth's poetry is a mature blend of both sound and meditative images. There is a noticeably deep and measured breathing heard under the main tone in each of his poems. This breathing seems not so much that of the poet, but like that of the Earth. The vibrations an earthworm might feel during a driving rainstorm might be something similar to this breathing. Nonetheless, when he speaks, we have to listen carefully, for often it is a matter of what he says so subtly that lures us deeper into his own imaginative blend of linguistic reality.

Kevin Sampsell runs Future Tense Books, a micropress in Portland, Oregon. His writing has appeared widely in newspapers, web sites, and literary journals. His books include *Beautiful Blemish* (Word Riot Press) and an upcoming collection of fiction from Chiasmus Press.

Davis Schneiderman is a multimedia artist and author of *Multifesto: A Henri d'Mescan Reader* (Spuyten Duyvil 2007), as well as co-author of the novel *Abecedarium* (Chiasmus Press, forthcoming) and co-editor of the collections *Retaking the Universe: William S. Burroughs in the Age of Globalization* (Pluto 2004) and *The Exquisite Corpse: Creativity, Collaboration, and The World's Most Popular Parlor Game* (forthcoming). His creative work has been nominated for a Pushcart Prize and accepted by numerous publications including *Fiction International, The Chicago Tribune, The Iowa Review, Exquisite Corpse, Other Voices,* and *Gargoyle.* Dr. Schneiderman is Chair of American Studies and an Assistant Professor of English at Lake Forest College, a contributor to the *NOW WHAT* blog (http://nowwhatblog.blogspot.com/), and a board member for *&NOW: A Festival of Innovative Writing and Art.* Find him virtually at http://davisschneiderman.com/.

Ben Slotky is the pseudonym of Michael Holocaust, the author of such popular children's books as *The Chocolate Robot Man* and *3-2-1 Christmas.* Slotky/Holocaust has published several stories previously, none of which were very good.

Carol Smallwood's work has appeared in *English Journal, The South Carolina Review, Iris, Main Street Rag,* and several others including anthologies. *Educators as Writers: Writing for Personal and Professional Development*, her 17th book, is just out from Peter Lang. She is active in humane societies and crafts.

A recipient of an NEA fellowship in poetry and the Edgar Allen Poe Award, **D. James Smith**'s poems and stories have appeared recently in *The Malahat Review, New Millennium Writings & The Notre Dame Review*. His books include the novel *My Brother's Passion* (Permanent Press, 2004) and two collections of poems, *The Dead Ventriloquist* (Ahsahta Press, 1995) and *Sounds The Living Make* (Lewis-Clark Press, 2007). He's also published four novels for teens (DK, 1999; Atheneum, 2005, 2006, 2007).

Joseph A. Soldati, a retired college professor, has published numerous poems and essays in regional and national magazines, journals, and anthologies. His chapbook, *Apocalypse Clam*, was recently (May 2006) published by Finishing Line Press. He is also the author of a scholarly work, *Configurations of Faust* (1982), a poetry collection, *Making My Name* (1992), and is co-editor of the bilingual volume, *O Poetry! ¡Oh Poesia'! Poems of Oregon and Peru* (1997). He lives in Portland, Oregon.

Dianne Stepp's poems have appeared in journals and anthologies, including *Willow Springs, Calyx, The Clackamas Literary Review, The Sonora Review, Portland Lights*, and *Regrets Only*. She is the author of a chapbook of poems, "*Half-Moon of Clay.*" A long-time therapist she specializes in couple's counseling in Portland, Oregon.

Brad Summerhill is a writer and college professor living in Reno, Nevada. His work has appeared in *South Dakota Review, Aethlon* and elsewhere. The Arkansas Arts Council and the Nevada Arts Council have recognized his fiction in the form of individual artist grants. His nonfiction has received awards from the Nevada Press Association and the Association of Alternative Newsweeklies.

Catherine Sustana is an Associate Professor of English at Hawaii Pacific University. Her work has appeared in *Alaska Quarterly, Arts & Letters, Crazyhorse, Quarterly West*, and many other journals.

Kelly Terwilliger's poems have appeared in journals such as *Hunger Mountain, Poet Lore, The Potomac Review, The Connecticut River Review, The California Quarterly,* and *The Atlanta Review.* In addition to writing, she works as a storyteller and artist-in-residence in local schools. She lives in Eugene, Oregon with her family and a lively flock of chickens.

Stacy M. Tintocalis is an assistant professor in the Creative Writing Program at the University of Alabama at Birmingham. Her fiction has appeared in *Cream City Review, Fiction, Event,* and *The North Atlantic Review,* among others. She is currently completing a collection of stories entitled *Honeymoon in Beirut.*

Victoria Wyttenberg received her MFA from University of Washington where she was awarded the Richard Hugo Prize, the Bullis-Kizer Prize. She is currently retired after teaching English at the high school level, four years at Grants Pass High School and 26 years at Sunset High School, in Beaverton. Her poems have been published in a variety of literary magazines, including *Alaska Quarterly Review, Calyx, Malahat Review, Poetry Northwest, Seattle Review, Poetry Canada.* She has a poem in the *Anthology of Oregon Poetry, From Here We Speak* and ten of her poems are published in the anthology *Millenial Spring, Eight New Oregon Poets.* She currently lives in Portland, doing some part time teaching and continue reading, writing, drawing, painting and gardening.

281

282

284

Printed in the United States
107443LV00002B/58-69/A

THE LITTLE ME
AND
THE GREAT ME

BOOK ONE　　》　　》　　THE SEVEN SECRETS

This is a book about ME

My name is

....

Presented to me by

....

in the hope it will point the way to a happy
and successful life

The "ME" Books

Published by the Partnership Foundation

Capon Springs, West Virginia

THE LITTLE ME AND THE GREAT ME

First of a series of books for children

Book No. 1 entitled

THE SEVEN SECRETS

by

LOU AUSTIN

*assisted by his wife and family
(including grandchildren) and a
host of friends, parents and
teachers; with particular thanks
due his daughter Claire Kay Bellingham*

Illustrated by
F. O. ALEXANDER

Other books in the "ME" series:
MY SECRET POWER
WHY AND HOW I WAS BORN

For Parents, Teachers
AND ALL WHO LOVE CHILDREN

Everywhere I go, *I** go too,
and spoil everything.
—Hoffenstein

This series THE LITTLE ME AND THE GREAT ME aims to revive an old but neglected truth: that there are two forces, two wills in every person: one — the will of the human self, the other—the will of the divine self. Between these two forces there is a continuous running battle.

You who are responsible for the child's mental and spiritual development can help him, early in life, to an awareness of the presence of these two forces within him. You will save him much needless frustration if, as he becomes aware of his ego, you teach him that there is within him not one, but *two* separate wills. Once a child understands that the Little Me (the will of the human self) and THE GREAT ME (the will of the divine self) are parts of his nature, he will realize that he has been given freedom to choose between the two.

It is a sad truth that one American out of ten suffers mental illness at one time or another, mostly because of the fallacy that he goes

*The Little Me

through life alone. The child is entitled to know of the presence within him of THE GREAT ME, as a living, working Partner.

Arnold J. Toynbee, the eminent historian and philosopher, wrote in March 1956:

"Since Man has been given freedom by God, Man is free to refuse to co-operate with God . . . When Man refuses, he is free to make his refusal and to take the consequences. When Man accepts, his reward for willing what is the will of God is that *he finds himself taken by God into partnership* in the doing of God's creative work. When Man is thus co-operating with God, Man's freedom is at its maximum, because Man is then realizing the *potentialities for which God has created him.* GOD HAS CREATED MAN TO BE GOD'S FREE PARTNER IN THE WORK OF CREATION." (*emphasis ours*)

When a child has been taught that God has given him freedom to choose between the two wills within him, it is not likely that he will become a problem to his parents or to his teachers.

Rather, the child will tend to develop his highest capacities and noblest qualities, making a real contribution to society. A child so taught will be helped in many ways: he will have 1) a greater, deeper sense of security; 2) a more sympathetic understanding of what motivates others and a sincere desire to help them achieve their best; 3) an awareness that the wants of the Little Me should not always be satisfied.

But perhaps more meaningful than any of these to the child is the fact that when he chooses to be THE GREAT ME, he is infinitely happier, things get done better and with less strain and worry, and people are drawn to him because he inspires the best in them.

Thus the child will learn from his own experiences that his true happiness lies not in the Little Me but in THE GREAT ME. And if the child is given this understanding, who knows but that grown-ups may be reached through him?

IMPORTANT FOR PUBLIC SCHOOL USE

This nation believes in God. The phrase "under God" as used by Lincoln, was recently unanimously adopted by Congress, in the Pledge of Allegiance. God is non-sectarian.

Because questions as to the nature of God may lead to sectarian interpretation, the child raising any such question should be referred to his parents and church for the answer.

This is a book about me

PASTE

PICTURE

IN THIS

SPACE

This is my picture

THIS is a book about me.

My name is . . . . *(child gives name)*

I am . . . . years old. *(child gives age)*

I have a great secret.

Only a few people know this secret.

Would you like to know my secret?

I will tell you.

7

First, take a look at me. What do you see?

You see me.

My name is .... *(child gives name)*

But you don't see *all* of me. You see only *one* ME.

Now here is the secret. There are really *two* MEs.

But you can see only *one* me at a time.

Sometimes when you look at me, you see what I call
  the Little Me.

But there is really *another* me.

I *know* there is *another* me.

And this *other* me is the one I want you to see.

This other me is a better me than the Little Me.

It is a *greater* me. I call it THE GREAT ME.

THE GREAT ME is always kind and loving.

THE GREAT ME does only kind and loving things.

The Little Me is not always kind and loving.

The Little Me wants things all for myself.

When another child plays with one of my toys, the
Little Me calls out "It's mine. I want it."

The Little Me always wants to be first.

"I'm first" the Little Me calls out.

The Little Me is selfish.

The Little Me thinks only of myself.

The Little Me does not think of others.

Could you love the Little Me?

If the Little Me does not get what I want, I cry.

The Little Me is not very happy.

Now I will tell you
another secret.

I can choose between the Little Me and THE GREAT ME.

I can be which one I choose to be.

I can be the Little Me or I can be THE GREAT ME.

It's all up to me.

Of course you know which one I will choose.

12

But first I must know how to get rid of the Little Me.

That is another secret.

Like magic I can change the Little Me into
    THE GREAT ME.

I will tell you how.

You know how to blow out a candle on a birthday
    cake?

Well, that's how I blow out the Little Me.

I just pucker up my lips and blow. *(child blows)*

Just like the candle goes out, out goes the Little Me.

The Little Me goes away.

13

And THE GREAT ME comes in.

Instead of being the Little Me, I am
THE GREAT ME.

And I am very, very happy.

I love everybody. And everybody loves me.

I'm kind to everyone. And everyone is kind to me.

THE GREAT ME does not say "I'm first."

THE GREAT ME says "You're first."

THE GREAT ME does not say "It's mine. I want it."

THE GREAT ME says "You may play with it."

THE GREAT ME makes everyone happy.

Everyone is happy because the Little Me is changed into THE GREAT ME.

THE GREAT ME thinks of others.

THE GREAT ME shares with others.

Everyone loves
THE GREAT ME.

Now I will tell you another secret.

I will tell you how *you* can become THE GREAT ME.

I have already told you how to blow out the Little Me.

You just pucker up your lips and give a good blow.
    (*child blows*)

Like blowing out a candle.

Out it goes. Out goes the Little Me.

15

Now here's the secret.

After I blow out the Little Me, I take a deep breath.

(*child breathes in*)

In comes THE GREAT ME.

No one can see THE GREAT ME coming in.

It's just like the air.

No one can see the air coming in.

So no one can see THE GREAT ME coming in.

But *I* know THE GREAT ME comes in.

I can *feel* THE GREAT ME coming in.

I feel happier. I feel like being kind to others.

I love others. I want to help others.

The Little Me does not want to help others.

The Little Me does not even want to help around the house.

The Little Me does not do things for my family.

The Little Me seems to love only myself and nobody else.

That's another reason to blow out the Little Me. *(child blows)*

17

THE GREAT ME likes to help around the house.

THE GREAT ME helps without being asked to help.

THE GREAT ME *loves* my family.

THE GREAT ME loves to play with other children.

And other children love to play with me when I am
THE GREAT ME.

THE GREAT ME makes *them* happy, too.

THE GREAT ME is not a show-off.

THE GREAT ME does not brag.

The Little Me *is* a show-off.

The Little Me is always calling out "Look at me.
   Watch what I'm doing."

People do not care to be around the Little Me.

That's another reason to blow out the Little Me.
   (child blows)

19

People love to be around THE GREAT ME.

They see how kind THE GREAT ME is to everyone.

How THE GREAT ME helps everybody.

They see how everybody loves THE GREAT ME.

That's why I want to be THE GREAT ME.

So I will remember to blow out the Little Me.

I will pucker up my lips and blow. *(child blows)*

Out it goes. Out goes the Little Me.

20

Then I will take a deep breath. *(child breathes in)*

In comes THE GREAT ME.

Now when you look at me, you don't see the Little Me.

You see THE GREAT ME.

My lips are smiling. My eyes are shining.

And I feel so much happier.

I don't want to be the Little Me any more.

I want to be THE GREAT ME.

When people look at me, I want them to see
THE GREAT ME.

21

When I am THE GREAT ME, I am very happy.

Of course, I cannot always be happy.

Nobody can be happy all the time.

Everybody has some unhappy times.

I know that I will have some unhappy times.

THE GREAT ME knows what to do when things
    are sad.

THE GREAT ME does not cry or worry.

When things are sad, THE GREAT ME looks around
    to help somebody else.

22

When **THE GREAT ME** helps somebody else,
THE GREAT ME feels good from the inside out.

The sad time passes away more quickly.

THE GREAT ME changes sad times to happy times.

The Little Me cannot change sad times to happy times.

Nobody is happy with the Little Me around, anyway.

So, if the Little Me sneaks in, I will give a good blow.
(child blows)

And the Little Me will go far away.

Then I will take a deep breath. *(child breathes in)*

And like magic THE GREAT ME will come in with
God's air.

And everybody will be happy again.

Would you ever choose to be the Little Me?

Would you like to be THE GREAT ME?

Isn't it wonderful to have people love you?

THE GREAT ME is wonderful.

I feel so good when THE GREAT ME comes in and stays with me.

I like to have THE GREAT ME stay with me always.

I like to have THE GREAT ME as my Friend.

I like to have THE GREAT ME as my Partner.

No matter what happens, THE GREAT ME is always with me.

Nobody can take THE GREAT ME away from me.
Nobody.

Nobody in the whole wide world.

But sometimes the Little Me gets in the way of
THE GREAT ME.

Then the Little Me shuts out THE GREAT ME.

But I can *choose* between the Little Me and
THE GREAT ME.

It's up to me. I can be which one I choose.

If nobody wants me around because I'm acting like the Little Me, I know it's my own fault.

And if everybody loves me and wants me around, it's because I chose to be THE GREAT ME.

So when the Little Me gets in the way, I will blow the Little Me away. *(child blows)*

Next I will take a deep breath. *(child breathes in)*

Then I will know that THE GREAT ME is right there with me.

Would you like to have THE GREAT ME as your Friend and Partner?

THE GREAT ME can make you very happy.

*   *   *

Now I have one more secret to tell you.

This is the *best* secret of all.

This is the *greatest* secret in the whole world.

Only a few people know this secret.

And because they know this secret, they are the happiest people in all the world.

I am going to tell *you* the secret.

I am going to tell you who THE GREAT ME is.

This is a great big secret, so get ready for it.

Here is the secret: *THE GREAT ME is God's Partner.*

Yes, THE GREAT ME comes from God.

So when I become THE GREAT ME, God becomes my
     Partner.

When I blow out the Little Me, God's Spirit comes in.

God's Spirit comes in when I breathe in God's air.

That's right. God's Spirit comes in like God's air
     comes in.

You can't see God. No one can see God, but God is
    there.

You can't see God's air either, but the air is there.

Yes, God's Spirit comes in like God's air that you
    breathe.

And God is THE GREAT ME's Partner.

That is why THE GREAT ME is kind and loving.

God is kind and loving.

That is why THE GREAT ME makes me happy.

God, my Partner, makes me happy.

When I breathe in God's air, God's Spirit comes in.

God is my Partner and Friend.

God guides and protects me. He looks after me.

God helps me. I try to help Him. We are Partners.

Isn't it wonderful to have God for a Partner and
    Friend?

People can tell that God is my Partner and Friend.

They can tell by the smile on my lips.

They can tell by the light in my eyes.

They can tell because I'm kind to everybody.

With God as my Partner, I am happy.

People around me are happy.

Those who are not happy, will learn how to become happy.

They will learn how to blow out their Little Me. (*child blows*)

They will learn how to breathe in their GREAT ME. (*child breathes in*)

Everyone has a Little Me. *Everyone* has a GREAT ME.

Even grown-up people have a Little Me and a GREAT ME.

But not everybody knows that.

Some people don't know they have a GREAT ME.

Maybe they can learn from me.

When someone else's Little Me is showing, I will not let my Little Me show.

When someone else wants me to follow his Little Me, I will not do it.

Instead, I will let my GREAT ME show.

When people see me, they will see THE GREAT ME.

When they see THE GREAT ME, they will think of God.

When people see that God is my Partner and Friend
they will want God for their Partner and Friend.

They will learn how to blow away their Little Me.

They will learn how to breathe in their GREAT ME.

I have one more secret.

You thought I had told you my last secret.

But I have one more. This is a great secret, too.

This secret is how I know that God is my Partner
and Friend.

Here is the way the secret works.

I give a good blow. *(child blows)*

Then I close my mouth and pinch my nose tight.
(child pinches nose)

Now I wait just a few seconds.

See what happens?

I have to let go of my nose. *(child removes fingers)*
Do you know why? Because God's air has to come in.
Because God's Spirit has to come in like His air.
That shows that I can't do without God.

That shows that God's Spirit must come into me.
I can't do without God's air. I can't do without God.
God wants so much to come into me, it seems He can't
    do without me either.

God wants to help me.   God wants me to help Him, too.

I help God when I am THE GREAT ME.

I do not help God when I am the Little Me.

God lets me choose between the Little Me and
    THE GREAT ME.

I can choose to be the Little Me.

I can say to God "I don't want you for a Partner and
    Friend."

Or I can say: "Thank you God for being my Partner
and Friend. Thank you for being my Leader."

It's all up to me.

When someone reminds me that I am acting like the
Little Me, I will quickly blow out the Little Me.
(child blows)

But I will not always wait for someone to remind me.

I, myself, will know when I'm acting like the Little Me.

I will know because I will be making someone
unhappy.

I will know because I'm not very happy either.

When I am the Little Me, even my Partner is sad.

But when I am THE GREAT ME, my Partner is glad.

So, I will remind myself to blow out the Little Me.
   (child blows)

I will breathe in THE GREAT ME. *(child breathes in)*

When I am THE GREAT ME, I am helping God.

That is why God made me. God wants me to work
   with Him.

God wants me to be His Partner and Friend.

Isn't that a wonderful secret?

I've told you a lot of secrets.

Sometimes you hear secrets you are not supposed to tell.

But the secrets I've told you, you *are* supposed to tell.

You tell these secrets just by *being* THE GREAT ME.

You don't go around saying "I am THE GREAT ME."

You just act THE GREAT ME.

People can tell from what you *do* that you are THE GREAT ME.

People can tell you are THE GREAT ME because you are kind. Because you help other people.

So, let's count up all the secrets I've told you.

First, there are two MEs, the Little Me and
THE GREAT ME.

Do you know the second secret?

The second secret is that I can choose between
the Little Me and THE GREAT ME.

The third secret is how to make the Little Me go far
away.

42

Do you know the fourth secret?

The fourth secret is that I can breathe in
THE GREAT ME.

The fifth secret is that THE GREAT ME is God's
Partner.

Do you remember secret number six?

Secret number six is that God is my Partner, and that
He is always with me.

The last secret is how I know that God is my Partner.

This is such a great secret that I just have to tell you
again.

I give a good blow. *(child blows)*

Then I close my mouth and pinch my nose tight. *(child
pinches nose)*

44

Pretty soon I have to let go of my nose.

Do you know why? Because I must have God's air.

I can't do without God's air.

Because I can't do without God.

God's Spirit comes in with the air I breathe.

God is THE GREAT ME's Partner.

If I forget to be THE GREAT ME and let the Little
Me sneak in, I will blow harder the next time.

THE GREAT ME will come in.

THE GREAT ME is God's Partner. God will be my
   Partner.

And when God is my Partner, I will do only
   kind and loving things.

*   *   *

I hope you like this story about me.

My name is .... *(child gives name)*

I want to be THE GREAT ME.

For I know I can be happy only when I make others
   happy.

And I can't make others happy if I am the Little Me.

When I am THE GREAT ME, everybody around me
   will be happy.

And I'll be happy, too.

All financial interest in this book, including royalties,
is assigned to The Partnership Foundation, a non-
profit organization, dedicated to furthering the concept
of the Partnership of man and Maker.

46

QUESTIONS

This story is about...................? *(child gives name)*

How many MEs do you have? What are their names?

Which ME would you rather be? Why?

Who decides which ME you're going to be?

When somebody grabs your toy, what do you do?

When somebody needs help, which ME helps?

Which ME is the happy ME?

Which ME tries to make others happy?

Which ME do you want your friends to see? Why?

If the Little Me sneaks in, how do you get rid of the Little Me?

Then how does THE GREAT ME come in?

Who is really THE GREAT ME?

Who is your Partner and Friend?

Is He always with you?

But who is it that sometimes gets in the way?

Which ME grabs the biggest piece of cake?

Which ME starts yelling when he can't do what he wants?

Which ME always tries to find something to argue about?

Which ME helps little brother or sister instead of picking on them?

In a game which ME do we all want on our team?

Which ME do you want to see in Mommy and Daddy?

Which ME do you think they like to see in you?

What is the best way to help others to be THE GREAT ME?

Does everybody have two MEs?

Does everybody know they have two MEs?

Can you remember the seven secrets?

Do you want to share these secrets with others? Why?

What happens when you blow out?

What comes in when you take a deep breath?

Who is the best Friend of all?

GOD IS WITH ME, THIS I KNOW

Words by
Lou Austin

Music by
William B. Bradb

God is with me, this I know, For The Great Me proves it's so;

God's my Part—ner help—ing me, I'll blow out the Lit—tle Me.
(CHILD BLOWS)

CHORUS

Yes, God is with me, Yes, God is with me, Yes, God is with me, The Great Me proves it's so.

I'll be happy all day long,
When The Great Me sings my song,
God's my Partner helping me,
I'll blow out the Little Me.
(CHILD BLOWS)

Chorus
   Yes, God is with me,
   Yes, God is with me,
   Yes, God is with me,
   The Great Me proves it's so.

I'm as rich as rich can be,
Rich in love 'cause God's with me,
God's my Partner, helping me,
I'll blow out the Little Me.
(CHILD BLOWS)

Chorus
   Yes, God is with me,
   Yes, God is with me,
   Yes, God is with me,
   The Great Me proves it's so.